Dirty Play

A Nolan Brothers Novel ~ Book Three

AMY OLLE

Copyright © 2016 Amy Olle

All rights reserved.

Ebook ISBN: 978-1-944180-04-4
Print ISBN: 978-1-944180-05-8

DEDICATION

To my mom for showing me how to be both soft-hearted and totally badass.

Chapter One

When it came to men, Haven Callahan had rules.

Hard, staunch, non-negotiable rules.

The kind etched in stone, locked in a tomb, and tattooed on the heart and mind.

Rule Number One: No sex on the first date. Not anymore.

Rule Number Two: No kisses on the neck. Neck kissing was her kryptonite. Her Achilles' heel. The warm brush of a man's mouth on the vulnerable spot beneath her ear or over the sensitive skin above her clavicle stirred something deep inside of her. Lust? Arousal? Passion? The perfect concoction of all three? Whatever it was, it drained her of her will to resist his tantalizing manliness, and before she intended, and *long* before he deserved it, she'd be handing over her heart to him to do with what he pleased.

Rule Number Three: No sappy declarations, grand

pronouncements, or talk of The Future. Marriage, children, cohabitation, weekend trips to Minnesota to meet his parents—all equally likely to make her break out in hives. All forbidden.

Rule Number Four: No relationship could be permitted to last beyond ninety days. Anything longer than three months and she was bound to agree to marry the jerk.

Marriage was not an option. Not for her.

A violation to any one of her rules and Haven immediately ended the relationship, often lashing out in a way to irreparably sever the bond. She didn't intend to be such a crazy bitch, but destroying the relationship beyond repair or recognition was the only thing that cleared her skin of the itchy hives.

Non-negotiable.

Sometimes, it was the only way to save her from herself.

Charlie knew Haven's rules, which was why she gaped stupidly at him now while the raucous Friday night bar crowd swirled around them.

"You think we should move in together?" Her voice pitched high above the din in the packed bar. "You and me?"

A sheepish smile touched the neat features of his face. "When Kaitlyn and Logan are married, you'll be moving out. I thought you could move into my place." He lifted his shoulders. "Permanently."

"Permanently?" Haven ran a hand down her bare arm to chase away the goose bumps prickling over her skin. "We've only been dating a month."

"Six weeks." Charlie's brown eyes warmed. "And it's been a great six weeks."

Now that Haven's roommate, Kaitlyn, had met the love of her life and agreed to marry the poor fool, she and her soon-to-be husband, Logan, were busy making plans for their future. Plans that didn't involve Haven living with them.

Haven made decent money working as a bartender, but it wasn't nearly enough to afford a place on her own in Seattle.

That didn't mean she wanted to live with Charlie.

Permanently.

"Charlie, you know how I feel about this. I—"

"Callahan!" her boss barked from the far end of the bar. "Less talking, more pouring."

Haven snatched a clean pitcher off the stack and thrust it under a beer tap. She wrenched the handle and golden liquid flowed into the container.

"Look, you don't have to answer right now," Charlie said. "Just... think about it."

She slid the pitcher across the bar to the waiting customer and accepted their debit card in return. At the cash register, she swiped the card.

Could she do it? Could she commit to one person? For ninety-one days, let alone forever and ever?

She was thirty-two years old, and Charlie was the almost perfect guy for her. Really, he was. He was nice, and he was cute, in a nerdy-scientist kind of way. Though not a scientist, he was an accountant who owned his own place, liked crossword puzzles and nature hikes, and used smiley faces in his texts. He was dependable and reliable.

Perfectly predictable.

What's more, he knew where her clitoris was located.

Granted, he attacked the sensitive spot as though it was an out-of-balance spreadsheet, but at least he cared about giving her orgasms. Not every guy was so considerate, she well knew.

Still, her stomach wrenched with knots when she returned the card to the customer and side-eyed Charlie, who watched her with sincere brown eyes.

Panic squeezed her throat. "The thing is... I'm not ready for such a big commitment."

The slash of hurt that chased across his face plucked a chord on her tone-deaf heart.

"I'm sorry," she said.

And she was sorry. She wasn't a completely heartless bitch, after all. No matter what her stepmother might say.

Haven pointed to the next customer, who shouted out his drink order. At the tap, she filled a pint glass with premium lager. When she turned back, Charlie scowled at her across the bar top.

"I don't know why you're making such a big deal out of this," he said. "I'm not asking you to marry me. At least, not yet."

The pint slipped from her hand and exploded on the concrete floor at her feet. "Ma-marry you?"

His thin lips pinched. "Is it so far-fetched?"

She gaped at him. "Yes. It's beyond far-fetched. We've been dating for a month."

On a curse, she snatched a towel from below the bar and dropped to her knees to sop up the broken shards of glass, beer soaking through her blue jeans. She flung the mess into the sink and plucked a clean glass from the rack.

At the tap, she thrust the pint under the nozzle and wrenched on the handle. When she handed the man his drink and change and he slipped away, she risked a glance at Charlie.

"I'm sorry if you think I misled you." She wiped her hands on a towel. "I told you I don't want anything long-term. I don't want to get married. Ever."

A light flashed in his eyes. "I thought this was going somewhere, but all this time, it meant nothing to you? I meant nothing to you?"

Did it bother her that she didn't feel something deep and profound for the man she'd been sleeping with exclusively for several weeks?

Maybe.

A little.

Okay, honestly, not really.

She'd planned it this way. She'd picked Charlie–so unlike any other guy she'd ever dated before–precisely because he didn't arouse her passions.

Passion was dangerous to someone like her.

"I told you–"

"I know, I know. The rules." Anger cluttered his tidy features. "Yeah, you told me, but then you spent the last six weeks sucking my dick and I thought things might've changed."

She swallowed her gasp and pushed a slow, sardonic smile to her lips. "Don't be such a romantic, Charlie. You're making it impossible for me to refuse you."

A trio of women shoved their way to the bar. Haven offered them a stiff smile and then set to work mixing three fruity cocktails.

Maybe it was time she added a few new rules. Or better yet, chucked the rules altogether and tried celibacy.

Who was she kidding? If celibacy were an option for her, she would've taken that route long ago. Trouble was, she enjoyed sex too much, and after a time, solo sex didn't deliver lasting satisfaction.

She craved what only a man could give her. A hard, warm body over hers. A masculine scent teasing her senses. The reminder that she still lived and there was yet some pleasure, maybe even some affection, to be found in this world.

She arranged the bright red concoctions on the bar before the women and accepted a debit card from one of them.

Charlie had the decency to appear ashamed when he pushed into her line of sight. "Haven, I'm sorry. It's just...

I'm frustrated and...."

Haven dragged the card through the card reader. "It's fine." While the machine churned, she scratched an itch at the base of her neck. Her fingertips detected the unmistakable bump of a welt. "But I think it's probably best if we move on."

He rocked back on his heels.

Haven ignored the guilt that swamped her and handed the woman her card.

Charlie's features twisted into a determined scowl. "No, you know what? I'm not giving up on you. On us."

Haven froze.

The women halted in their retreat and turned round eyes on the suddenly impassioned Charlie.

"We're good together."

Haven shrugged. "We're okay—"

"And you're scared. That's all this is."

"I know I'm scared. I admit that, but it doesn't change anything—"

"However long it takes you to get over this phobia, I can wait."

She licked her suddenly dry lips. "Oh, no. Please, don't—"

"If it takes a year, or two, then so be it."

"Charlie, listen to me—"

"And then, when you've come to your senses, I'm going to marry you, Haven Callahan. Mark my words."

Synchronized sighs of contentment eased from the trio of women.

Haven shrank back and wiped viciously at the beads of sweat on her forehead.

Charlie's mouth kept moving as he spoke words she couldn't hear over the hammering of her heart. The pounding thundered through her veins, echoing inside her skull with sickening thuds.

"No." The denial leaked through the narrow opening

of her throat.

He remained undeterred. "...and then we're going to live happily ever after. For the rest of our lives."

His words struck with the force of a physical blow.

For. The. Rest. Of. Our. Lives.

She was shaking her head. "I won't marry you." *Or anyone else.* "I'm completely fucked-up, Charlie. You need to move on or you'll be waiting forever for a future that won't ever come. Never, ever."

It was cruel. She often was cruel, because it beat the alternative of going all-in on somebody, loving them with her whole heart, only to find out they couldn't see it through to the end. They couldn't stay, couldn't stand by her, with her, and when they left, she'd have nothing but a broken heart and a renewed determination not to let herself be so vulnerable ever again.

With panic screaming through her, she somehow managed to walk, not run, to the end of the bar, past her snarling boss, and exit the barroom through a set of swinging doors. At her locker, she retrieved her jacket and purse, and kept right on walking out the back door.

Outside, the city sidewalks were crowded with late-night revelry. Fear nipped at her heels, and she craned her neck to glance over her shoulder. She increased her pace. Her spine stiff and straight, she dodged bodies.

She was desperate to be away from the place where Charlie had threatened to claim her future, and the heels of her ankle boots struck the concrete sidewalk with jarring jolts. Soon, she struggled to draw painful gulps of cold December air into her aching lungs.

She plunged into the apartment she shared with Kaitlyn and slammed the door shut behind her. Pressing her back to the heavy wood, she sucked in greedy swallows of air. Her cheeks were wet, but she didn't have time to think about why.

Kaitlyn and Logan, snuggled under a blanket on the

sofa, regarded her with curious gazes.

Haven forced a weak smile. "Hey, guys."

Logan squeezed Kaitlyn's shoulder and the expression on her pretty face shifted from inquisitive to reluctant.

She stepped out from under the blanket. "Um, do you have a minute?"

Haven willed her panicked heart to slow. "Sure. What's up?"

But she already knew.

"Logan and I, uh, we found this great place in South Newcastle. We put in an offer, and we just found out the house is ours."

"Congratulations." Haven's voice sounded strained and tight to her own ears. "When do you move?"

"At the end of the month, when our lease here is up. I'm sorry—"

Haven waved off Kaitlyn's next words. "Don't be sorry. You should be happy."

Naked relief swamped Kaitlyn's features, and her soft smile brightened into a full-wattage grin. "I am happy. So, so happy."

Haven gaped at her roommate for a moment. Kaitlyn did, in fact, look happy. Stupidly happy. But how could that be? How could it feel good to depend on someone else? To be completely vulnerable to another person?

Pleading exhaustion after a grueling work shift, Haven sought the sanctuary of her bedroom.

In the shower, where she hoped to wash away the hives before any more formed, reality crept in. Had she just walked off her job? The tentacles of fear coiled tighter around her throat.

After her shower, she dressed in yoga pants and a tank top. Her body trembled, the compulsion to run still reverberating through her, and she paced the bedroom like a caged animal. Had the room always been so small? Or were the walls actually closing in on her?

She needed space. She needed to put some distance between herself and the fear.

By now, she knew the fear never really went away. She scratched at a fresh hive.

It was true that she couldn't outrun the fear, but she could outsmart it. Distract it and confuse it until it lost sight of her amidst the chaos she created.

Chaos. Chaos was her ally. Where to start?

Run!

She could run. Leave Seattle.

At the thought, the vise squeezing her chest began to ease.

Yes, that was it. She needed a fresh start. She'd find a new town, a new job, a new life. This one free of men. Well, for as long as she could go without, anyway. A billion distractions awaited her somewhere.

But where? Her gaze swung to the map hanging on her bedroom wall, stuck with hundreds of pins marking the places she'd visited or lived over the past decade.

Yanking open the drawer of her nightstand, she fumbled for her dart case. Her fingertips brushed over the faded photograph, but she pushed aside the photo of Ryan with his disapproving brown eyes and grasped the sleek black leather case.

In front of the map, she poised with a metal dart between her thumb and forefinger, raised it before her face and, closing her eyes, let the arrow fly.

It struck the wall with a satisfying thud. She sidled closer and peered at the spot on the map pinned beneath the sharp point.

She frowned. Atlanta, Georgia?

Biting down hard on her bottom lip, she wondered how her foul mouth and sarcastic disposition would go over in the South.

She sighed. Oh well, the dart had spoken.

Georgia would give her the sizable wedge of distance

she required.

Plus, it was nowhere near Milwaukee.

She plucked her cell phone off her nightstand and settled on the bed to do a little research about her soon-to-be new hometown.

She'd browsed for several minutes when the phone chirped with an incoming e-mail. Reading the name of the sender, Haven grew instantly alert.

Emily Cole?

She sat upright, the memories rushing forth.

Her college roommate, Emily, had been an incredibly shy but impossibly sweet girl. She and Haven, opposites in so many ways, nonetheless became fast friends. By the time they'd reached their senior year, Emily had become the only real friend Haven had ever known. A true friend who didn't compete with her for boys or call her a slut behind her back.

But Emily left school a semester early, and shortly after that, Haven's life took a dramatically different turn.

With a tap on the screen, Haven opened Emily's message and started to read.

Emily expressed her regret that she hadn't e-mailed Haven more often over the years, but in two weeks, she was getting married and she wondered if Haven could come to the wedding. Then she apologized for the last-minute invitation, noting that it was a bit sudden.

She went on to write how much she'd love it if Haven could attend, though she totally understood if Haven was unable to make the trip to the remote island in northern Michigan on such short notice.

Haven sat back in bed. "Holy crap," she said to the empty room. Despite herself, she laughed. A wedding, huh? Seemed to be the day's theme.

She reread the e-mail, a smile playing at the corners of her mouth. Emily wrote the way she spoke, in a rush of tangled uncertainty. Except without the stutter.

Of course, Haven hated weddings. The last one she'd attended, for two of her coworkers, she'd broken out in hives on the way and ended up sneaking out halfway through the ceremony.

But at that moment, Haven didn't hate the idea of attending Emily's wedding. She wanted to see her friend and she was beyond curious to meet the man Emily, a girl too afraid to talk to boys in college, had fallen in love with and agreed to marry.

Though not exactly on the way from Seattle to Atlanta, Michigan fit her requirement for a change, and it'd put a fair distance between herself and the suddenly smitten Charlie.

She typed a reply. *I can't wait to see you and meet your guy! Maybe we can find the time to get into a little trouble, for old time's sake?*

Then she hit Send.

Chapter Two

Two weeks later, Haven peered through the tiny window at the blur of snow and ice pelting the airplane's aluminum exterior. A wall of dark clouds engulfed the tin aircraft and when the turbulence shook the wine from her plastic cup, she sucked down the beverage in one terrified gulp.

Miraculously, they managed to land safely in Chicago, but to a noisy refrain of cancelled flights and delays. The next twenty-two hours were a special kind of hell for her. Travel delay hell.

She slept on the airport floor at the gate to her connecting flight, which finally touched down in Traverse City, Michigan a day later and an hour after the start of Emily's wedding ceremony.

Haven picked up her car rental and set off for Thief Island. But the snowplows, overwhelmed by the storm, didn't have the roads cleared, and what should've been a forty-five-minute drive along Michigan's scenic western coastline instead became a harrowing slog through enough snow and ice to bury the car, along with her body, so completely that neither of them would be found until the spring thaw.

By the time Haven boarded the car ferry out to the island, Emily's wedding ceremony would have ended. The boat lurched and pitched in the choppy waters of Lake Michigan and when they reached land thirty minutes later, Haven resisted the urge to drop to her knees and plant a kiss on the solid scrap of earth.

Dressed in the blue jeans and sweater she'd first donned almost two days before, Haven decided to drive straight to the Winslow Inn to change before heading to the restaurant where Emily and her guests had gathered to celebrate her marriage.

With Emily's instructions, Haven easily found the stately home perched atop a hill overlooking the lake. Storm clouds darkened the early evening sky and warm lights from within the massive house glowed softly through the windows.

The front door swung open as she climbed the steps, and a handsome college-aged kid named Max showed Haven to a second-floor bedroom. After he'd left, she flipped on the bedside table lamp and hoisted her suitcase onto the wrought iron bed.

The room boasted high ceilings, wide-plank hardwood floors, a stone fireplace, and a set of French doors to frame the view of a darkening sky and churning lake waters. Haven seriously contemplated starting a fire and crawling beneath the shabby-chic quilts to sleep away the nightmare that was her trip.

With a weary sigh, she dug out a crumpled black pencil skirt and white wrap blouse. She hung them on the bathroom door while she showered, hoping the steam would loosen some of the wrinkles.

After her shower, she did a quick blow-dry of her hair, then put on a slapdash of makeup and her slightly less rumpled clothes before climbing back behind the wheel of her car to make the return drive to the quaint downtown she'd passed through on her way to the inn.

Darkness had settled over the island and as she neared the heart of Main Street, a tiny breath of wonder slipped between her lips. Decked out for the upcoming holidays, large pine wreaths hung from the vintage streetlamps while strings of golden Christmas lights zigzagged down the street, connecting the lampposts to one another.

She found a parking spot across the street from the lone Irish pub. Snow piled high along the sidewalks, and the freezing fluff and slush seeped over the edges of her heels to soak her nylons as she crossed the street.

A blast of warmth and noise greeted her when she ducked inside, and she drew up at the wall-to-wall bodies packing the pub's interior. Emily had described the post-ceremony gathering as a small family dinner, not the rousing revelry Haven saw before her.

She squeezed between the crush of bodies, winding her way across the dimly lit room to the massive mahogany bar. She peered into the faces of those she passed by, keeping watch for her friend. At the bar, she rose up on her tiptoes and made a more thorough scan of the room.

That's when she saw him.

A dark-haired man seated on a barstool at the opposite end of the bar. He wore a black tuxedo that hugged his broad shoulders and set off his dark coloring. His thick hair, cut short on the sides and longer on top, lay in playful disarray while a shadow clung to his square jawline. Brilliant white teeth flashed in his tanned face when he laughed at something the man next to him said, and Haven experienced a dizzying rush of pure appreciation.

Whoa.

Her breathing hitched a little higher.

The man at his side, also in a tuxedo, shared a likeness, but Haven didn't get the chance to examine their similarities before a form appeared before her, blocking her view of the men.

"What can I get you?"

With a start, she looked up at the bartender, who also wore a tux. His vivid blue eyes glittered in his taut, youthful face, so at odds with the shock of his grayish-white hair.

Suddenly warm, she removed her wool coat. "A white zin, please." She laid her coat atop her purse on the bar.

Against her will, her gaze slipped back to the careless-haired man.

To find him watching her.

Dark eyes of an indeterminate color eased over her face. No traces of humor touched his features, and the intensity of his gaze whipped heat into her cheeks. Blindly, she reached out for... something, and her hand knocked into the wineglass the bartender had set in front of her. The glass teetered and she lurched to steady it with both hands.

The hot guy's puffy mouth curled with a slow, knowing smile.

Haven plucked a bill from her purse and thrust it at the bartender.

He held up his hands. "Drinks are free. Enjoy."

She dropped the cash into a tip jar, snatched up her things, and twisted away from the bar.

With the desperation of a castaway seeking a life raft, she searched the faces in the crowd for Emily. When finally she spotted a flash of bright hair and a bulbous white gown, Haven plunged into the mass of people and fought her way to the booth in the back of the pub.

She didn't allow herself another glimpse of the dark-haired man with the hot gaze.

A sexy groomsman was exactly the kind of chaos Haven did not need.

☙

Jack Nolan wasn't a romantic guy.

Some thought him intense, and he supposed that much was true. His emotions ran high and hot, and he'd learned a long time ago to let his passion guide him.

As a power forward in the National Hockey League, he wore it all on his sleeve, and that passion, along with a tireless work ethic, unwavering discipline, and a borderline insane willingness to put his body in harm's way, had fueled him to a lucrative, decade-long career at the highest level of his profession.

No, Jack didn't have the time or the inclination for romance, but even he grasped what a colossal shitstorm his brother's wedding had become.

Already a hastily thrown-together affair, the sudden emergence of a blizzard on the eve of the nuptials managed to further inconvenience everyone. Meanwhile, the youngest Nolan brother, Leo, who after months of being missing in action, not only bothered to show up in time for the wedding, but proceeded to get drunk and drive his car into a tree. The groom, a local cop, managed to track down their wayward little brother, but in the mayhem, he missed the start of his own wedding by more than an hour.

Things went downhill from there.

Leo passed out in a church pew and provided a serenade of drunken snores throughout the rushed, tension-filled ceremony, and when the family arrived at the eldest brother's pub for a private dinner over an hour past the scheduled time, tired, hungry, and on edge, they found the place packed with people. Island folk, wishing to get a look at the woman who'd finally snagged Jack's popular, outgoing brother Luke.

Now, from his vantage point on a stool at the bar, Jack watched one townsperson after another trap the obviously miserable groom in shallow conversation while the bride retreated to a corner by herself.

"How the hell did he coerce her into marrying him, anyway?" Jack posed his question to his older brothers, Noah and Shea. "She seems smarter than that."

From the barstool beside Jack, Noah slipped him a sidelong look. "I don't think there was all that much coercing involved."

"It's the face, isn't it?" Jack said, referring to Luke's uncommonly good looks. "Damn. I used to be that pretty, before I broke my nose."

Shea, leaning with both elbows propped on the bar top, shook his head. "Was before then. When ye took that puck to yer teeth."

"You got hit in the face with a puck?" Noah's dark-eyed gaze dropped to Jack's mouth. "Your teeth are perfect."

"Are now. It happened five or six years ago."

"When did you break your nose?"

Jack frowned, chasing the memory. "I was playing with the North Stars, so I must've been seventeen or eighteen."

"You must've had a good doctor." Noah examined Jack's face. "I can't even tell you broke it."

"Neal made sure we were taken care of."

"Who's Neal?" Noah sipped his Guinness.

"Neal Thompson," Jack said. "I lived with him and his family when I played in the junior league."

Having moved overseas when Jack was fourteen, Noah hadn't been around when Jack's career in hockey took off after a scout spotted him playing and extended an invitation to him to play for some bigwig's junior league hockey club.

So at fifteen, Jack had moved to Detroit to live with Neal Thompson, a former NHL player and guardian to several kids like Jack, young boys with a natural talent and enough hoped-for potential that they might one day turn into the next hockey star.

"How long did you live with them?" Noah asked.

"Just until I went to State." Jack rolled his shoulders, trying to shake off the uneasy tension that arose with the memories. "Three years, I guess."

At first, Jack had hated being away from his brothers, but his family didn't have money, and with an ex-convict for a father, his future was less than certain. So he moved six hours away, suffered years of homesickness and grueling, ball-busting workouts for a chance to make something of himself. To make the name Nolan mean something more than ex-convict, drunk, or deadbeat.

He'd done it for himself, and for them.

A thoughtful frown puckered Noah's brow. "If Neal oversaw your medical treatments, he was your guardian then?"

Jack inclined his head. "That's right."

Noah's gaze shifted to Shea. "You were okay with that?"

A subtle current passed between the men.

"It was the opportunity of a lifetime." Shea straightened to his full height. "He had a real shot at doing something great, so I convinced Dad to sign over guardianship." After a pause, Shea added, "I'd do it again, if given the choice."

"Judging by the results, it's probably safe to say you made the right decision."

Noah wasn't the only brother who knew so little about Jack's life. As much success as he'd had in his hockey career, there'd been a price, and nowhere was that price more evident than in an awkward conversation with any one of his four brothers.

Ready for a change of topic, Jack scowled at Noah. "What's with you and Luke throwing these pretty redheads in front of me? You know I have a thing for redheads."

With mention of his new wife, Mina, a satisfied smile spread across Noah's face. "Why do I get the feeling that you're not exactly pining for female attention?"

Shea snorted. "Maybe because every available woman here tonight has tried to capture his notice at some point and he hasn't gifted any one of them with his attention?"

Jack gritted his teeth. In the last three hockey seasons, he'd survived a lockout, an injury, months of rehab, a re-injury, more rehab, and at present, an increasingly pesky overreliance on painkillers.

The passing of his thirty-second birthday two months back had only served to remind him that time was not on his side. Hockey required everything he had just to stay competitive, but the sad fact remained that over eighty percent of his peers would retire by the age of thirty-three. Unless he proved to be an exception, going forward, every year would get a little harder. His body would grow a little weaker. A little slower.

It'd already begun. The recovery from his last injury, a minor groin pull, had taken twice as long as he'd expected. Now in his thirties, he was a half step slower than he'd been in his twenties, and his speed would only continue to deteriorate. Injuries would only accelerate the process.

It all added up to one thing: sooner rather than later, he'd cease to be a professional hockey player.

Then what?

He had no answers for that question. All he saw before him was emptiness. A future without passion or the need to push himself and his body beyond the point he ever thought possible. He'd go back to being a regular guy.

One of those Nolan boys. Not the oldest or the youngest, not the genius or the beautiful one. He'd be the one who used to play in the NHL. Or worse, he'd go back to being the idiot brother.

This year, and the next few after, was likely all he had left. If he was going to continue making it in the league and stave off retirement a few more seasons, his singular focus needed to be on hockey.

So instead of prowling the bar, he bared his teeth to Noah. "I don't have time for women right now."

While Shea slipped away to tend to a thirsty partygoer, Noah chuckled.

"You don't have to make time for women," he said through his laughter. "It's a bit like a pit bull taking your balls between her teeth. When it happens, she becomes the single most important thing to you."

But Jack was no longer listening to his brother.

A woman had detached from the swarm of bodies crowding the bar to emerge at the far end. He'd never seen her before, though he wasn't sure how he knew that with so much certainty. He no longer knew most people living on the island, and those he was supposed to know he often didn't recall having met.

But her, he would've remembered. Her long dark hair shimmered with lighter strands of caramel and honey, and her buttery smooth skin glowed in the dim lighting.

As Jack stared, her wide mouth fell slightly ajar and her huge dark eyes fixated on him. She blinked, as though confused or dazed, and the tip of her pink tongue slipped out to take a tiny taste of her full bottom lip.

His balls tightened.

She startled, as if coming to, and her hand knocked into her glass of wine. With goalie-like reflexes, she steadied the wineglass and, snatching up her things, whirled away from him.

Jack's gaze dragged down the length of her body, admiring the way her skirt stretched tight across the generous swells of her hips and her lush, round ass. Long legs and shapely calves pulled him down, down, to the fire engine-red high heels on her feet.

He swallowed hard. He'd never been one to be swayed by a woman's style choices—a naked woman always won out over one clad in a bikini or some silly lingerie—but those shoes screamed "fuck me!" and though he knew he shouldn't, Jack very much wanted to oblige.

Luke appeared at his elbow then, a nasty scowl marring his perfectly formed features. "Have either of you seen my wife?"

Jack pointed to the booth in the back corner of the pub and Luke twisted around. He started forward, only to draw up sharply when Emily spotted the brunette with the hot ass approaching her table and a radiant smile lit up her small face.

The first smile Jack had seen on her that day. Her fucking wedding day.

The air wheezed from Luke's lungs with a low hiss.

"Who is she?" Noah gave voice to the desperate question banging around inside Jack's chest cavity.

Luke gave his head a small shake. "That must be her friend. I forget her name."

The two women embraced before sliding into the booth. Soon they chatted away. Jack had been around his brother's new wife only a couple of times, but he'd never known her to be much of a talker.

By the slightly stunned smile on Luke's face, he suspected her sudden animation was as much a surprise to him as it was to Jack. Luke's smile lingered when he lifted his pint to his lips and sipped his drink.

Just then, someone slapped him on the back. "My man, congratulations."

Luke coughed. "Thank you," he croaked.

The man had a large middle and a receding hairline. "We've been wondering where the hell you been lately. Should've known you were holed up with some female."

While the man ribbed Luke some more, Jack's focus remained riveted by the woman in the red shoes. A frenzied storm made up of lust and need, and a fair bit of curiosity, whipped inside him.

He'd been a pro athlete for ten years, a college star before that, and in that time, he'd seen it all. Hookups and STDs, escorts and prostitutes, groupies and gold-diggers. Domestic abuse and infidelity. Unhappy marriages, unhappy mistresses, and messy breakups, complete with paternity tests and custody battles. He'd heard accusations of every kind, some true, some false, all with the potential to be reputation-destroying, or even career-ending. Each and every scandal had come with a media write-up of all the varied and perverse details, from penis size to kinks and fetishes, and performance issues.

Having watched successful, seemingly intelligent men risk everything they'd fought years to achieve for a blowjob from some skeezy stripper in a seedy back alley, Jack had chosen differently.

He'd yet to meet any one of their women and think she was worth the trouble, let alone the risk to his career.

He wasn't a saint, or a prude, but he was discriminating. Cautious.

Even so, as he watched the unknown woman with Emily, the fire coursing through his veins implored him to throw it all away, all the caution and common sense and restraint he'd ever held on to, for nothing more than the chance to discover her name.

Chapter Three

Haven approached Emily with an apology on her lips. "I'm so sorry I'm late–"

Emily scrambled to her feet and threw her arms around Haven. "It's so good to see y-y-you," she whispered, squeezing tight.

At the fierce desperation in Emily's deep-tissue hug, Haven's heart pinched. All the angst and frustration she'd experienced in the past twenty-four hours melted into an inconsequential puddle on the floor.

She slid into the booth. "I almost gave up. This place is nearly impossible to get to."

Emily sat across from her. "I'm sorry it's b-been so awful for y-y-you."

Haven lifted the wineglass in her hand. "I'm almost recovered from the trauma."

Emily laughed, as Haven had hoped she would.

She leaned forward with a conspiratorial smile. "So tell

me, which one is he?"

A blush touched Emily's cheeks. With a quick scan of the room, she pointed to the bar where another mouthwatering piece of tuxedoed man candy stood beside the hottie with the probing gaze.

Haven's mouth fell slack. "Holy shit, I'm just gonna say it—your husband is freaking hot. Does he have any brothers?" she teased.

Emily held up her hand. "F-Four of them."

A pang struck Haven beneath the breastbone. "Wow, four brothers?" The old wound, scarred and calloused over after so long, hardly hurt anymore. "Are they all as hot as Luke?"

Emily blushed. "Luke stands out, but y-yes, they're all good-looking and w-wildly successful. One's a w-world-famous professor." She craned her neck and rocked forward and back. "He's the one next to Luke. W-We like him. He's smart and funny, and super sweet."

Haven straightened, trying to peer around a cluster of bodies passing by their table at just that moment. She leaned back, and when the path cleared, she caught a glimpse of *him* standing beside Emily's groom.

He was a college professor? The tuxedo skimmed his tall frame, lean except for the wide span of his shoulders. With his imposing size and carelessly tousled hair, his appeal was so much more than the summation of his pleasant features and dark coloring. He had an aura. Edgy and confident. Compelling. And he was smart, too?

Haven licked her lips. He was the total, delectable package.

Too bad she'd given up sleeping with men she met in bars years ago.

She sipped her wine while Emily spoke. "O-one brother quit law to run this p-pub and o-one is a p-p-professional hoc—"

Someone bumped Haven's elbow and wine sloshed

over the rim of her glass onto her skirt. She bristled, but froze at the expression that came over Emily's face when a woman with bottle-blonde hair dropped into the booth beside her.

"So, Emma." The woman snickered. "Have you met my friend Kate?"

Emily's features morphed from wary to panic-stricken.

Kate, a leggy blonde with large breasts and dewy skin, bore a striking resemblance to a Victoria's Secret catalog model, even down to her wide-set, cornflower-blue eyes.

Which blazed with envy as she gazed at Emily.

Kate sank into the booth next to Haven. "Congratulations." The word held a teardrop of heartbreak in it. "I didn't know you and Luke were even dating."

Emily's throat worked. "Oh, w-well, uh... w-w-we... uh...."

Were these women the reason for the desperation in Emily's hug? Was she so in need of a friend, any friend, that she'd even take one as pathetic as Haven?

"It was a bit of a whirlwind romance. Love at first sight." The words spilled out of Haven. "I mean, what's not to love, am I right, *Emily*?" She couldn't resist hanging the heavy emphasis on her friend's name.

A Cheshire cat smile curled Bottle-Blonde's lips, and she raised her pint. "How about a toast? To love at first sight?"

Haven bit down ruthlessly on her tongue. This was Emily's wedding day. She would not ruin it by informing one of the guests that she was being a bitch. She would keep her mouth shut no matter what, because she didn't let her passions rule her anymore.

With the look of someone about to swallow poison, Emily lifted her glass.

Blondie squinted at the champagne flute in Emily's

trembling hand. "Wait, is that water? Why are you drinking water at your wedding reception?"

Riotous color rushed into Emily's cheeks.

Haven winced with Emily's pained expression.

Just as Blondie's scandalized gasp pierced the air. "*Oh. My. God.* Are you pregnant?"

The color drained from Emily's face, her honest features confirming the accusation. Her mouth moved wordlessly and her toffee-brown eyes filled with watery panic.

Haven's heart wrenched for her friend.

The bitch chortled. "So *that's* why he married you."

❦

Jack couldn't pull his gaze off the woman. Thus, he watched the tension arise between the quartet, and his sister-in-law's smile disappear with it. When the peachy color drained from her face, an eerie calmness came over her friend whose name he didn't yet know. The dark-haired beauty remained stock-still in the booth, like a jungle cat poised to pounce on her unsuspecting prey.

Jack glanced over at Luke, who remained surrounded by people, his line of sight to his wife blocked.

Noah and Shea, engaged in a robust debate about the proper mechanics involved in pouring a pint of Guinness, didn't seem to notice their sister-in-law's growing misery.

Jack pushed a heavy sigh through his lips. He wasn't a hero.

Not a romantic and not a hero.

Still, he had a reputation in the NHL as an enforcer, and if his sister-in-law needed someone to step in and deliver a hit for her, Jack was her man.

He slid off the barstool, and as he picked his way

across the crowded barroom, someone called out his name in friendly greeting. He turned his head toward the sound—

A sharp cry rang out. His head snapped around in the direction of Emily's booth as chaos erupted.

The overprocessed blonde lunged across the table and pounced on Jack's woman, who deftly wriggled out from under the assault.

Then it was all thrashing hair and long, writhing limbs. Curvy body parts bounced and swayed in glorious, carnal combat. The tight skirt strained over his woman's luscious ass, which clenched and jiggled with her epic struggle.

Gaaawdddaaamn.

With a piercing shriek and the devil's scowl, the blonde relaunched herself and Jack snapped out of his lust-filled stupor. He charged forward and hooked his arm around his woman's waist, hauling her back from the fray.

She was fierce and fiery in his arms.

"Holy shit." Jack gasped for air. "I think that's the hottest thing I've ever seen."

The woman twisted in his arms, craning her neck to look up at him. A gasp burst from her. Her ample breasts, which rested atop his forearm, rose and fell with her labored breathing as she gazed up at him with huge, dark eyes.

"I might say the same thing," she said, her cheeks flushed pink with exertion.

If he had been the romantic type, he might've fallen in love with her then and there.

His hold on her tightened. "I don't believe we've met. Hi, I'm Jack."

"Hi, Jack. I'm Haven."

Haven. Hot name to go along with that hot ass.

"You *bitch.*" The blonde seethed. "She threw her drink

at me."

Haven blinked her wide, doe eyes. "I'm so sorry, I don't know what happened. The glass slipped right out my hand."

The blonde coiled with tension, and secretly, Jack prayed that she would reengage.

Instead, she pressed a palm to her cheek and, with a feeble huff, stalked away.

Haven peeked up at him from beneath the long sweep of her eyelashes. She tipped her chin in the direction her vanquished foe had fled. "Sorry, but she was mean to my friend."

Jack's gaze swept over Emily, whose misery had turned to stunned disbelief as she openly gaped at them.

"Your friend is my new sister-in-law," he said. "So I thank you."

Haven's laugh came out on a puff of air. "Are you single, Jack?"

Without releasing his hold on her, he reached up and brushed a strand of hair out of her eyes. "As a matter of fact, I am, Haven." His fingertips stroked her silky-soft skin and a shock of electricity shot through him.

Her breath caught. "Are you going to let me go, Jack?" Her voice dropped to a husky whisper that squeezed his balls.

His gaze fastened on her mouth. "No, I don't think I will."

He might hold on forever.

"Emily, where are you?" a voice boomed over the pub's sound system.

Jack looked up as Emily turned toward the front of the pub. His gaze followed the path hers had taken, over the wall of the crowd to Luke, standing on the small stage, a guitar strapped to his body.

"C'mon up here, sweetheart." Luke teased the bars of a song on his instrument. "Let's show these jackasses how it's done."

The color leached from Emily's face. She swayed slightly, but stiffened and remained upright.

Jack's hold on Haven relaxed, though he couldn't quite bring himself to let her go completely.

"Em, are you okay?" Haven asked.

Emily didn't respond, nor did she move. She stayed rooted to the spot, motionless and pale as a porcelain statue. One by one, people turned to stare at her, and with each set of eyeballs that landed on her, Jack could feel the panic mounting within her.

She was going to bolt, and if he were perfectly honest, Jack wasn't certain his brother would have a wife when it was all said and done.

He dropped his arm, though the other lingered loosely around Haven's waist. He leaned closer to Emily, close enough that she might steal a bit of his strength.

"What do you say, Em?" He forced a hitch of playfulness into his tone. "One of us should go up there and kick his ass, don't you think?"

A startled laugh—or was it a sob?—burst from her. Toffee-brown eyes clamped onto his face.

His mouth pushed up at one corner. "Is it going to be you or me?"

Her brows pulled together with the faintest hint of a determined scowl. She might've moved, or did he only imagine it?

Then—there, she did it again. She took one tiny, infinitesimal fraction of a step forward.

Then another.

Suddenly, Luke appeared before her, his hand outstretched. She hesitated, and her pain-filled gaze locked onto her husband's face.

Luke's throat worked, and then, finally, she placed her hand in his. As Luke pulled Emily through the buzzing crowd toward the stage, Jack heaved a relieved sigh.

He looked down to find Haven still nestled against his body, gazing up at him with shimmering brown eyes. Something soft and slippery danced in their warm depths. Not lust or attraction—well, not solely. Gratitude? Admiration?

Whatever it was, his body hummed with appreciation of it. Like the lit fuse of a firecracker, it sizzled through his veins with a delicious crackle. At any moment, it might blow.

He welcomed the destruction.

C3

His eyes were the most unusual color. Neither green nor gold, the color vacillated between the rich jewel tones. They ensnared her.

As she stared into their kaleidoscope centers, her body pressed against the length of his long, well-muscled frame. With his arm still wrapped around her waist, his other hand slid down her arm to the fine bones of her wrist, where he pressed the tips of his fingers to her throbbing pulse point.

He entwined his fingers with hers as overhead the chords of a melodious ballad began to play. Neither Jack nor Haven spoke, just gazed into each other's eyes as they began to sway gently with the music. Jack's palm smoothed in tight, tiny circles on her lower back as Emily's sultry, fragile vocals intermingled with the strong, clear tone of Luke's voice.

Together, they sang. A love song, or a lover's lament, Haven didn't know. The words didn't matter. Their song poured over and around her and Jack, locking them together inside a solitary sphere. An insulated shelter that hummed with their awareness of one another.

Her gaze devoured the interesting angles and fine

contours of his features, and his crisp, spicy scent soothed her senses as they swayed and yet barely moved to the music. His hands on her body stoked the flicker of heat rising inside her. Heat and something else.

Something more.

Something calming, comforting.

Her heart swelled with the chorus. His head bent low, and her pulse skittered.

Then his mouth met hers in a kiss. Nothing sloppy or out of control, just the barest brush of fire.

At the gentle friction of his lips against hers, a delicious tension began to build low in her belly. Her tongue slipped out to take a tiny lick of his lower lip and a dizzying rush swooped through her.

He tasted like freedom.

She clutched at the lapel of his tuxedo and his hands came up to cup the sides of her face. When he broke the kiss, he didn't move his hands.

"Haven...." He swallowed hard.

"I know." She felt it, too, this thing zinging between them.

The crowd sent up a wild cheer and Haven jolted, having forgotten the others. Jack's arm slipped protectively around her waist.

A confused pucker crinkled the spot between his brows. "I can't explain it, but I can't bring myself to let you go. Haven."

The sound of her name on his lips sent a delicious shiver shuddering through her. "I don't want you to let me go, Jack."

A sensuous light flickered in his eyes. "What are we to do, then?"

"Keep holding on, I guess."

His arms tightened around her as another song began to play. "I can do that."

She couldn't catch her breath as he gently rocked her

in time to the music. The haze of instant, all-consuming lust enveloped her and she got lost in studying his face. In the dim lighting, she didn't at first notice the small scar above his left eye, or the one catching the corner of his puffy bottom lip.

Her lust-addled mind grappled with the information. Had he been a fighter as a child? Small and picked on? He did have four brothers, after all.

Suddenly, she wanted to know everything about him.

Her fingers danced over the warm skin at the back of his neck and toyed with his soft hair. "Are you close to your brothers?"

He seemed surprised by her question at first, but then a frown turned down the corners of his mouth. "No, actually. Not as close as I'd like." A frisson of vulnerability rippled over his features. "I travel a lot for work and don't see them often."

A college professor traveled a lot? Honestly, she knew little about the job. She'd started to ask him when his hand shifted from the dip of her waist to the curve her hip.

Her thoughts scattered. There was nothing scandalous about his touch, but she sensed he hovered at the edge, his desire and restraint a potent mix that caused her heart to beat at a frantic pace.

A body bumped into her from behind. With a slight turn, Jack angled his big body around her, protecting her like a shield.

"Would you like a drink?" He spoke low next to her ear.

She shook her head. She didn't want anything that involved leaving the security of his arms, and she didn't want a single drop of alcohol to dull or alter the full force of her experience inside his embrace.

She lifted her chin and looked into his face. "I want...."

He tilted his head. "What is it? What do you want?"

"I want you... and I...."

The gold light in his eyes flared.

"I want us...."

His grip on her hip tightened. "Say more." He cleared his throat. "Please."

"We're both single, and sober." She didn't understand why her voice trembled. "If we wanted to... get closer, just for tonight, is there any reason we shouldn't?"

His Adam's apple bobbed. "Are we talking about a hookup?"

Haven blushed. She never blushed. Maybe it was the heat swirling in his kaleidoscope eyes. Or the way he thought to protect her, and Emily. Or maybe her heart had fixated on him the moment she glimpsed his obvious longing to be closer to his brothers.

He had a good heart, she was certain of it, and she wanted to reach out and touch it. To experience its softness and warmth, for a time. She wanted to recall what it felt like to love and live, and take her pleasure in the heat and strength of a man like him. Something she hadn't allowed herself to do in a very long time.

"Y-yes. A hookup. One night, no regrets."

A cool shadow chased across his face. "I don't sleep with women I've just met."

Haven flinched. Neither did she sleep with men she'd only just met. Not anymore.

There was a time in her life, when she was lost and lonely and more than a little troubled, that she'd sought sex with unfamiliar men to fill the hole near her heart, but those days were far behind her.

She enjoyed sex. Good sex, that was. Sex with those men, men she didn't know and who didn't care that they didn't know her, wasn't good sex. Not because they were strange to her, but because she'd had sex with them for all the wrong reasons. Reasons that had too little to do with their merits and everything to do with her lack of self-worth.

Sex, she enjoyed. *That* sex, she regretted. Regretted that she'd given them everything. Her respect. Her vulnerability. Her heart. She gave it all away, though they didn't deserve any of it.

Haven didn't think she'd regret sex with Jack, and if the rioting in her veins was any indication, she'd definitely enjoy it, but the last thing she wanted was for *him* to have regrets about *her*.

Through the heat of mortification on her cheeks, she managed a weak smile. "I understand. I didn't mean to—"

His hand flattened on her hip, splaying to cover the upper swell of her bottom with possessive intent. He pulled her body tight against his. "But somehow, the rules don't apply to you."

Chapter Four

The wild fluttering beneath her breastbone dropped to her stomach even as her runaway thoughts sputtered to a stop.

"You have rules?"

One of his broad shoulders lifted beneath her hand. "More like guidelines, but I prefer to know a woman before I sleep with her."

"You don't know me."

He peered into her eyes. "Don't I?"

His words pierced her, setting off a torrent of tiny tremors. "Maybe we need a few new rules. Just for us. Just for tonight."

"What did you have in mind?"

"We'll use protection."

"Of course," he said easily.

"We'll spend one night together." Fighting the pull of his poignant gaze, she forced out her next words.

"Tomorrow, we walk away."

It was the perfect compromise, even if her heart wanted to rebel. Especially if. She sensed she was skating into dangerous territory with him, and a hookup didn't violate her silly rules. There'd be no chance of losing her heart to him, not in one night. Nor could there be discussions about a future that didn't exist for them.

He gave his head a small shake. "No." His palm smoothed over her back, which had the effect of quieting the protest that built in her throat. "Something tells me one night with you won't be enough."

"I won't commit to anything long-term." The words launched from her. "I can't."

He eyed her closely. "I'm here for a few days. Can you give us two or three nights, or is that too long-term for you?"

A shaky breath of relief shuddered through her.

"You're really serious about this." His tone, while gentle, held a hint of amusement. "I think I might be offended."

"Don't take it personally." She managed a self-deprecating smile. "I can't commit to anything. Not a job or a hometown. Not even a brand of shampoo."

His head dipped, nuzzling close to her ear. He inhaled deeply. "I like this one."

Gooseflesh prickled over her skin.

"Any other rules?" His lips brushed the sensitive spot beneath her earlobe.

Of its own will, her head dropped to one side, giving him better access. "No slapping or hair pulling."

He stiffened.

The words surprised her, too, and her spine stiffened.

Dammit. The neck kissing threw her off.

She dragged her gaze up from the strong column of his neck to his face. "I don't really like rough sex. I had a bad experience once."

His expression darkened and his hold on her tightened, more protective than sexual. "I'm sorry."

"It was a long time ago." His touch, unbearably gentle, soothed her. "And it doesn't have anything to do with us now. Does it?"

He appeared as though he might argue, but finally he shook his head. "No."

"Oh, and no more neck kisses."

His mouth quirked with a dry smile. "How specific."

"I can't think straight when someone's kissing my neck."

"That's the point. You shouldn't be thinking at all."

She frowned, puzzling over his words. "What about you? Anything you don't want me to do?"

Penetrating green-gold eyes captured hers. "I don't want you to do a single thing you don't want to do or that makes you uncomfortable. At all. I think if we follow that one rule, we'll do just fine together."

A tangle of emotions rushed over her. Relief mingled with hunger, and something else that made her chest ache with the fullness of it all. She'd never spoken about the painful parts of her past with a guy before, and she didn't know why she'd told Jack now. Except she trusted him. She felt safe with him.

Safe enough to go somewhere secluded with him.

The liquid warmth simmering low in her belly spiked with need. She should've tried the honesty bit sooner. It was a heady rush, and thoroughly arousing.

"Where are you staying?" The low timbre of his voice sloped through her.

"At Emily's inn." She hesitated, but only briefly. "But we can go to your place, if you want."

He studied her closely. "I think we should go to the inn." His hand at the small of her back, he turned and motioned her ahead of him as they left the dance floor.

She took a step just as a waitress bustled through the

crowded space carrying a tray filled with drinks. The waitress stumbled and lurched. The tray teetered. Jack's hand shot out and caught her by the elbow before she went down, but not before the tray dipped and the cocktails slid to the edge where they hovered a moment before toppling over. Onto Jack.

Pink and red liquid soaked through his white shirt.

A strangled screech wrenched from the waitress. "Omigod, I'm soooo sorry." She pitched forward with a towel, shoving it into his chest. "I'm so so so sorry."

"It's okay." Jack held his hands out at his sides while she mauled him with the towel. "Nicole, it's okay."

"I can't believe I did that." Her wide eyes filled with tears and her voice cracked as she repeated, "I can't believe I did that."

At the first tear to leak down her cheek, Jack plucked the towel from her grip, placed both of his hands on her shoulders, and guided her to a nearby table.

When she plopped down in a chair, he glanced at Haven. "Will you sit with her for a minute?"

"Sure." Haven approached the table as Jack plunged into the crowd.

Nicole's dark eyes latched on to Haven. "Do you think he's going to tell his brother?"

"I don't—"

"I can't lose this job." Nicole twisted in the chair, trying to catch a glimpse of Jack.

"He won't get you fired. I promise." She didn't know how she knew that, but she did.

Nicole wilted. "I can't believe I dumped that tray on him."

Haven had done it. Hadn't everyone who'd ever worked in a busy bar? At some point, the mix of dim lighting and drunk people caused spills to happen. It was an occupational hazard.

Nicole rubbed her forehead. "I'm just so tired. This is

supposed to be my night off. My son's at home sick with a cold and the babysitter keeps calling."

Jack reappeared, his slow smile warming Haven from the inside out. He set a soda and two slices of cheese pizza on the table in front of Nicole.

"Here we go. Why don't you eat and head home." He shot Haven a look of apology. "We'll finish up."

Nicole stared at the pizza. "You brought this for me?"

"Shea tells me you aren't even supposed to be working tonight." Jack shook off his tuxedo coat. "That you just came in to help him out when the whole town surprised us."

Haven's heart swelled. She was right about Jack. His concern for the waitress that'd dumped a tray of drinks on him proved it.

Nicole lifted the soda to her lips and sucked down a greedy gulp. "I need the hours. Shea's doing me a favor letting me work overtime."

"Then we're even." He removed his tie and unfastened the top button of his dress shirt. "If you leave now, you might be able to say good night to Brandon."

Haven repressed a dreamy sigh. This man, this moment, would never happen again. He was a once-in-a-lifetime opportunity. And there was no way she was going to let him slip away.

Nicole started to stand. "Let me help."

"Honestly, it's not necessary." He pulled the wet dress shirt away from his body and tossed it over the back of the chair with his coat. A black tribal tattoo danced up one forearm and disappeared under the sleeve of his white undershirt, though a sliver of the black ink peeked out from under the pristine white neckband to lick the side of his neck. "We're about to shut it down. The bride and groom have disappeared and the rest of us are ready to call it a night. You go home. We got this."

At his inclusion of Haven in his family "we," her heart

fluttered.

A piece of pizza poised before her, Nicole smiled. "Thanks, Jack." She bit into the gooey pie.

When Haven pushed to her feet, Jack's gaze found hers as he rounded the table.

He sidled close. "I'm so sorry about this. Give me a half hour or so, and then we can get out of here."

A delicious shiver chased up her spine at the seductive drop in his tone.

"It's okay." She surveyed the crowd. "I'll start here, if you want to take the tables in the back?"

"I can't ask you to help. You're a guest."

An unfamiliar flash of insecurity struck her, but she ignored it and told him the truth. "I've worked in a bar for the last ten years. I was a waitress for three years before I started bartending. I can help you."

She watched him closely, curious to see if a college professor would suddenly experience a change of heart about hooking up with a bartender/waitress.

His soft smile caught her by surprise. "Thank you." Then he tossed her a dry towel and backed away. "Let everyone know its last call."

They set off in opposite directions to work their tables and a half hour later the crowd had thinned by half. A pretty redhead Jack called Mina jumped in to help clear tables while Noah and Shea worked away in the back rooms, closing down the bar and the kitchen.

At one of the larger tables, Haven loaded a tub with dirty dishes when Jack appeared close at her side.

Once, a man of his size would've scared her, but somehow Jack, in all his maleness and vitality, didn't. Maybe it was because he was a college professor, or because she'd told him something of her past and he'd made her a promise.

"This should do it." His chest muscles rippled beneath his T-shirt as he lifted the basin she'd filled. "Let me go wash these, and then we can go."

His potent gaze tangled with hers and her heart hammered as though she stood at the cliff's edge staring down the impossible drop-off. Was she really going to go through with it?

Everything in her—all that she was and all that she was not—begged her to go anywhere with him, the desire so strong it felt necessary. Inevitable. She couldn't walk away, not before seizing this moment with him.

Outside, the storm had pushed on and brilliant stars poked through the black canvas of night sky. Having lived in big cities all her life, she'd never seen so many stars. Jack caught her staring up at them, her mouth slack. The smile in his eyes possessed a sensual fire, and as she gazed back at him, she began to wonder if this island was enchanted by some special magic.

At a black car, he grabbed a duffel bag from the backseat and then they crossed the snow-covered street together to pile into Haven's rental car. Though the road conditions, made difficult by the storm, required all her focus, in the cramped sedan her acute awareness of him heightened. His scent, his solid warmth. The way he watched her from behind hooded eyes.

By the time they reached the inn, her nerves were strung tight and her body hummed with need.

The house-turned-bed-and-breakfast was quiet and dimly lit when they entered through the front door. Upstairs, she led Jack to her bedroom, closing the door softly behind them. She'd left on the table lamp, and its faint glow cast a cozy warmth over the room.

She removed her coat and a chill chased through her. Jack crossed to the fireplace and flipped the switch on the wall next to the mantle. A soft flame flickered to life in the stone enclosure.

In the quiet, they stood on opposite sides of the room and gazed at one another in the shimmer of firelight for a time.

"Haven."

That was all he said. Only her name.

The aching want in her unfurled.

With trembling hands, she reached for the knot at her side where her wrap blouse tied. When she finally managed to pull the fabric free, she let the shirt slide off her shoulders and fall to the floor.

The column of Jack's throat worked when he swallowed.

She hooked her fingers into the waistband of her skirt and inched the stretchy fabric down over her hips. Soon, she stood before him in only her bra and panties.

His hungry gaze devoured her.

A hitch of insecurity struck her with a sharp lash. She ate too much, drank too much, and the leanness of her youth had faded in recent years.

But she saw no judgment or disappointment in his questing gaze. Indeed, the way he looked at her, like a starving man who'd spotted a wedge of chocolate cake, accelerated the rhythm of her heart into a frenzied pulse.

Reaching behind her, she unhooked her bra and let the garment fall away from her body.

His appreciative gaze latched on to her breasts. They were large and for the most part a nuisance, but men sure seemed to like them. A lot.

He removed his tuxedo jacket and laid it on the accent chair in the corner of the room. Then he yanked his white undershirt over his head. Her breath caught.

The tribal tattoo on his forearm unfurled up his arm, over his bicep and shoulder to lick the side of his neck. Even with his clothes on, she'd been able to tell he was fit, but unexpected muscle definition cut across the plane of his abdomen and full, round pecs.

This guy was a college professor? If her professors had been half as glorious, she never would've left school.

She went to him and, standing before him, smoothed her hands over his muscled torso. He took her face in his hands and bent his head low to take her mouth in a soft, lingering kiss.

Her fingers found the waistband of his pants and together they worked the fastening.

She slid the tuxedo pants away from his body and gazed down at him. Good Lord, the man was simply glorious. The cotton fabric of his underwear struggled to contain his bulge and his big, powerful thighs.

She licked her lips. Seriously, he made tight white boxer briefs look sexy as hell.

He touched her chin and nudged her face up. "You okay?"

She nodded, unable to form words just then, her thoughts fracturing the moment she caught sight of his delicious bulge.

Her hand slipped down to find his, and she pulled him with her as she backed up to the bed. Sitting on the edge of the mattress, she pulled him closer. While he stood before her, she eased his boxers down over his hips and thighs.

His heavy erection bobbed free.

A groan of longing reverberated in the back of her throat. He was big. Possibly the biggest she'd ever been with. She wanted to taste him—and did. A tiny, tentative lick with the tip of her tongue.

His sharp intake of breath sent a thrill zinging through her, but then he pulled back.

His hand slipped to her nape. "Thank you, but I want this to last longer than the next two minutes."

She laughed.

Had she ever laughed while naked with a man?

At one time, she knew a thousand ways to please a man, and she tried to recall some of them then, for she very much wanted to please this man.

On the bed, she twisted around and, with a glance over her shoulder, placed her knee on the mattress.

His hungry gaze latched on to her bottom. He drew the waistband of her panties down over her hips. Her heart racing, she arched her back and his palms smoothed over her naked globes.

A growl sounded in the back of his throat and his hardness pressed between her legs. He wrapped his solid warmth around her and hooked an arm around her ribcage, holding her tight against him while the flat of his other hand smoothed over her abdomen, and lower.

With feathery strokes, his fingers brushed along her slit. While he worked her body, low, incoherent sounds piled in her throat. She grew lost in the feel and smell of him wrapped around her, and in the pulsating sensation at her core.

His husky voice, thick with want and need, whispered something near her ear. Then she felt his hands between their bodies, sliding a condom into place.

It brought her back to her senses.

She rolled onto her back and parted her legs before him. The unique light in his eyes flared. He gazed down at her while his erection stood proud against his abdomen and his chest rose and fell with his breathing.

The throbbing between her thighs threatened to pull her behind the veil of lust once more, so she arranged her features into a once well-practiced face. Her lips slightly parted, her eyelids heavy, she traced tiny circles on her stomach, above her mound, with one tantalizing finger.

Jack's hand smoothed up the length of her thigh and his clever fingers teased at her opening. He pushed a finger inside her and stroked her folds in a slow, smooth rhythm. With his lashes half-lowered, his hungry gaze riveted to the place where he worked her body, his expression intent and penetrating.

The world began to recede beyond the haze of her arousal and she struggled to pull herself back from the fog. She arched her back so that her breasts jutted upward to appear fuller, perkier, when she wrapped her legs around his waist.

He lowered himself over her and the tip of his penis nudged at her entrance. She tilted her hips to take him more fully. He went deeper and held, waiting for her body to yield to him by slow degrees.

Then he started to pump. A startled gasp of pleasure tore from her, which she concealed with a lusty moan. The excruciating friction drove her to the brink, so she reached between their bodies to cup his balls. She moaned his name and guided him toward release with her expertise.

But he refused to travel too far without her.

He cupped her breast and brushed the pad of his thumb across the sensitive bud. Then his tongue followed with a slow, feathery lick. A jolt of electricity arced from her heart to her core.

She didn't know what was happening to her, but she pulled her legs open wide until her muscles ached, her body desperate to give him the access he wanted.

He slid in and out of her with increasing urgency, and she reached up to brush a lock of his dark hair off his forehead. Her chest ached, but she didn't care. This guy was worth the pain.

With every thrust, tremors rippled through her thighs and groin. The exquisite tension built until the luscious slide of sensation between her legs crested with pure, explosive pleasure. She buried her face in the crook of his neck and clung to him while the waves crashed over her.

"Sweet Jesus," he muttered into the side of her neck. Then, shoving deep and holding there, he roared out her name and came.

They remained joined while their labored breathing

slowed, until finally Jack lifted his head and peered down into her face.

Satiated and powerless, an unguarded smile teased its way to her lips.

"Thank you." He dropped a soft kiss on her forehead. "But next time, we do it for real."

Chapter Five

She sputtered, "Wh-what do you mean?"

"Don't get me wrong. That was amazing. You are amazing." He pressed his mouth to her shoulder, over the spot where her clavicle had been broken. "But that wasn't real sex."

He left her body, and she shuddered at the sensation of loss. Rolling off her, he pushed up off the bed.

She thrashed to a sitting position. "You thought that wasn't real sex?"

He disappeared into the bathroom a moment and then reemerged to collect his underwear from the floor at the end of the bed.

The long shaft of his manhood still plump, he tugged his boxer briefs over his hips. "That was porn sex. It looked great, it felt fucking fantastic, but it's not real sex."

He'd stunned her to speechlessness. She hadn't been speechless since she was a troubled teenager craving attention.

"I-I-I don't understand you." With the plaintive ring in her voice, she even sounded like that troubled teenager.

His gaze clamped on her face, he moved to the edge of the bed and wrapped his hand around her ankle.

"Real sex is out of control." His thumb traced circles around her anklebone. "It's losing your mind and forgetting about everything that doesn't serve the purpose of getting you off." Lifting her leg, he sat on the bed. "It's total surrender. To me." He kissed the bottom of her foot. Then his hand on her knee gently eased her legs apart. "To your body." He kissed the soft skin on the inside of her thigh. "To us."

Positioning himself between her thighs, his glittering gaze found hers over the soft swell of her stomach. "I want to have real sex with you, Haven. The porn sex only convinced me of that. I want more. I want all of you."

She swallowed audibly. "But, I-I-I told you, I can't give you... all of me."

"I don't want your forever, sweetheart. I want your body, and I want it without conditions or qualifiers."

Protests jammed in her throat.

"I only want your pleasure." He dipped his head and took a tiny taste of her.

With his slow lick, a dizzying rush sloped through her. She dropped back against the pillows, opening her legs wide to accommodate his broad shoulders.

His hands slipped beneath her bottom and he lifted her. Her sensitive flesh quivered while his hot mouth tasted her with the most delicious nibbles and nudges.

Sensation flooded her and her hips began to move. He gripped her waist and his tongue coaxed a throaty moan from her. His hands moved to the inside of her thighs, where his fingers forged a path along her soft skin upwards to her center. The slide of one finger stroking inside her sent her pulse pounding at a painful gallop.

Somehow, his mouth, his touch, managed to be both gentle and possessive at once.

Her moans turned greedy and she turned her head into the pillow to muffle them while her hips rocked against him, chasing the height of ecstasy his mouth pledged.

Her world narrowed to the feel of him between her legs. The soft scrape of his stubble against her skin. The slow lick of his tongue. Her hot, wet heat.

With her orgasm, her thoughts fragmented, scattering to the far corners of her mind.

All thoughts, that was, except one.

He didn't want real sex, whatever the hell that was.

He wanted her soul.

☙

The mix of Haven and firelight worked to cast a spell over him. He'd never felt so relaxed, so peaceful.

So horny after sex.

The hours melted into one another, night into day and back to night, and his need for her never lessened. His want of her never slackened, but only grew sharper and more frenzied.

He straddled her legs and his hands glided over her bare back, rubbing the muscles.

Her soft groan brimmed with sweet agony and his cock jumped at the sound.

He loved her sounds. The sultry mews and husky moans. With each new squeak and sigh he coaxed from her, he wanted more. More of her body, and of her ravenous hunger. He wanted to touch every part of her. Know everything about her.

"How do you know Emily?"

Lulled by his kneading touch, she took a moment to

answer. "We were college roommates."

He loved her voice. Throaty, with a seductive rasp.

"What college did you go to?"

"Arizona."

Using the heels of his palms, he kneaded the large muscles of her back. "What did you study?"

"Business and law."

"Uh-oh. You didn't tell me you're a smart girl. I don't think this is going to work out between us after all."

"I dropped out before I got either degree. That's kind of my thing. I can't commit to seeing anything through to the end."

He kissed her shoulder. "You're pretty good at seeing climax through to the end."

Her husky laugh grabbed him by the balls.

"I think Emily was the only girl at that university who was nice to me."

His hands massaged the upper swells of her luscious, perfectly round ass. "The others were jealous."

A derisive snort escaped her. "No. I was trailer park trash. Totally beneath them."

Not liking her depiction, a frown pulled at his features. She misunderstood his silence.

"Don't worry. I left the trailer park years ago."

"That's not what I was thinking."

He worked her muscles in silence for a time.

"What were you thinking?" she finally asked.

"I was thinking how much we have in common."

"You grew up in a trailer park?"

"I grew up in a shitty house in the shitty part of town with an ex-con for a dad."

Rising up on her elbows, she looked at him over her shoulder. Judging the truthfulness of his words, he gathered. Then, beneath him, she rolled onto her back.

Reaching up, she brushed a lock of his hair off his forehead.

Her concern was sweet, but unnecessary. His dad had spent three years in prison before he was released and returned to their lives. Not long after that, Jack moved away to focus on his future playing hockey.

He'd escaped the taint of Daniel Nolan, and now he was nothing like his idiot, loser dad.

Jack was driven, disciplined. He'd taken a God-given talent and turned it into a lucrative career, and once he lifted the Stanley Cup above his head, he'd relish the ultimate proof that he was nothing like his piece-of-shit old man. No one could call him a loser then.

He'd have the rest of his life after hockey to work on the idiot part.

Under him, Haven gazed up at him with huge brown eyes. Naked and fully exposed to him.

His starving gaze drank up every inch of her body. He took his time, savoring the sight of her voluptuous flesh. Cataloguing every curve and dip. Her body was the most incredible he'd ever touched. Soft and feminine, lush, with ample breasts and hips. So fucking lush.

He'd grown tired of twig limbs and boy hips. Weary of floatation devices passed off as breasts. He'd been starving for something more. Someone exactly like Haven. There was nothing fake about her fleshy tits, all warm and jiggly, or the large, dusky pink areolas surrounding her nipples. Or the dark fuzz between her thighs.

The hollow of her neck filled with soft shadows.

His fingers went searching. "You broke your collarbone."

"Hmm. How did you know?"

He traced the clavicle from her neck to her right shoulder. "I can see it didn't heal evenly. What happened?"

In the firelight, her dark eyes shimmered. "I was in a car accident. The seat belt broke the bone."

His elbows on either side of her head, he brushed a strand of her hair off her forehead. "How old were you?"

"Sixteen."

He dropped a kiss to the spot where the bone hadn't fused properly.

Her fingers threaded through his hair. "It was a long time ago," she whispered.

Lifting his head, he peered into her dark and rather delicate oval face. "You had a hard time of it, a long time ago."

When she wriggled under him, he shifted to allow her to lift her knees. Her legs fell open around his naked hips.

His cock settled tight against her hot heat, pulling a soft groan from him. "So tell me, why don't you do commitment?"

"Probably the same reason you don't." She wiggled under him.

His hand found the dip at her waist. He splayed his fingers wide and smoothed his palm up her side. "Because you've given, and continue to give, everything you have to your career and there's no room in your life for anything else?"

A smile teased her wide mouth. "Okay, maybe we have different reasons."

His thumb brushed the impossibly soft skin on the underside of her breast. "Like what?"

"Like, it's just easier that way."

He toyed with the hair at her temples. "What's easier?"

She swallowed, and one shoulder lifted in a half shrug. "It's easier not to fall in love, and if you're not in love, it doesn't hurt so much when they... leave."

At the quiet vulnerability in her voice, his heart gave a little pinch.

"Sounds like a great plan," he said. "How's it working out for you?"

She laughed.

God, she had a great laugh.

"Right this moment, it's working out great."

She waggled her hips in a way that caused his hard shaft to rub tighter against her core.

Nuzzling her ear, he reached over her head and snagged a packet off the night table. Then he pushed to his knees and rolled the condom into place.

She watched him, and when her pink tongue came out to lick her bottom lip, he almost blew it, right then and there. Then she lifted her knees and showed him her heart.

Her moist curls glistened above her firm, succulent lips. His erection straining painfully, he reached for her, dipping his fingers into the pooling honey at her opening.

He forced himself to take it slow. He wanted to savor her. Linger over her decadent curves. Explore all the ways her body found pleasure. Make sure there was no room in her mind for thinking or worrying. Only feeling.

He would fuck her senseless.

If they were to have only this night plus one more together, the memories needed to last him a lifetime.

He lowered himself over her and took his time licking and tasting. He suckled the lush buds of her nipples, pebbled with her arousal. His teasing drew soft whimpers and gasps of pleasure from her, and whipped the heat and tension in him into a feverish compulsion. For more. For everything. For all of her.

His heart beat in time to the throbbing between his legs when he held her hips and pushed inside of her. A groan tore from him as her body swallowed him. He waited until her tightness could take more and then pushed further.

"Jack." Desperation and longing filled her voice. "Please."

He drove home.

Home.

She cried out his name and clawed at him. Her eagerness demolished his last restraint and he slid in and out of her hot heat with desperate, frenzied plunges. Her breasts bounced with his pounding thrusts, and the reckless moans in the back of her throat tightened his balls and spurred him on faster, harder.

In all his life, he'd never lived in one place long enough to grow an attachment, but gazing into her eyes while he thrust fully, finally, inside her, he found his home.

He came in a shattering torrent as he cried out. Tremors racked his body and he ground against her sensitive clit so that her body gripped his with the unmistakable spasms of her climax.

He stayed inside her afterwards, his mouth and hands resuming their exploration of the lush peaks and valleys of her body.

It was true that he hadn't made a habit of picking up strange women in bars, or at weddings or any place else. The risks were too great. He wasn't a saint, but neither was he a walking STD. He didn't sleep around and he didn't do commitment, but he sure as hell liked to fuck, and fucking Haven was turning out to be better, hotter, than he could've ever imagined.

Lost in her soft heat and carnal curves, he hadn't once thought about the painkillers.

Ↄↄ

Having eaten all the food Jack had pilfered from the pub, hunger finally drove them from bed. They waited until the house was still and dark before they snuck downstairs and raided the kitchen.

Back in the bedroom, they lounged in bed, snacking on fresh fruit and an assortment of baked goods.

"Omigod, did you try the cookies?"

White teeth flashed in his dark face. "I've had them before. My brother made them."

"Which brother? Don't you have four of them?"

"Luke."

"Emily's hubby?" She sampled an oatmeal raisin cookie and moaned. "Lucky girl."

Haven wanted to ask him about his brothers, what they were like and if he might, one day, travel less for work so that he could be closer to them, but it smacked too much of caring and she didn't want to care about Jack.

Anything more pulling them together would be bad. Dangerous.

"I'm a terrible friend," she said instead. "I haven't seen Emily in years and not only do I miss her wedding, but then I disappear with one of her groomsman afterwards."

He rubbed her bare foot. "Emily's busy with her new husband. Believe me, girl talk is the last thing on her mind."

If Luke possessed a fraction of what Jack brought to the bedroom, she could imagine that was true.

Later, while Jack showered, she wandered over to the French doors. A nearly full moon illuminated the breathtaking landscape and the vast, undulating waters of Lake Michigan. It reminded her of the place where she'd grown up, on the other side of this same lake that looked like a sea.

She hadn't been home in a couple of years, which was the way she liked it. However, she did miss the smell of the freshwater sea and the crisp air near the lake. She'd tried to replace her love of the water by living near the ocean, but it wasn't the same, and not just because of the saltwater and sharks.

Where she'd grown up, on the sunrise coast, she'd often gazed out at the majestic lake and wondered what lay beyond the horizon. When her family fell apart, that longing intensified. She'd never understood the odd way her heart longed to know what lay across the sea.

The bathroom door opened and Jack emerged on a cloud of steam, a white towel wrapped around his lean waist.

That is, she'd never understood her heart's longing until now.

Was it possible, all along, that she'd craved this moment, on this little island, with this man?

He moved to stand behind her, pressing the length of his large body against hers. She leaned back, sinking into his solid warmth. Neither spoke for a long time, only watched the whitecaps rise and plunge toward shore under the moonlit sky.

With one fluid motion, he dragged the chaise lounge around to face the window so they could sit and watch the view. He sat, and she nestled her bottom between his powerful thighs, reclining against his broad chest.

When his arms came around her, his hand brushed the skin where her robe gaped.

She felt his arousal throb near her backside, and a luscious ripple of need sloped through her. Her hands moved to his thighs, pushing the towel away so she could touch his warm skin.

His hand slipped beneath her robe and covered her breast, his calloused palm rubbing over her beaded nipple. The electricity from his touch arced downward to arouse an acute aching between her legs.

She laid her head on his shoulder as his hand roamed down her body. Her knees fell apart. His mouth near her ear, his short rapid breathing fed her pleasure as his hand pushed through her curls to locate the heart of her. A moan rose in her throat with the first slow, leisurely lick of his fingers along her slit.

Caught deliciously between his hand and his body, she swiveled her hips, chasing after the delicious tingles.

Helpless to his touch, she clutched his thighs and pumped her hips.

Her muscles clenched while, inexplicably, emotion clogged in the back of her throat.

"Jack." The ragged whisper wrenched from her.

"What is it, baby?" His deep baritone shivered through her.

She shook her head and squeezed her eyes shut when the orgasm crashed over her. There were no words beyond that.

Just Jack.

The only word she'd ever known. The only word she would ever speak again.

That was it.

Just... Jack.

Chapter Six

The soft ringing tugged her from deep slumber. She blinked open her eyes.

Darkness engulfed her, and for a moment, she forgot where she was—until she felt the solid body beside her.

Jack.

Another jingle disturbed the stark quiet in their room and she recognized her cell phone's ringtone. Her heart kicked against her breastbone while she fumbled for the phone on the nightstand. She tipped the device and squinted against the harsh glare of its light.

Her heart stuttered when she read her stepmother's name on the display screen.

Instinct screamed at her to decline the call even as her brain registered the time on the phone's digital clock—5:22 a.m. A nauseating knot of terror wrenched her stomach.

Beside her, Jack stirred. She flipped back the covers

and slipped from the bed.

Heart thrumming, she accepted the call. "Hello?" she whispered.

"Haven? Is that you?" Kristen's voice sounded shrill. "Haven?"

"Yes, it's me. What's going on?"

"It's your dad." Kristen's next words shattered Haven's world. "He's been in an accident."

Haven's knees gave out and she plopped down hard onto the stuffed ottoman.

"We're at the hospital. The police are here and—"

"The police?" Haven's mind struggled to keep up. "Why are the police there?"

"I don't know." Frustration mixed with hysteria in Kristen's voice. "They say he was drinking."

"He's been drinking again?"

"He's hurt."

"How long has been drinking?"

"Why aren't you listening to me—?"

"How long, Kristen?"

Silence crackled through the phone speaker. "Since the summer."

Haven squeezed her eyes shut.

"He wants to see you."

Haven sucked in a sharp breath through her nose. "I won't come."

"Stop it. Stop it right now." The snap in Kristen's tone dissolved into sobs. "You have to come. I don't know what to do and there's no one else."

Her stepmom's pitiful wails reminded Haven of the time they were in second grade and Kristen had fallen off the swing on the playground. She'd cried huge crocodile tears and begged Haven to stay with her while the nurse cleaned and bandaged the bloody scrape on her bony knee.

Eleven years later, when the girls were eighteen,

Kristen had married Haven's dad. Needless to say, Haven's relationship with her dad and stepmom was complicated.

"I can't," Haven said. "I'm sorry."

She wanted to snatch back the apology. Why should she be sorry? Because he was her dad? Well, she was his daughter, and that hadn't compelled him to rush to her side when she'd needed him.

"He asked to see you, Haven."

"He did?" She cringed at the hopeful ring in her tone. "What did he say?"

"He wants to talk to you about something. Something important. I don't know what. He's not making any sense. He's drunk, or drugged, or in too much pain—God, Haven, will you just come on already? We need you."

Haven wanted to argue with Kristen, but she became aware of Jack sitting up in the bed, his green-gold eyes fixed on her.

"I'll see what I can do," she hedged. "Maybe in a few days—"

"No. There isn't time."

"What do you mean? How badly is he hurt?"

"I don't know. I don't know anymore." Kristen's words garbled. Her exhaustion and fear reached through the phone to wrap tentacles around Haven's throat. "I can't think and.... Haven, please, just come, okay?"

Haven stared blindly at the closed bedroom door for many long moments while the weight of attachment pressed down on her. "I'll be there as soon as I can."

"Thank you, thank you. I'll let him know. He'll be so relieved."

Kristen disconnected the call before Haven could argue with that last comment.

In the silence, she stared at her cell phone's dark display screen. She wiped away imaginary fingerprints. Then she set the phone aside with undue care and risked a glance at Jack.

He sat up in bed, his back against the headboard. "You have to go."

She ducked her chin and nodded.

The sheets rustled and soon his bare feet came into her line of sight.

He crouched before her, bringing their faces level. "You okay?"

"I'm fine." She swallowed the hard lump in the back of her throat. "I can't keep our deal. I'm sorry."

His hand found hers. Turning her palm face up, he lifted her hand to his lips and pressed a kiss into the heart of it. "Another time, then."

They both knew it was a lie. That, barring some insane twist of fate, they'd never see each other again.

Hot pressure formed behind her eyes. "Sure."

Instead of spending one more day, and night, with Jack, she'd be traveling to Milwaukee. Though a straight shot across the lake, the ferries that ran between Michigan and Wisconsin would be unable to make the crossing until spring. Which meant she'd have to drive around Lake Michigan.

First, she'd have to get off the island.

"What time does the first ferry leave?"

"Seven."

"Perfect." Her voice wavered. Clearing her throat, she stood. "I'm going to grab a shower."

She stepped under the water's warm spray, hoping to wash away the stormy jumble of emotions freaking her out. She'd never felt quite like this before. Haven recalled how, in college, Emily and the other students living with them in the dorms had talked about missing their friends and families at home. Haven hadn't understood the sappy melancholy they'd described.

Until now.

Which didn't make any sense.

She wrenched the shower nozzle, cutting off the flow of water.

When she emerged from the bathroom, Jack disappeared behind the door. The sound of running water accompanied her as she dressed in blue jeans and a wheat-colored wool sweater, then moved around the bedroom, gathering up her scattered belongings.

A white undershirt lay atop his duffel bag and she paused to finger the soft fabric. She lifted the shirt and his unique, spicy scent clung to the material.

The odd compulsion to steal, which she hadn't indulged in years, overcame her then. With a glance over her shoulder, she swiped the cotton T-shirt from his bag and stuffed it inside her suitcase.

She yanked the zipper closed as the bathroom door swung open and Jack reemerged, his dark hair sticking up on end and a towel wrapped snug around his lean waist.

She thrust a thumb at the bedroom door. "So, I'm going to head out."

"Wait, I'm going with you." At his bag, he removed a pair of blue jeans.

"Oh, that's not necessary—"

He silenced her with a look. "It's not up for debate."

She pulled her bottom lip between her teeth as he pulled a sky-blue T-shirt over his head and shoved his arms through the armholes.

"Besides," he said, "the ferry is a few blocks from where I left my car."

The sun had not yet peeked over the horizon and the world remained cloaked in dusky darkness as they loaded their suitcases in her rental and climbed into the frigid interior.

They rode in silence along the winding lakeshore road back to town, which remained perilous with patches of ice and wide, blowing snowdrifts.

Jack directed her to the car ferry lot and she pulled into an empty parking spot.

They sat in silence a moment. Through the windshield, seagulls circled overhead.

"I should've told Emily I had to go."

"I'll see her later. I'll let her know."

He reached across, slipped his hand beneath the curtain of her hair, and pulled her close. "Thank you, Haven."

She swallowed convulsively.

He kissed her long and deep, his mouth all slippery friction and hot silk. His grip on her neck tightened, as though he might refuse to let her go.

Unable to catch her breath, she broke the kiss. She wanted to say something smart-mouthed, but nothing came to her, so she faced the front.

"Good-bye, Jack."

A moment passed where she thought he might say more, but instead, he reached for the handle and a blast of winter air struck her when he climbed from the vehicle.

Her heart aching, she backed out of the parking spot and steered the car around to the short line of vehicles waiting to board the ferry.

In her rearview mirror, Jack stood watching her car pull away.

A biting sorrow kicked in her chest and only served to convince her it was for the best she left him now. If it hurt this badly after only two days, she could only imagine how painful it would've been to say good-bye after they'd spent another day together.

Yep, she'd avoided a disaster.

A catastrophe of epic proportions.

She should be happy to be so lucky. Jack was trouble for someone like her. Someone who gave her heart to anyone who showed her even the slightest affection.

In high school, she'd earned a reputation as a slut. She'd truly earned it. She was, in fact, a slut. After Ryan died, her parents had withdrawn into their own pain and, starved for attention, Haven mistook sexual interest from boys for something more.

She gave herself to them freely because, at sixteen, she was too young to understand that intimacy didn't equate to love and respect. She flirted and chased after them, prepared to give it all away for nothing more than an hour of their attention. Along with her body, she gave her heart to all of them.

She was a heart slut.

Past tense.

These days, no one touched her heart. Not since Ryan died.

Which was why Jack belonged in her rearview mirror, before her foolish heart decided to love him forever.

愸

The stench of disinfectant and despair slammed into Haven when she entered the hospital.

Nausea choked her as she rode the elevator to the fourth floor, and as she walked down the long corridor in search of her dad's room, memories taunted her from the shadows.

She rubbed at the phantom twinge on her clavicle, one of several broken bones she'd suffered in the car accident that'd confined her for three weeks to a bed in this very hospital.

It was where she'd lain when they confirmed what she already knew. That Ryan was dead.

Her steps slowed as she approached the room number Kristen had texted to her, but she didn't enter.

When Haven was young, her dad had delivered pizzas

for a living while her mom attended college. When Haven was five, he'd opened his own pizzeria, and a couple of years after that, her mom quit her job at the high school to help him run the restaurant.

In the summer of Haven's eleventh year, some fancy food critic voted her dad's pizza the best in Milwaukee. Business took off and soon, her parents opened a second, and then a third restaurant. Every year after that for the next five years, they opened a new restaurant in the state, and it was only as her family moved into the upper middle class that Haven realized they'd been poor before.

Then Ryan died.

In the year after his death, Haven rarely saw her dad, who threw himself into working and drinking while her mom lay in bed, crying. By Haven's seventeenth birthday, her parents had divorced, because the idea that love overcame all or healed the worst kind of pain was an utter joke.

Shortly after the divorce, the pizza chain, which her dad had won sole custody of, went national, and he spent the next couple of years amassing a fortune. With his newfound wealth, he acquired a sprawling mansion in Milwaukee's most affluent neighborhood, vacation homes in Aspen and Napa Valley, a helicopter, a professional hockey team, and a trophy wife.

Meanwhile, Haven's mom struggled to get out of bed, which meant she also struggled to find and keep a job, any job, and the fixer upper they'd moved into after the divorce never quite managed to get fixed up. Eventually, they were forced to move on, and Haven's notions of refinished hardwoods and neutral paint colors turned to dreams of escaping the trailer park where she and her mom had landed.

Now, Haven inhaled a bracing breath and stepped through the door.

Her dad lay in the hospital bed, his eyes closed and his

thin body covered in a white bedsheet. His hair had more salt than pepper now, and puffy bags sat under his eyes.

How old was he? Fifty-six? Fifty-seven? Not nearly as old as he appeared.

Kristen popped up out of the recliner beside the bed. She'd pulled her expertly colored blonde hair into a messy ponytail, and a conspicuous coffee stain marred her rumpled designer blouse between her breasts. Full, perky breasts Haven didn't recall her having the last time they saw each other for the holidays nearly two years before.

"Thank God, you're here." She flung a snow-white parka over her shoulders.

Her dad's eyes, red-rimmed and bloodshot, blinked open. "Hey, pumpkin."

"Hey, Dad." Haven sidled around the side of the hospital bed. "How are you feeling?"

"I've been better."

"What did the doctors say?"

"They think I'll live. Unfortunately." His voice sounded thin.

Weak. One quality she couldn't recall seeing in him before.

She resisted the urge to smooth a hand over his forehead. "When can you go home?"

"Wednesday at the earliest, but probably Thursday or Friday." Kristen snagged her Kate Spade purse off the floor. "I've got to run."

"Wait, what?" Haven shot a panicked look at her dad. "You're leaving?"

Kristen sailed across the room. "I've got to pick up Braden. He's stuck at practice."

Kristen and Haven's dad had two boys together, Braden and Chance, who must've been around ten and twelve years old by that point. Haven wasn't close to her half brothers. She hardly knew them. It hurt too much to know them.

At the hospital room door, Kristen blinked large green eyes at Haven. "Can't you sit with him until I get back?"

"Uh... how long will you be?"

"Not long. I have to grab the boys something to eat, and take a shower. And I need a nap, but then I'll be right back."

"I can't stay...." Haven's protest died on her lips when Kristen disappeared through the door.

She pasted a stiff smile on her face and wiped a clammy palm on the thigh of her blue jeans.

"You don't have to stay," her dad said quietly. "What I have to talk to you about won't take long."

Haven frowned with her weariness. She'd assumed, years back, that her dad had disinherited her. So why would he make her show up in Milwaukee simply to confirm what she, and everyone else, already knew?

On the small TV mounted to the wall at the foot of her dad's bed, a sports talk show played. She dug through her purse for her cell phone. If she had to guess, Kristen hadn't updated her dad on the day's scores.

"I need a favor," her dad said.

The recliner's vinyl squeaked when she perched on the seat edge. Her head bent over the device as she browsed to the hockey scores.

"I need you to take over the team for a while."

Her cell phone hit the floor. "*What?*"

Her dad held up both hands, a tangle of wires rustling with his movement. "Only for a couple of months."

Haven was shaking her head. "No. Uh-uh. No way. Absolutely not."

"Haven, I need you to listen to me."

The gravity in his tone cut off her protest.

"I need help." A slight quiver wobbled his bottom lip. "I've got a problem with alcohol. I'm going to spend Christmas with Kristen and the boys, but next week I'm checking into rehab."

"Good." She approached the bed. "Dad, that's good."

He watched her with sad, serious eyes. "I gotta do sixty days this time."

She rushed forward. "Whatever it takes, Dad, you can do it. I know you can."

"The thing is, I need help. I need you to oversee a few things with the team while I'm away."

"Dad, I can't." Terror choked out her guilt. "I can't drop everything and move to Milwaukee." Memories clogged in the back of her throat. "I have a life I need to get back to."

A life she'd just hit the reset button on, but a life nonetheless. Sort of.

"You're a waitress."

"Bartender."

The line of his mouth pinched with disappointment. "Then it's settled."

"Dad—"

"You can move into the apartment downtown. Kristen and the boys will be at the house and won't bother you."

She swiped at the bead of moisture collecting on her forehead. Their conversation had passed ridiculous. What he called an apartment was a penthouse overlooking Lake Michigan, and the team was a professional hockey club, full of professional hockey players. Only an act of God could convince her to set foot in that arena.

"Isn't there, uh, something else I can do to help you out?"

"Kristen's taking care of the rest." His mouth formed the downturn of disappointment once more. "But she can't do it all. The restaurant and the boys are more than enough for her to handle."

"I'm flattered, Dad. Really, I am, but I'm not qualified to run a hockey team."

He waved off her worries. "I'll tell you everything you need to know to keep from burning the place down while I'm away. We're in last place in the league, so there are no expectations for you. I just need you to show up and act busy for a few hours every day, and make sure Darby is doing his job."

"Who's Darby?"

"Darby Poitiers. He's my general manager."

"He isn't doing his job?"

"He's doing everyone's job."

"Great. Get him to take over for you. Hell, your secretary would be a better pick than me."

But her dad gave his head a hard shake. "You heard me say we're in last place? Darby's got work to do. His work, no one else's. We're breaking in a new coach, and the list of injuries has grown longer than my prenup." He pulled a rumpled napkin from the blankets. "We've got a couple of trades in the works I need you to follow up on for me. Here." He held the napkin out to her. "Take this with you tomorrow when you go to the arena."

She recoiled. "Tomorrow?"

"I wanted Hansen, but he balked. Try again to get him, but if you can't, here's a list of alternates." The napkin dropped to his lap. "We have needs at every position so you can't go wrong, but focus on defense. Darby promised to get us an elite defender in the off-season, but then he loaded up on offense instead. I know he's got his mind set on the shooter from Toronto, which probably isn't a bad idea if Bryce can't stay out of trouble, but a defense-minded player has to be the priority right now."

His words twisted and jumbled in a hopeless tangle inside her head. Overriding the chaos was the certainty she couldn't go near that arena. Those players. She hadn't attended a hockey game in nearly ten years.

Panic took hold. "You can't just pick me. You need to

find someone who knows what they're doing."

"I'm the owner of this team." He bristled at the perceived insult. "I can do whatever the hell I want."

Haven gaped at him a moment. "Are you seriously telling me there isn't one person inside your entire organization better prepared to do this job than me?"

He hesitated. "Look, it's complicated."

"What's complicated?"

"It doesn't matter."

Their gazes locked. "It matters to me. Tell me, or I'm walking."

His head lolled back on the pillows. He stared at the ceiling for one long, excruciating moment.

"Someone's been feeding information to the press." His throat worked when he swallowed. "Someone on the inside. It's not that big a deal—there isn't much to hide aside from the fact we can't steal a win, but the truth is I don't know who I can and cannot trust right now."

A curse slipped from her.

"I've never asked you for anything." Emotion thickened his voice.

It was true, he hadn't asked for her help in anything ever before, but that didn't mean she'd given him nothing. She rubbed the ache forming between her eyebrows.

Her dad's next words shattered any semblance of peace she might've held on to.

"Ryan would've done it."

The tremors started in her center and resonated outward. For a long, perilous moment, she struggled to hold herself together, the last thread of her composure threatening to unravel. "Ryan's dead, Dad."

He winced as though her words caused a physical slash of pain. "That's why it has to be you. I need *you*, Haven."

It was the closest he'd ever come to a declaration of

love.

He actually hadn't said he loved her at all, she was well aware, but needing someone was kind of like loving them, wasn't it?

"Did I mention I'll pay you?"

Her head came up. "What, like a salary?"

"A healthy salary."

"How much?"

When he told her, she wasn't able to hide her shock. For two months of work, she'd receive more money than she'd earned the previous two years bartending.

She'd be able to afford her own place.

An image arose in her mind, as clear as the shrewd calculation in her dad's eyes. Of a house. A little Cape Cod with a garden and a panoramic view of Lake Michigan.

A pang of longing struck her beneath the breastbone.

"Fine." She snatched the napkin off the bed. "Tell me what to do."

Chapter Seven

"Jack, peas?"

Jack paused with his fork poised before his lips. "Sure." He smiled at Evelyn and, returning his fork to his plate, accepted the bowl of peas she held out to him.

The smile held as he scooped peas onto his plate. Neal's wife, Evelyn, lived to stuff food into the bellies of her three children and the numerous kids her husband had brought into their home over the years, Jack included.

Neal plucked a dinner roll from the breadbasket. "How was the wedding?" With his crooked nose and chipped front tooth, he had the face of a champion.

A face Jack hoped to have one day.

"The wedding was nice."

The statement didn't begin to capture the chaos of the ceremony, or the two nights he'd spent in Haven's bed.

He'd thought about her constantly since she left him.

The morning after they'd parted ways, while on his flight back to Nashville, he'd worried about her and whomever she'd rushed off to see. That afternoon, while he'd waited for his appointment with the team doctor, he told himself it was for the best that she left when she did. The truth was, if he'd had her one more time, he might not have been able to let her go. It didn't matter that he knew next to nothing about her. Hell, he didn't even know her last name.

He knew she had a soft heart but pretended not to, and he knew her body.

When the doctor cleared Jack to play, Haven dominated his thoughts as he returned to his apartment, repacked a bag, and headed to the airport to meet up with the team for their chartered flight to Detroit ahead of their game the next night. By the time he sat down to Evelyn's home-cooked dinner, his concern for Haven had warped into a sharp ache of longing.

He wanted to see her again.

After years of guzzling keg beer, she was like a fine wine, and he wanted another taste. Desperately.

But wine wouldn't get him closer to his goals, he reminded himself for the two-hundredth time or some such shit. He should be happy if he never saw her again.

A frown pulled at his features.

Evelyn sipped her wine. "What did you think of your brother's bride? This was the first time you met her, wasn't it?"

The Thompsons had met Jack's brothers only once, the day they came to pick him up and take him to their home in the Detroit area. But they inquired about them often, as though determined to prove to Jack that they never intended to replace his family.

Though that's exactly what had happened.

The old sliver of guilt wriggled under his skin.

He couldn't say he regretted his choice. Hockey was

his life. As a dyslexic, Jack had struggled in school, and in life, before he discovered hockey. On the ice, the world finally made sense to him. It was the one place he excelled, and he wouldn't have given that up for anything.

"The bride is a sweetheart, and I'm sure my brother doesn't deserve her," Jack teased. "He must've charmed her with his cooking and good looks."

Neal winked. "Worked for me."

Quickly spotting the learning disability Jack had hidden from his own family, Neal had hired tutors who specialized in working with dyslexics. He oversaw Jack's hockey career as well as his education, and Jack credited Neal with the bachelor's degree he'd earned from State and the large sums of money now sitting in his bank account. In every way that mattered, Neal was the father Jack never had.

Evelyn smiled sweetly. "It wasn't your cooking or your looks that attracted me to you, dear. It was the fact that you did the dishes."

Neal's dark eyes glinted with humor. "I'm sure it had nothing to do with the fact that I was the leading scorer in the league at the time."

Evelyn's cascade of laughter was contagious. "I can promise you it did not. I knew nothing about hockey before I met you."

Jack chewed around his smile. "Speaking of hockey, how's the new job going?"

A former player, Neal was in the midst of his first season as the General Manager in Detroit.

"Front office is definitely different than the player perspective." A dry smile turned up one corner of Neal's mouth. "It's a lot more brutal."

A bitter laugh escaped Jack. He could well imagine. The egos of multimillionaire businessmen surpassed even those of pro athletes.

"No, but seriously, I can't complain. It's a good

organization," Neal said. "The staff is incredible, and so far Martha's been great to work with."

Martha Fillmore, the team's owner, was the type of owner every club dreamed of having—a ninety-year-old widow unafraid to part with large sums of money who left the running of the team to her innovative, competent, well-paid staff.

"Sounds like a great gig," Jack agreed.

"It could certainly be worse." A frown touched Neal's features. "We could be Milwaukee."

A soft gasp slipped from Evelyn. "Did you hear about Hank Callahan?"

The biggest scandal to hit the league in a year?

"Yeah, I heard." Though he'd caught only the bare-bone details before he switched off the TV.

He preferred to stay removed from scandals and rumors. It only made his job harder if he had strong opinions about the spoiled, self-centered owners and executives running the league.

Besides, he'd heard all he needed to know about the incident. "Sounds like Callahan's lucky he didn't hurt anyone."

Evelyn murmured her agreement. "At least he's going to get some help. I hope it all works out for him."

"Rumor is his daughter's taking over while he's in rehab." Neal shook his head. "I don't envy her."

A frown pulled at Jack's features. "I didn't know he had a daughter."

"She hasn't been around the organization much, from what I hear. It's unclear what her background is, but I don't think it's in hockey."

Jack shot Neal a sour look. "Since when did an owner need actual credentials? All they really need is money."

Neal chuckled. "True enough."

In his career, Jack had seen every type of ownership, from the young entrepreneur who partied with the players to the seasoned businessman who treated the team as though it were just another capitalist venture. Some took ownership in hopes of a gold rush, others for the adrenaline rush. Very few understood fandom, a vastly different beast than consumerism, or possessed the skills necessary to run a successful pro sports organization.

Never was that more painfully obvious than when they handed the reins to the team over to one of their children who, more often than not, had been given every opportunity in life but never earned anything.

As a player, all he could do was hope whoever the owner was, they learned fast or failed faster and moved on. It was entirely out of his hands. A fact that often pissed him off.

Across the table, Neal and Evelyn's gazes caught and held. Then Evelyn turned her big blue eyes on Jack.

Jack grew still.

Neal sat back in his chair and regarded him across the table. "I wanted to talk to you about the possibility of a trade."

"A trade?" Jack's knee banged against the table leg. "You mean, me?"

"We're looking to make some moves, and I think you'd be a perfect fit for what we're trying to do in Detroit. We'd like to get a deal done this week. I haven't talked to Roger yet," Neal added, referring to Jack's GM in Nashville. "And I won't contact him if you don't want me to."

Jack gaped at Neal while he struggled to comprehend the meaning of the man's words. Was he really offering Jack the opportunity to play in Detroit? Alongside his mentor and father figure?

It was the team Jack had dreamed of playing for since he was a homesick sixteen-year-old living five hours from home. It was that dream he'd latched onto to fuel himself through grueling 4:00 a.m. workouts and a brutal schedule that often had him playing ten games in three cities in a five-day period.

One of the original six teams in the league, Detroit had history, tradition, name-recognition, and a track record of making the playoffs every year for the past twenty-four years. With two future Hall of Famers on the current roster, they sat in first place in the league, and while there were no guarantees in sports, at present the shortest, most direct path to a Stanley Cup ran through Detroit.

"Jack?" Neal shifted in his chair. "What do you think? Are you ready to play in Detroit?"

Jack cleared the unexpected emotion from his throat. "Yes, sir. More than ready."

Evelyn yelped and slapped Neal's raised hand in a high five.

Neal reached for his wine glass. "Here's to winning a lot of games together."

Jack took a healthy swallow of his chocolate milk, and amidst their celebration, he didn't hear the back door open. He didn't notice the woman until Evelyn, spotting her, scrambled to her feet with a surprised gasp.

"Oh, sweetie, I didn't know you were coming for dinner." In the kitchen, Evelyn pulled a plate down from the cupboard. "Come, join us. Look, Jack's here."

The woman pulled up, and her soft blue eyes landed on Jack's face.

Jack choked on a pea.

At first, he hadn't recognized her. Not the mile-long legs or the silky spun-gold hair that hung in luxurious waves down her back. Definitely not the soft blue eyes that shone like jewels amidst the perfection of her delicate features.

He blinked stupidly. "Sutton?"

The last time he'd seen Neal's daughter, she was a

gangly preteen with braces and a crippling shyness. The outrageous beauty before him now bore little resemblance to that girl.

"Omigod, Jack." Sutton plopped down beside him. "It's good to see you. What are you doing here?"

A waft of her flowery scent teased his nostrils. "We're playing Detroit tomorrow night. Just stopped by and your mom insisted on feeding me."

An agonized groan reverberated in Sutton's throat. "You made cheesy potatoes?"

Evelyn held the dinner plate to her chest. "Is that bad?"

Sutton shot to her feet and backed away from the table. "Do not let me eat those."

Neal waved his fork at the table. "A couple bites won't–"

A strangled sound erupted from Sutton. "Do not tempt me."

Evelyn scowled. "Jack lets me feed him."

Sutton planted a kiss on her mom's cheek. "Sorry, Mom. I'll eat after the photo shoot. I promise." She whirled on Jack. "Are you around for lunch tomorrow? There's this new place downtown I've been dying to try." She ducked her chin and peeked at him from beneath the sweep of her long eyelashes. "You wanna come with me?"

Unease rippled through him. He shoveled a forkful of peas into his mouth and took great care to chew them thoroughly. Risking a glance at Neal, whose features remained inscrutable, Jack wondered what was more likely to irk the man, agreeing to go on a lunch date with his daughter, or refusing her?

He chewed the peas to dust.

"It's right next door to the new arena, so you won't have to rush around at all before the game." She worried her bottom lip while she gazed at him with large, hope-filled eyes.

He gulped. "Uh... yeah... sure. Lunch would be great."

Chapter Eight

Haven ignored her cell phone as it vibrated across the sleek coffee table in her dad's "apartment," which turned out to be a top-floor penthouse with twenty-foot ceilings, marble flooring, and wall-to-wall windows framing dramatic views of historic downtown Milwaukee to the west and the expanse of Lake Michigan to the east, and painted hot-pink polish onto her toenails.

The phone went silent for approximately two seconds before going off again.

Unhurried, she returned the cap to the bottle, screwed it on, giving it an extra twist, and then she accepted her dad's call.

"Where the hell are you?"

She sat back and, feet on the table, inspected her work. "Oh, I'm just settling in—"

"Not at the arena. You're a no-show so far this morning."

At least some of the strength had returned to his voice.

"How do you know that?"

"I talked to Mel."

"Who's Mel?"

"You'd know if you'd bothered to show up."

Haven winced. "Good point." Then, because the thought of setting foot inside that arena made her stomach lurch, she heaved a dramatic sigh into the phone. "I guess this isn't going to work out, huh? Oh well. Sorry to let you down, Dad. Feel better."

"It's too late for that, Haven Marie."

"But—"

"You're not getting a dime out of me if you don't show up. Get your ass down there. They're waiting for you."

The connection went dead.

Her stomach in knots, she left the penthouse an hour later and headed east toward the Milwaukee River. The bright midmorning sunshine chased the chill from the cool December air and danced across the facades of modern skyscrapers and historic buildings.

The charm of the new-old, coastal-urban city was lost on her as she made the nine-block walk through the dense, narrow streets of Juneau town where her dad's apartment building was located to the west side of town. She crossed over the river, and the massive steel and glass arena loomed large before her.

She arrived at the north entrance, as her dad had instructed, but the burst of courage that'd carried her across town dissolved like snowflakes on her tongue. She spun away from the doors, only to abruptly turn back and then away once more.

One of the doors opened and a woman with spiky yellow hair and a round middle poked her head out. "Ms. Callahan?"

Haven swallowed the terror rising in her throat.

"Yeah?"

The woman positioned her body to prop open the door as her shrewd blue eyes slid over Haven.

A bartender's wardrobe didn't have a lot to offer by way of professional office attire, so Haven had dressed in the black skirt and white blouse she'd bought to wear to Emily's wedding. Except she'd thrown a bulky winter coat over the ensemble and had ditched the red heels in favor of her winter boots.

The woman's plump face remained expressionless when she turned. "Follow me."

Haven lunged to catch the door before it fell shut.

In the empty concourse, she caught up to the surprisingly quick-footed woman. "I'm sorry, who are you?"

"I'm Mel." Large peace sign earrings swung from her earlobes.

"Nice to meet you, Mel." Haven stuck out her hand.

The woman thrust a file folder into her palm.

"What's this?" Haven asked, cracking open the folder.

"I pulled together some information for you." They approached a bank of elevators and Mel pushed the button. "There's a list of staff by department, a team roster with salaries against the cap, last season's stats, and some advanced metrics that may prove helpful to you."

With a soft ding, the elevator doors slid open to reveal three men crowded in the tiny car.

Big men. Huge. Athletes, no doubt.

A shudder rippled through her.

Mel plunged into their midst. "Hello, gentlemen. On your way up?"

"Yes, ma'am."

Mel turned and the gazes of everyone inside the elevator fixed on Haven.

Who remained firmly planted on the other side of

those doors.

"Gentlemen, this is Ms. Callahan. Ms. Callahan, this is your team captain, Mr. Marleau, and Misters Tierney and Donovan."

Haven offered a weak smile, which faltered when the elevator doors lurched.

One of the men's massive arms came out to block the elevator doors from closing. "Going up, Ms. Callahan?"

On wobbly legs, Haven stepped inside the steel trap.

Mel punched the number to the third floor and the heavy doors closed them in. "How are we doing today, boys?"

One man turned a charmer's smile on Mel. "Better, now that we've bumped into you."

Mel snorted.

The man beside Haven shifted and his arm brushed against her shoulder. An innocent touch that sucked the remaining oxygen from Haven's lungs.

Dark memories spiraled through her.

She shuffled closer to Mel, longing for her familiar turf behind the fortress of a bar. There, she wielded the power in the bottle of alcohol in her hand. She was in control.

Here? Not so much.

The elevator cart jerked to a stop. The doors pulled open and Haven shot from the enclosure like a cork from the champagne bottle.

Mel breezed past her and set off across the bustling reception area. "Later, boys."

The men headed in the opposite direction from Mel.

"This way, Ms. Callahan."

Haven scurried after Mel, who led her down a long corridor lined with offices. As they passed by, Haven peeked through the open doors to find people huddled over laptops or engaged in animated conversations.

A bead of moisture broke out on her forehead and she

wriggled out of her heavy winter coat.

At the last door on the right, Mel slowed her steps. She reached for the handle.

"Wait." Haven's hand clamped over Mel's fist. "Please."

Twin pools of deep blue stared at her with a mix of shock and curiosity.

"I can't do this," she whispered.

Mel's eyebrows inched upward. "Your father says you can."

"He's wrong. He's wrong about me."

"He says you have a strategic mind."

"No—I don't know, maybe." Haven shook the cobwebs from her muddled thoughts. "He doesn't know me. I'm... a flake. I'm incompetent and unreliable and...."

Alarm stole over Mel's expression. "You attended college on a scholarship. You earned an MBA."

Haven swallowed convulsively. "I dropped out."

Mel's hand dropped to her side. "You're a fan of the super fan, at least. You've studied hockey your entire life."

"I hate hockey." The confession burst from her. "I haven't watched a game in years."

The color leached from Mel's face. Then the line of her mouth thinned. Squaring her shoulders, she drew up to her full height, which was about six inches shorter than Haven's five-foot-seven frame. "I guess you better start watching, then."

She wrenched the handle and shoved open the solid wood door.

An older man standing at the head of an oblong table stopped speaking midsentence and turned to look at them. As did the dozen or more other men dressed in dark suits seated around the vast table.

Their expressions ranged from curious, to cautious, to hostile.

They waited.

Expectant. Of what, she didn't know, though she was

certain she'd disappoint them.

Someone coughed.

Beside her, Mel spoke in a low voice. "This is your team now, Ms. Callahan. You can do this." Her voice held a conviction Haven knew she couldn't possibly believe. "Don't forget to breathe."

With that, Mel gave her a small push in the back, and she stumbled forward into a stream of sunlight pouring in through the wall of windows. She blinked against the harsh glare and stepped farther into the room.

The man at the head of the table eyed her as though she were a bug. "Ah, you must be Haven."

Haven smoothed a clammy palm down the front of her black pencil skirt. "That's me."

"I'm Darby, General Manager and Executive Vice President of Hockey Operations." He pointed to the man at his right. "This is Coach Cal Chambers."

He continued around the table, naming the men and their titles. Assistants and executives of things she'd never heard of, coaches and specialists, it all jumbled into an inseparable tangle in her mind.

All but one tiny tidbit.

"It you're the vice president, who's the president? Shouldn't they be here?"

A rumble of annoyance vibrated in the back of Darby's throat. "That'd be you."

"Oh." Her frayed nerves unraveled.

"Hank is this team's owner and president." Darby turned his back to her. "For the next sixty days, we'll operate as though nothing has changed. Whether Hank's here or a thousand miles away, sober or high on his next grandiose scheme, you all have a job to do and I expect you to do them."

His words penetrated the fog of panic closing in on her. Maybe it was the way he belittled her dad.

Or the pointed look he gave her when he said, "You

don't need an owner or anyone else to tell you that. You have me, and I'm here to make sure each and every one of you is held accountable."

A deafening silence settled over the room when Darby lowered himself into a chair.

One by one, all gazes strayed to her.

The walls inched closer, crouching over her like angry beasts.

"Uh... thank you. I... thank you." Her heart thundered in her ears.

The tension in the room wound tighter, until the strain became unbearable.

She pushed a hard puff of air between her lips. "Okay, can someone just tell me what the fuck I'm supposed to say?"

A smattering of surprised laughter carried around the room, releasing some of the pressure.

"Say anything you want." Bitterness edged Darby's tone. "This is your show."

"Okay, well...." She fumbled for her purse. "My dad mentioned something about a trade. Have you talked about that yet?"

Men straightened in their chairs and hunched over electronic devices on the table in front of them.

"I like Miller out of Toronto." The man spoke with a thick accent, Russian or Eastern European.

Her hands trembled as she unfolded the flimsy napkin.

"I'm not paying to buy out his contract," Darby said. "Gauthier's looking for a home."

Unable to steady the napkin long enough to read the names scrawled in her dad's handwriting, she abandoned the effort.

"We have sharpshooters in Donovan and Avery." The man's gravelly baritone sounded strained, as though he'd abused or torn his vocal chords. "We desperately need a defenseman."

"The best defense is a relentless offense."

A torrent of fervent chatter followed Darby's declaration.

The knot in her stomach wrenched and she turned from their aggression. Crossing to the bank of windows, she peered out at the cityscape while they argued strategy and discussed players she didn't know anymore.

Someone lashed out, a hostile bite to their tone, which was met with equal anger.

Dizziness gripped her and she pressed her damp forehead to the glass.

"He's an energy guy," the gravel-voiced man said.

"He has good size. Six three, two fourteen," someone added.

"I thought he was injured."

"It's a minor thing."

Cars eased down the busy city street. Haven ached to be on the other side of the glass. In one of those cars. Driving away from this place. Not stuck in a too-small room with too-thin air and all these too-fiery men.

More than that, she wanted to be away from this city and back on that island. With Jack. A big man who didn't incite terror in her.

"His speed is a game changer. He's got big powerful thighs, and his hockey IQ is off the charts."

The room tilted and she laid the palm of her hand flat against the window to try to stop herself from sliding off the edge of the earth.

"He's got a dangerous slap shot and plays suffocating defense. If he—"

"Him." The word leaked from her.

A beat of silence fell over the room.

"Get me him," she said to the window.

"How long has he been back from injury?"

"He has some rust to shake off. Nothing to worry about."

"We might be able to get him cheap."

"Detroit's interested. They might've already struck the deal."

"No." With the pressure sitting on her chest, her voice sounded weak. "I want him."

"We don't need another right side forward," Darby argued. "Lovejoy will be back from suspension next week, and Tierney can move over."

She faced the men. "I said I want him."

"We have other needs. Bigger needs." Darby sounded bored. "What about Theroux?"

Bile rose up and she careened toward the door, doing all she could to walk, not run. "The guy with the thighs, he fills our needs. He's the priority."

"Look, I know you think you're helping, but why don't you leave this to us?"

She mimicked the scowl on Darby's grizzled features. "Do what you want with the others, but get me my guy."

Bolting from the room, she raced down the hall until she spotted the women's restroom. She ducked inside and barricaded herself in the first stall. The air wheezing through her lungs stung. She collapsed back against the door and stared up at the ceiling, straining to pull in enough oxygen.

It'd been years since her last panic attack. Therapy had helped, but only one thing ever stopped an attack.

She had to flee. Run. Get away, far away, as fast as she could. Only then would she be able to breathe again.

α

Jack glanced at his cell phone lying next to his lunch plate.

The previous night, he'd talked to his agent, Graham, and let him know there might be a deal brewing to trade

Jack to Detroit. Such deals might take hours or days, but Jack was cautiously optimistic he would get the call that day. At any moment.

Across the table, Sutton picked at the scraggly plate of lettuce she called a salad.

It had occurred to Jack to try to get out of his lunch date with Neal's daughter. He had no enthusiasm for it, and when he saw the restaurant she'd picked, one of those places where people went more to be seen than to eat, any obligation he felt vanished.

Still, lunch with a beautiful woman beat sitting in a hotel room trying to ignore the gnawing urge to take another pain pill. Haven remained the most powerful distraction from the cravings, and since they'd parted, the sheer strength of his will had proven stronger than the lure of those fucking pills.

So far.

Every day he won the battle, it'd get easier. He knew that much from witnessing several teammates go through the same struggle over the years.

It was a common enough thing, this cycle. Years spent pushing their bodies to stay competitive, even as the players seemed to get bigger, stronger, and faster. The inevitable injury. The pressure to get back on the ice. To perform at a pre-injury level. Pills to cope with the pain, and the pressure, to get them back in the game quicker. A cycle that was easy to fall into, but hard as hell to break.

A fresh start with a new team in a new city might be exactly what he needed to put it all behind him.

For now, he forced his mind back to Sutton.

Damn, but she was beautiful. Tall and long-limbed. A little too close to rail thin for his tastes, but supple. Along with her golden-streaked blonde hair and soft blue eyes, she compelled the gaze of everyone in the room.

While strangers gawked, Jack contemplated all the ways Sutton's striking appearance differed from Haven's dark, quiet beauty.

He pointed to her salad. "How is it?"

"Great." But a scowl touched her features.

He lifted an eyebrow.

She sighed. "I don't think there's anything I wouldn't do for a slice of pizza."

He laughed. "Then why didn't you get pizza?"

"Because it goes straight to my hips and they're putting me in a string bikini tomorrow," she said, laughing with him.

Jack thought she could use a little more on her hips, but he didn't think she needed to hear his, or anyone else's, opinion about her weight.

Instead, he took a drink from his water glass and tipped his cell phone so he could read the display.

No call from Graham.

Noise at a nearby table drowned out Sutton's soft voice.

He leaned forward. "I'm sorry, what did you say?"

"I said I had a crush on you." Pink stained her cheeks. "From the time you came to live with us."

The confession knocked him back in the chair. "I didn't know that."

She rolled her eyes. "You didn't know I was alive."

"In my defense, you were twelve the day I turned eighteen. If I'd noticed you, that would not have been cool. At all. In fact, it would've been criminal."

A smile lit up her face. She really was breathtaking.

His phone vibrated on the table.

Her blue eyes swung to the device. "Is that him?"

Jack had told Sutton about Neal's plan and warned her a call might interrupt their lunch.

He nodded. "Mind if I take it?"

"Of course not." She waved her hand. "Pick it up. Pick it up!"

Smiling, he did as she ordered. "Hey, Graham, what's

going on?"

Jack and Graham had been together since the beginning. Jack trusted Graham, and Graham understood Jack. Aware of Jack's dyslexia, Graham never e-mailed or texted. Instead, he always picked up the phone and talked to Jack directly.

"It's been a hell of a morning." Graham's voice rode high and breathless.

An answering rush of adrenaline kicked in Jack's chest. This was it, the moment he'd been waiting for, working for, as long as he could remember.

"Let me hear it."

"You've been traded—" Graham paused to catch a breath. "—to the Renegades."

The words slammed into Jack.

"The Renegades?" He shook his head, trying to clear away the fuzz. "What about Detroit?"

"Detroit was in on you early, but Milwaukee came in with an offer they couldn't refuse. Two first-round draft picks, a third- and a fifth-round pick...." Graham rambled off the list of sparkle and bling attached to Jack's trade, but Jack wasn't listening.

Nothing could bedazzle the pile of shit he'd just stepped in.

Milwaukee?

His mind scrambled to recall what he knew about the struggling franchise.

The team owner was a drunk.

They'd finished last in the league the last two seasons—not the division, but the entire league—and were working on a three-peat.

They'd squandered a first-round draft pick, twice, and pissed away the loyalty of a rabid, hockey-loving fan base.

They played in the absurdly named Hank's Pizza Haven Arena, and he was going to have to play for them.

In an arena named after shitty pizza.

They were bad. Historically bad.

"I've been traded to Milwaukee." The words dropped off his tongue like cinder blocks.

"You'll be a free agent at the end of the season," Graham was saying. "Detroit will pick you up then."

Jack reared back in his chair. "I'm a rental player?"

"Milwaukee wanted you bad. They coughed up a big chunk of change to get you."

Graham told him the dollar figure, and Jack drove a hand through his hair. The money was nice, but *fuck*.

He'd had it all right there in front of him, and it'd just slipped through his fingers. The dream, the Cup, the self-respect that came with playing for a competitive club. All gone.

Because of fucking Milwaukee.

Chapter Nine

Haven tossed and turned in restless sleep while her mind played with scenarios of fleeing. Fleeing town, fleeing the state, fleeing the country. But when the sun broke over the horizon and streamed into the penthouse, she climbed from the bed and shuffled to the spacious marble-tiled bathroom.

After a shower, she dressed in the black slacks and a button-down white cotton shirt she often wore when bartending. She paired the ensemble with the red heels and a red belt, hoping it appeared as acceptable office attire, but not really knowing for sure.

She'd not be fleeing town today. She couldn't. Not this time.

Well, not just yet anyway.

The day before, while she'd crouched in the bathroom stall, someone had entered the restroom. The clip-clop of a woman's heels had echoed in the small chamber, and soon two tiny feet appeared under the door outside Haven's hideout.

"You can come out anytime." Mel's voice held the authority of a military general.

Haven had ignored her, knowing Mel would give up on her and leave. Eventually.

But Mel didn't leave.

Haven had tried waiting her out. She must've remained holed up in that bathroom stall for forty minutes or more. When she finally emerged, disgruntled but curious, Mel's keen gaze had swept swiftly over her. Then the older woman had crossed to a sink and wet a paper towel under the water's soft spray.

She held it out to Haven, who took the cool towel and pressed it to her forehead.

Mel tilted her head to one side. "I think that's enough for today, don't you?"

Haven had nodded before going to the sink and cranking the nozzle.

While the water flowed, Mel watched her in the mirror with troubled eyes. "Will I see you tomorrow?"

Haven opened her mouth to tell Mel there wasn't a chance in hell of that happening, but their gazes clashed in the mirror and the words wouldn't come.

Instead, Haven shut off the water and straightened away from the sink. "Yep."

So now, less than twenty-four hours after she'd emerged from that bathroom stall, Haven slipped into her winter coat and boots and set off in the direction of the river.

When she arrived at the arena, she rode the elevator to the third floor. With a ding, the doors slid open, but a large man with light brown hair waiting to enter the car hamstrung her exit. They sidestepped one another and as they passed, his light brown eyes caught hers.

An odd expression crept across his face, something

like recognition, except without a friendly smile or even the barest acknowledgment.

A shudder passed through her.

Then the elevator doors closed on him and she turned as Mel greeted her. In the no-nonsense manner Haven was fast becoming familiar with, Mel showed Haven to a large office beyond the reception area.

At the door, she stumbled to a stop.

The space was larger than her bedroom in Seattle. Maybe larger than the entire apartment she'd shared with Kaitlyn.

A wall of windows ran the length of the room and the largest flat-screen TV she'd ever seen hung on the opposite wall before a leather sofa, twin club chairs, and an oversized coffee table. At the far end of the office sat a dark wood desk surrounded by matching bookcases, which held no books but instead were stuffed with framed photographs and various sports paraphernalia.

Mel closed the door behind her as she slipped out of the room, leaving Haven alone in the cavernous office.

Haven removed her coat and laid it over the arm of one of the club chairs. Moving around the desk, she sank into the ginormous leather chair, but her feet didn't reach the ground.

Her head hanging over the side of the chair, she fiddled with the settings when the office phone rang.

She bolted upright. The phone rang again, and cautiously she reached out to pick up the receiver.

"Hello?"

"Ms. Callahan, Mr. Callahan is on the line for you."

"Uh, okay—"

Her dad's voice crackled over the line. "I think this is the first time I've ever found you where I expected you to be."

"Hi, Dad. Checking up on me?"

"Damn straight, I am. I heard about the new player

you picked up last night. A veteran forward with strong defensive skills. That's a good get, Haven. I like it. I like it a lot."

A tiny bloom of pride sprouted in her chest. "Thanks." She ducked her chin to hide the smile she couldn't stop from forming. "How are you feeling?"

"Well, they finally sprang me from the hospital, so I guess I'm doing better."

The folder Mel had given her yesterday lay on the desk and she flipped it open. "When do you leave for California?"

"Tomorrow morning." Wariness tinged his voice. "I wanted to give you the number where I'll be so you can reach me. You ready?"

Scrambling, she found a sticky note and pen in one of the desk drawers. "Ready."

He relayed the phone number and she wrote down the digits to the rehabilitation center where he'd be spending the next sixty days. "I won't call unless it's catastrophic. You focus on getting better."

"That's the plan."

"I'm glad you're doing this, Dad." She cleared her throat to cover up the unexpected surge of emotion. "Any last-minute advice?"

"Oh, let's see." Her dad grew quiet for a moment. "I guess I'd say, don't get too close to the players. They're employees and this is business. Things are a lot easier if you don't know them as actual people. Remember that, and you should be fine."

"That's the one thing you don't have to worry about." She'd rather lick the ice clean after a game than "get close" to a professional athlete, let alone a hockey player. "Take care, Dad."

She returned the receiver to the cradle. Not sure what she should be doing, she leafed through the documents in Mel's folder and became quickly engrossed in the stats and figures contained within. So engrossed that she didn't break until her stomach let loose with an angry growl near midafternoon.

The corner of one bookcase housed a mini-fridge and microwave. She rolled over to the fridge and pulled open the door. A gasp slipped from her when she saw the contents. Among a twelve-pack of Diet Coke and a box of Chinese takeout, she counted eight half pints of Grey Goose, small enough to slip into the breast pocket of a suitcoat.

She took a Diet Coke, tossed the leftovers and the vodka in the garbage, and slammed the door closed.

As she sipped from the can, a sharp knock on the door startled her. She jerked and a splotch of soda sloshed from the can and splattered onto her white blouse. A bull's-eye directly between the breasts, where the fabric tended to gape.

Mel swept into the office, a young man with chestnut-brown hair and horn-rimmed eyeglasses in tow.

"Ms. Callahan, this is Mr. Martin. Your father appointed him the new Director of Communications this morning."

That explained the terror glimmering in his dark eyes.

She offered him a commiserating smile. "Please, Haven will do."

"Wyatt." He shoved a loose-leaf sheet of paper to her. The corners quivered. "This is the press release we sent out regarding Mr. Callahan's car accident and your appointment in his absence."

She cringed when she took the paper from him. "How has the coverage been?"

The past two days, she'd been too afraid to turn on the TV.

Wyatt's beat of silence confirmed her fears.

He nudged his glasses up the bridge of his nose. "The press conference will help, I think."

"Press conference?" The sharp punch of panic struck in the center of her chest. "What press conference?"

"The one starting now." Mr. Martin's eyes darted between Haven and Mel.

Mel peered at him over the rim of her reading glasses. "Did you send notice to Sabrina?"

Wyatt frowned. "Who? No." His throat worked.

"Next time you schedule something, e-mail Sabrina with the information and she'll add it to Ms. Callahan's calendar."

"I have a calendar?"

"Yes." Mel's round features pinched. "Mr. Martin, will you show Ms. Callahan to the media room?"

Haven reared back. "I don't want to go to a press conference."

Wyatt blanched. "They're going to introduce the new player, and Coach Chambers is going to take some questions."

"The new player? He's here already?"

"Arrived an hour or so ago." He pointed to the sheet of paper in her hand. "We'd like you to read the statement on the back."

Haven's heart dropped to her stomach. "All I have to do is read it?"

"I don't advise you to say a single word more than what is on that paper."

ℂℤ

With a sinking sensation, Jack watched the Milwaukee Renegades' media room fill with reporters and beat writers. He recognized a couple of the national guys and suppressed a groan.

The national writers didn't show up often, and when they did, it meant either the team was winning, or they were embroiled in scandal.

As this was the Milwaukee Renegades, an organization allergic to winning and in the midst of perpetual turmoil, Jack understood the reason for their appearance. Even so, the steady stream of bodies cramming into the room struck him as remarkable.

He supposed it probably shouldn't. Other than winning, nothing drew more clicks than a downward spiral of incompetence and self-destruction.

Entangled in the logistical nightmare of relocating to a new city in a twenty-four-hour period, he'd so far managed to dodge the gory details. The move had been smooth, in large part because he'd so far avoided the hassle of a wife and kids and, thus, the nuisance of relocating them as well. Within hours, everything was set and he was ready to go.

He'd arrived at the arena around noon, one day after his trade, where he met with the coaches and a few players. He knew Cal Chambers from his work with a minor league affiliate team and respected the hell out the young coach. Though his tenure with the Renegades was off to a rough start, Jack gave the man and his staff an open mind. He listened as Coach explained his vision for the team, and Jack's role in achieving that vision.

Jack liked what he heard. He liked to play the kind of hockey Coach's scheme favored, and the man's excitement to have Jack onboard appeared genuine. So much so that soon, some of Jack's initial disappointment began to fade.

Maybe his trade wouldn't turn out to be the train wreck he feared. He was a professional, after all. A seasoned warrior. The Renegades organization didn't define him. The game did. He'd do everything in his power to win games, as he'd always done, and he'd collect a damn good paycheck for doing so. When opportunity arose, as it also always did, he'd be ready to seize it and take his career to the next level.

Then the Renegades' GM, Darby Poitiers, joined them, and it all seemed to turn to shit.

Coach's clear vision became murky, and the solid foundation he'd described weakened under Poitiers's heavy qualifiers and nebulous strategies. When Poitiers mentioned the press conference, which was set to begin in a matter of minutes, the entire staff seemed flummoxed.

Amidst scrambling bodies and a terse exchange wherein they decided to introduce "the new guy" to the media, Jack's disappointment snowballed, picking up traces of anger and disgust as it rolled downhill. He despised incompetence, never more so than when it meant innocent bystanders, such as himself in that moment, would suffer.

He arrived in the Renegades' media room, determined to get through the hellish task of a disorganized press conference and a meet-and-greet with the front office staff, so that he could return to his real work—figuring out what the fuck he was going to do now.

ೞ

Bodies already packed the second-floor media room when Haven arrived with Wyatt. Large pieces of equipment littered the floor like landmines. While Wyatt moved to the platform at the front of the room, Haven slunk off to one side.

As she backed up to the wall, her heel caught on a cord. She stumbled and came up hard against a large body. Hands gripped her arms, steadying her, and when she twisted around, she collided with a broad, suit-clad chest.

Dazedly, she looked up.

Into green-gold eyes.

His set features melted with recognition. "Haven?" His fingertips brushed her cheek. "It's really you."

A jolt ricocheted through her.

"Jack." His name fell from her lips like a prayer. "What are you doing here?"

She tilted her head toward his warm touch, but he was already pulling away.

Wyatt's voice crackled through the microphone. "Thank you, everyone, for coming out today. I'd like to introduce you to the newest member of the Milwaukee Renegades, Jack Nolan. Jack? C'mon up."

Jack's hand dropped away from her face. "Wait for me, please. I have to...."

He bounded up onto the stage.

She stared after him, her mouth slack, as he moved to stand at the podium.

He stooped to speak into the microphone. "I want to thank the Milwaukee Renegades organization for this opportunity. I look forward to continuing my career in this great, hockey-loving city."

She fell back, coming up hard against the wall.

Jack Nolan.

She'd slept with Jack Nolan. Last weekend.

Her Jack was Jack Nolan, the same man now standing up on that stage. A hockey player. A hockey player on her dad's team.

Her team.

Wyatt stepped up to the mic. "If anyone has any questions?"

Hands shot into the air and Wyatt pointed to a reporter.

"How's the groin, Jack?"

The best sex of her life, with the most tender, special man she'd ever almost wanted to kind of sort of fall in love with, was with a professional athlete employed by her father?

Jack's smile mimicked the heartbreaker's smile he'd used on her. "I don't think I know you well enough yet to answer that question, Matt."

Laughter drifted through the room.

"No but honestly, I'm feeling great," Jack said. "I'm ready to play."

Beneath the glare of artificial lights, his dark hair shone and his bright eyes blazed in his beautiful face. The pleasant arrangement of his features resembled her Jack, but the cool professional standing behind that podium didn't match her memory.

She couldn't catch her breath, as if she'd fallen and had the wind knocked out of her.

How had this happened?

She recalled Jack's touch, his soothing heat and reassuring strength. Incredible strength. Seriously, his body was rock-hard. The muscles chiseled. A memory flashed through her mind of how the muscles of his abdomen rippled when he moved over her.

Then she remembered his comment about how much he traveled for work. A pro athlete would travel a remarkable amount. A college professor? Probably not so much.

Her head dropped back and landed against the wall with a thud. *Well, hell.*

Another reporter called out a question. "Yesterday, rumors swirled of a possible trade to Detroit, but by the end of the day, you'd been sent to Milwaukee. What is that like, to go from possibly playing for one of the best teams in the league only to end up on the roster of a struggling Renegades team?"

Jack's features took on a grim set. "I'm excited for a chance to win hockey games."

Wyatt stepped forward. "We have time for one more question."

"Hi, Jack. Kyle Gregory from the Milwaukee Gazette. Ten years ago, you were the thirty-seventh player selected in what was widely considered the weakest draft in a decade. Did you think then that you'd experience such a long career in the league?"

When Jack's disquieting gaze fastened on Kyle, the man stumbled over his next words. "And what are your remaining g-goals before r-retirement?"

Except for the muscle that ticked in his jaw, Jack stood still as an ice sculpture. "Thirty-eighth."

"Excuse me?"

"I was the thirty-eighth player selected in the draft that year."

Kyle looked down at his tablet. "It says here—"

"Corey DeBoer was the number one overall pick, taken by Boston," Jack interrupted. "Brandon Crawford went to Phoenix second. Montreal took Ben Braden and Nashville took Joe Stakoviac."

While Jack continued, Kyle, and several other reporters, listened with their heads bent low over their phones and tablets, their fingers swiping and tapping frantically.

"Pick six was Marcus Chumra to Detroit, seven was Dylan Montgomery to Vancouver, and eighth was Johan Fredrickson to Minnesota."

A camera flashed.

Jack went on naming players and the teams that'd selected them. A soft buzz built among the reporters as they murmured to one another, fact-checking Jack's list. By the time he reached the mid-twenties, the buzz in the room had swelled to a steady drone.

He stumbled once, at number thirty-four. "Columbus picked the kid out of Denmark. Henrik...."

"Nilsson," someone called out.

"Henrik Nilsson. That's it. San Jose had the thirty-fifth and thirty-sixth picks, and they took Jacob Bartoleme and Mikko Kucherov. I forget which was which." Then Jack's gaze found Kyle. "And the thirty-seventh pick was Casey Reynolds to Toronto."

He started to straighten away from the podium, but bent forward once more. "And to answer your other question, yes, I have goals before I retire."

Jack moved to the edge of the platform as Coach Chambers stepped up to the podium. He spoke about Jack's skills as a player and about the team's recent string of losses.

She barely registered his words over the hammering of her heart, which tripped and fell into an erratic rhythm when Jack's brilliant gaze locked on her, a confused frown playing over his features.

Coach tossed out a nonanswer to a reporter's question about how he planned to turn the season around, and then Wyatt was moving toward the podium.

He bent to the microphone. "Thank you, Coach. Ms. Callahan will make a brief statement and take your questions."

The effort to walk seemed agonizing. She crossed the platform as though trapped inside one of those dreams where she couldn't move her legs, and the more she tried, the harder it became, until the struggle and the panic frightened her awake.

Except she didn't wake up, and with the intense awareness of a nightmare, she noted the moment Jack's face darkened. Curiosity and confusion twisted into shock, and then something else. Something uglier.

She turned away from him and into the harsh brightness of the media's lights. Behind the blinding glare, fuzzy forms and faces swarmed.

She hated how her voice shook when she read Wyatt's prepared statement. Two sentences that conveyed very little.

Then the questions started.

"Will your dad face criminal charges?"

A camera flash went off.

"I... I don't know."

"Should the commissioner decide to take disciplinary action, will Hank accept his punishment?"

"He's seeking help for his problem. I believe that proves his willingness to accept the consequences of his actions."

The questions came at her like arrows across the bow.

"Is Hank planning to sell the team?"

"Are you his successor?"

"Is it true an oil tycoon wants to buy the team and move it to Canada?"

Memories swamped her of the last time she'd stood in front of the media and tried to defend herself. "My dad has no plans to be away from the organization longer than is necessary for him to receive treatment."

Her gaze darted to the shadows in search of Wyatt. She found him standing beside Darby. He must've recognized the plea in her eyes, for he lurched forward, but Darby's hand on his arm stopped him coming to her rescue.

"Your father has the worst record of any owner in the conference in a decade." It was a statement. "What will you do differently?"

"The focus right now is getting Coach Chambers the players he needs to win hockey games." Some of the strength returned to her voice. "My dad trusts Darby Poitiers to do his job, and so will I. Unless or until proven wrong."

"What qualifications do you have to run an organization of this size?"

Her nerves unraveling, she drew a deep breath and pushed it out between her lips. "Not many."

Her response elicited a few gasps, quickly hushed.

Oops.

"What do you think of your dad's decision to leave you in charge?"

"I'm happy to help in any way I can."

"But don't you think this is one more thing he's done to embarrass the organization? Fans and shareholders are beyond frustrated at this point."

Haven bristled. The fans were frustrated with her dad? They should try being his daughter. Still, it was one thing if she'd written Hank off, but it was an entirely different beast if anyone else thought to do so. He was her failure, not theirs.

"I think he's putting his health and his family first for the next sixty days, and that's a good thing for everyone involved, including the Renegades organization."

"When will Bryce Lovejoy be back from suspension?"

Wyatt all but shoved her out of the way. "Sorry, folks. That's all we have time for."

The camera lights went dark and bodies began filing toward the exit.

Feeling dazed and bruised, she blindly followed Wyatt off the platform. "Who's Bryce Lovejoy?"

"Starting forward," Coach Cal answered when Wyatt scurried away. "He's serving a six-game suspension."

Darby shook his head. "It's an excessive punishment. We're appealing the league's decision."

"What did he do?" she asked.

A glower tarnished Coach Chambers's well-formed features. "He beat up his girlfriend in a nightclub parking lot. Surveillance cameras caught the whole nasty incident on tape. All thirty-eight seconds of it."

She swallowed the wrench of nausea that hit her.

Darby bridled. "You're making it sound worse than it was."

Haven wished she were surprised to hear Darby defend the jerk. "Only six games? He stays suspended."

Darby's face turned red and ruddy, but before he

could demean or debate her, she turned her back to him.

To find herself pinned beneath a paralyzing green-gold gaze.

Chapter Ten

They didn't speak, waiting while the few remaining reporters shuffled out of the room.

Believing she'd never see him again, she drank in the sight of him. Long, dark eyelashes framed his vivid eyes, made brighter against the canvas of his smooth, swarthy skin. The familiarity of his face soothed her, and a slow, steadying breath seeped from her.

Until she registered his dark scowl.

When they were alone at last, the air took on a hostile chill. She'd been identified as a threat.

"Did you plan this?" Wounded accusation laced his voice. "This thing between us, was it a setup?"

She gaped at him. "Did I...? You think I planned this?"

In response, one of his dark eyebrows lifted.

A lash of hurt and anger struck her. "Are you serious? You think I flew across the country, in a blizzard, to seduce you, somehow knowing my dad would get drunk, crash his car into a convenience store, and put me in charge of his hockey team, where I could then acquire you in a trade deal and show up at this press conference to make a fool of myself?"

A flicker of doubt flitted over his face, though he remained silent.

"I can assure you, I did not plan this." The annoying quiver returned to her voice. "I don't want this. Any of it."

"Then why did you lie to me?"

She drew up at the accusation. "What did I lie to you about?"

"You said you were poor. But you're not. You're... you're... rich." He spat the word.

"I'm not rich. My dad is."

His bitter laugh rankled. "It crossed my mind to worry you might be a puck bunny, but you're a thousand times worse. You're a puck princess."

She flinched. "You told me you were a college professor."

His brows slammed together. "I never once said that."

She crawled through the jumbled chambers of her memories. Emily had said Jack was a professor. She recalled her pointing across the bar, and Haven had peered through the crowd to see Jack and another man....

A man with the same dark hair and striking features.

Oh, no. Was he–?

"Noah is the professor." Jack's hard gaze was unrelenting. "You know, the guy *married* to Emily's cousin."

"I was in town a few hours before I was in bed with you," she snapped. "I didn't have time to sort out the family tree."

"Or you knew exactly who I was and what you wanted from me."

"If I'd known you were a hockey player, I never

would've slept with you." Her fingernails bit into the flesh on her palms.

A smirk twisted his full lips. "That's a bit superficial."

"If you'd known I was Hank Callahan's daughter, would you have slept with me?"

His smirk vanished. "Not a chance in hell."

She should have felt some small sliver of satisfaction. Should have, but didn't. "Now who's being superficial?"

"That's different."

"How?"

That muscle ticked in his jaw. "Everyone on that island knows I'm a hockey player."

She flung her arms wide with frustration. "I never once set foot on that island before that day. How was I supposed to know? You don't have hockey hair!"

A quizzical pucker formed between his eyebrows. "What the hell is hockey hair?"

"You know, the hair." Her hands swept over her head. "Long and flowy. You don't have it."

"And you don't act like a stuck-up rich girl. What's your point?"

"That's because I'm not a rich girl," she ground out. "And my point is, I'm just as unpleasantly surprised by all this as you are."

He searched her face for several heartbeats, and then he cursed. "So we were both fooled?"

"No, not fooled." She lifted her chin. "We both got exactly what we wanted from each other—a no-strings-attached hookup."

"Honey, we got more strings than a damned puppet."

She frowned. "You make it sound so ugly."

"Look around you." His voice rose with the sweep of his arms. "This is ugly."

"It's only temporary." She couldn't banish the defensive ring from her tone. "In sixty days, I'll be gone and you can go back to pretending I never existed."

"What do we do until then?" His expression softened a little. "Pretend we never met before this moment?"

A band of butterflies banged around in her stomach. Did he think they had any other choice? That they could just pick up where they'd left off on the island? In bed together?

The butterflies crash-landed somewhere near her naval.

"It's not that far from the truth." She folded her arms over her abdomen. "What happened last weekend was a mistake. Just a moment, or... ten moments, of weakness. But it's over now. Like it never happened."

He crossed his arms to match her stance. "I wasn't weak."

Her arms dropped to her sides. "Fine. I was the weak one and I seduced you to my own purpose. Does that make you happy?"

"Depends. What purpose was that again?"

She hesitated. "I'd just broken up with my boyfriend."

His eyes narrowed to dangerous slits. "I was your rebound guy?"

No, he was her escape.

The thought startled her. To hide it, she lifted one shoulder. "You were my breakup guy."

"What the hell is a breakup guy?"

"I had an ex-boyfriend I wanted to forget. Sleeping with you was a hell of a distraction, let me tell you."

One corner of his puffy mouth tilted upward. "That's the only reason you slept with me? To forget—what was his name?"

"Ch-Charlie."

"Charlie." Icicles dripped with the name. "I feel so cheap."

She blushed. Seriously, what was happening to her? She never blushed. Ever. "You should. I used you."

"Because of Charlie?"

His eyes were laughing at her, as though he knew the truth. That since the moment she'd laid eyes on him, Charlie hadn't once visited her thoughts. Not once.

"Right. Because of...." Oh, crap. What was his name? "Because of him."

Jack's gaze, hot and intense, roamed over her face, caressing every inch, drinking in every nuance and trait. Butterflies took flight.

Then, with a suddenness that left her cold and dizzy, a chill froze the warm green-and-gold jewel tones in his eyes and he gave his head a shake, as if throwing off a shroud of fog.

"Look, none of that matters now." He fixed her with a dark look of mistrust. "You need to fix this. I'm supposed to be in Detroit right now."

"Detroit?"

"It's where I was supposed to be traded before you stepped in and ruined everything."

His words took a gash out of her heart, though they didn't hurt as much as the way he looked at her. As though she were nothing more than a nuisance to him. A regret he wished to scrub from his life.

The same way the boys in high school had looked at her after she'd had sex with them.

The soles of his shoes scraped against the floor as he moved to stand closer. He pushed into her space, towering over her.

The slippery slime of fear slithered down her spine.

"I won't play for this team, Haven."

Anger flared in her chest. How dare he—the one big man she could recall who didn't frighten her—try to use his size to intimidate her.

She lifted her chin. "You'll play. I own you, Jack. Or, m-my dad does."

Fiery gold flashed in his eyes. "No one owns me. Not you, and definitely not your daddy."

"So, we're to be enemies now?" Even through her anger, the thought made her sad.

A flicker of some emotion alighted in his eyes but vanished too quickly for her to identify it.

He eased away from her. "You're my boss. Beyond that, we're not anything."

∽

The next day, Haven didn't go to the arena. It was Saturday, and it was Christmas Eve. In her nightshirt, she sipped from a coffee mug and stared out at the wide expanse of the churning winter sea.

She stared hard, but no matter how long she stared, from so far up and away, the lake's calming magic was lost to her. She couldn't feel the reassuring lull or the moving strength that'd poured over her on the island.

The rest of the day, she tried unpacking the few belongings in her suitcases, but it felt too much like committing to this joke of an idea that she could take over ownership of the Renegades, so halfway through, she abandoned the effort.

The old familiar melancholy tried to take ahold of her, and several times throughout the evening she had to remind herself that she liked being alone. It'd taken years to get used to being alone after Ryan's death, but now she relished the isolation. Preferred it, even.

Really, she did.

But even if she didn't love it, Ryan had been gone fourteen years, and if he couldn't be the one there with her, she didn't want anyone else taking his place, in her life or in her heart.

The next day, bright sunlight ushered in Christmas morning. Haven set the coffee brewing and, as she did every Sunday, she reached for her cell phone.

She tapped the series of digits and when she heard the soft pitch of her mother's voice, she forced a cheerfulness she didn't feel into her own tone.

"Hi, Mom. Merry Christmas."

"Hi, sweetie. Merry Christmas to you, too."

She pulled a coffee mug down from the cupboard. "What are you doing today?"

"Oh, just taking it easy. Going through some pictures."

The ball of dread in Haven's stomach gave a wrench.

"Do you remember the year you two got bikes for Christmas?" Her mom's soft laughter sounded light and tinkling. "And you rode them all through the house because the snow was too deep to ride outside."

"I remember that. My bike had green streamers and a picture of Scooby-Doo on the seat."

Neither of them spoke for a moment and through the connection, Haven heard the soft creak of the plastic photo album as her mom turned the pages.

"He was so handsome, wasn't he?"

Haven swallowed the lump trying to form in the back of her throat. "Yeah, he was."

"And so smart. I don't know where he got that, but he was so bright."

"How are you, Mom?" Haven poured coffee into her mug. "Are you feeling okay?"

"I'm fine, just fine." After a beat of silence, her mom asked, "What was the name of his best friend in kindergarten? The little boy from Sheboygan?"

"Jonah."

"Of course. Jonah." She laughed. "I was up all night trying to remember his name. I wonder what he's doing these days...."

Another crinkle reached Haven through the phone. Her heart ached.

"Mom, I have to get going. I just wanted to call and say Merry Christmas."

"Oh, all right, dear. We'll talk again soon."

"Okay." Haven's voice cracked. "Love you, Mom."

"Love you, too, baby."

Silence dropped like a sledgehammer in the sprawling penthouse.

Restless, she paced the apartment, picking up and setting down the odd piece of abstract art or an article of her scattered clothing. By the afternoon, the walls were closing in on her.

Her mind kept trying to latch on to the sad memories, so she switched on the TV in hopes of distracting herself. Instead, she found the airwaves were flooded with sappy sentimental crap about families with parents that didn't drink too much and call each other nasty names, and children who actually wanted to spend the holidays with them.

It was too ridiculous to be believed.

She ticked through the channels, landing eventually on a sports talk show. It'd been recorded a day or two before, as the two analysts squaring off across a large desk spoke of a football game that'd taken place three days prior.

The analyst with dark, wavy hair turned to the camera. "Now on to this week's winners and losers. Let's start with the losers, shall we?"

Beside his big head, a picture of Haven's dad popped onto the screen. It was a close-up of his face, and he appeared dazed and disoriented, with an angry gash on his forehead leaking a trickle of blood.

"Oh, boy," the other analyst said. "Do we have to talk about this guy?"

"Yes, Jerry, we do. Hank Callahan, owner and president of the Milwaukee Renegades, got drunk and ran his Escalade through the storefront of a Quickie Mart in downtown Milwaukee. But that's not the craziest thing he did this week."

"What's the craziest thing?" Jerry asked obediently.

"He left control of his hockey team to his daughter."

Jerry held up a hand. "C'mon, Dave. What's so crazy about that?"

The picture in the background changed to one of her from the press conference, her white blouse straining over her breasts.

Jerry ate his smile. "She seems smart."

Dave stared into the camera while his shoulders shook with repressed laughter. "Let's roll the clip."

The camera cut to the Renegades' media room, and the shaking visual steadied on Haven at the podium.

In the background, the reporter asked his question. "What qualifications do you have to run this team?"

The line of Haven's mouth twisted in a smirk. "Not many."

They paused the film on her face and the two analysts reappeared on either side of her image.

"What's wrong with that?" Jerry wanted to know. "It was a joke."

"She has no experience!" Dave shouted.

"You think it'll make a difference? This is the Renegades we're talking about, after all."

Dave crowed. "You know what, Jerry, that's a great point." Dave peered into the camera as the image of her dad reappeared next to her smirking face. "Nonetheless, Hank Callahan gets my biggest loser stamp for this week. The guy deserves to be locked up."

With an obnoxious sound effect, a red X stamped onto her dad's head.

"Give the guy a break, Dave. He's in rehab. He's trying. Shouldn't he get the chance to fail at his recovery before we lock him up and throw away the key?"

Dave's expression morphed into the epitome of somber seriousness. "Of course he should, Jerry. And let me be clear. I don't believe Hank Callahan should go to jail for having a problem with alcohol. He should go to jail for being the worst owner of *all* the owners of *any* professional sports team *in the history of sports.*"

Both analysts roared with laughter.

"Can't argue with you there," Jerry said through his snickering.

She flipped off the TV. Her stomach roiled with nausea.

They thought this was funny? Haven didn't recall her dad drinking when she was young, but he'd struggled with alcohol since Ryan's death. They'd all struggled, in one way or another.

She wondered how much Chance and Braden understood what was happening to their family. At ten and twelve years old, probably an awful lot. Had they seen Dave and Jerry's little act? Did the other kids at school tease them?

She wondered if Bryce Lovejoy had made the show's list of losers. How did beating up a woman you supposedly love compare to the sin of losing a game? Or, as it were, a whole bunch of games?

Anger took root inside Haven. She wanted to shout at those mean men. Shake them until they understood the hurt they were causing. Mostly, she wanted to tell them to shut up.

But there was only one way to silence the haters.

Win.

The surge of angst and anger deserted her.

Welp, that wasn't going to happen.

She flopped onto the sofa and lay staring up at the ceiling.

But what if they could win?

Truthfully, she knew too little about the team to know if winning was within the realm of possibility for them. Were the personnel in place simply underperforming, or were there larger issues? Could they make a few more trades and plug enough holes to float the boat? If they could just sneak a few more W's into the score column....

She pushed to her feet and crossed to her purse hanging on the back of a dining chair. Maybe the answers were in that folder Mel had given her.

But the folder wasn't in her purse, and then Haven recalled that when she'd fled the arena Friday after that horrible press conference, she'd forgotten to grab it from her dad's desk. If she was going to get any idea what was wrong with this team, she needed that folder.

Wrapping herself in her heavy winter wool coat, she plunged out into the frigid day. She expected the streets to be quiet, and mostly they were, though families packed the ice rink in midtown and a couple of nearby restaurants remained open to sell hot chocolate and provide a respite from the biting cold.

She circled around to the arena's south end, where she'd been given card access to an employee-only entrance, but she found the large garage doors raised. She slipped past the charter bus idling in the garage, craning her neck to search for clues to the reason for the bus's presence.

As she climbed the steps to the employee entrance, the heavy steel door swung open and a gigantic man stepped out onto the landing. Then a larger man followed, and another.

They filed out, surrounding her. Dwarfed by their size, the panic it'd taken years to get under control welled up, squeezing her chest and closing the back of her throat.

She stumbled along, bumping into one large chest and off another like a pinball. She gulped for air and tried to scurry out of their path.

Then a massive chest, and two large hands, came around her. She whirled and looked up into green eyes flecked with gold and rimmed in black.

Kind, kaleidoscope eyes.

"Jack."

His clean, spicy scent tortured her senses, and with it, a punch of longing struck her beneath the breastbone.

He set her away from him. "Hey, boss."

He made it sound like an insult.

With the pain of a slow heartbreak, she returned to herself. "Wh–What are you doing here?"

The words were out before her mind registered his tailored charcoal gray suit, the long hockey stick in one hand and the black duffle bag slung over his shoulder.

"We're on our way to the airport. Road trip." He spoke with a businesslike manner that wrenched her heart. There was no playfulness in his tone. Only an impersonal practicality.

"Right. A road trip. I knew that." She scratched the tip of her nose. "Where are you going?"

His eyes narrowed. "To Buffalo."

"Buffalo. That's right. Should be cold there, huh?"

"We're not going to Buffalo, Haven." He shook his head. "You didn't even read the schedule?"

"I did." It was almost the truth. She'd glanced at the long list of games remaining on the regular season schedule, but it spanned three months and the dates and cities were too numerous to grasp. "I just... forgot the details."

He started to turn. "Whatever you say."

"I didn't ask for this." She blurted the words.

With slow increments, he turned back.

"I don't want this." She hated the catch of vulnerability in her voice. "I asked my dad, begged him, to pick someone else, but he picked me."

"Why?"

"I don't know why. Maybe he was still drunk."

"No, why would you beg him not to pick you?" He hitched his bag higher on his shoulder. "Do you know how many people would kill to be in your position?"

"Did you watch that press conference?"

He shrugged his broad shoulders. "It's the media. Who cares about them? Every fan has dreamed of playing god of their team for a couple of months."

"I am not a fan. I don't even like sports."

His long eyelashes fluttered. "What do you mean, you don't like sports? You don't like hockey?" Confusion puckered his brow. "You a football fan?"

"No, I don't like *any* sports."

He shuffled his feet. "You mean professional sports. You like the unpredictability of the college game better."

She made a noise. "I detest college athletics."

"You go to a liberal arts school or something?"

"What is so hard for you to understand? I do not like sports."

He recoiled. "You really don't like sports." He shook his head. "That's just not right."

"Would you focus?"

Fire flashed in his eyes. "Oh, I'm focused. I even read the schedule."

"Why are you so mad at me?"

"Why am I—" He pulled up. "No. You know what? Forget it." He turned his back to her and strode toward the bus.

"I don't want to forget it. What were you going to say?" she called after him. "Jack, please."

His steps slowed, and a few feet from the bus, he stopped. Finally, he faced her. "I get it, okay. You didn't ask for this and you don't want it. But the thing is, Haven, you got it. It's yours, along with the fate of a whole bunch of people. People who've given their lives to this game. Families whose livelihoods depend on it, who are now depending on you." The warm passion in his voice iced over with his next words. "It's your now. So what the hell are you going to do with it?"

Without waiting for her answer, he climbed onto the

bus, and through the tinted windows she lost sight of him. With a hiss, the bus doors closed and the large vehicle rolled out.

Leaving her all alone again.

Exactly the way she liked it.

Chapter Eleven

Jack welcomed the road trip. Airports and hotel check-ins, arena walk-throughs and team meals, while tedious, kept him singularly focused until game time, where he relished the animosity of the home crowd and the fire brought by the opponent seeking to defend their home turf.

Unfortunately, neither the mundane nor the hostile was enough to banish Haven from his thoughts. Not his yearnings for her delicious body, nor memories of the wounded expression that'd marred her pretty face when he'd accused her of plotting against him and snapped at her for not knowing where or even that the team was traveling.

Maybe he wasn't being fair, but what the fuck did fairness have to do with any of this? She held his fate, and the fate of every other player on this team, in her hands, and she couldn't be bothered to read the fucking schedule?

Maybe, if he were completely honest with himself, he'd acknowledge what was really pissing him off. That what had transpired between them felt like a betrayal. A dirty hit. She'd told him she grew up poor, like him, and he'd believed her. Not only was she not poor, she was the daughter of a fucking billionaire.

He'd never been stupid around women, and he sure as shit never let one dupe him. Until Haven fucking Callahan.

By game time, Jack was eager to hit someone.

The team captain, Mathieu Marleau, hadn't played in eight weeks while he recovered from knee surgery, and the alternate captain, Bryce Lovejoy, was in the middle of a six-game suspension. The team played as one might expect a leaderless band of beer-leaguers to play.

Their timing was off and the refs whistled them offside a number of times throughout the game. On the other end, poor communication led to defensive breakdowns that gave Los Angeles too many opportunities to put the puck in the back of the net. They took advantage twice before the clock ran out on the first period.

In the second period, Jack worked on opening communication between his teammates. On the bench, he kept up a constant stream of chatter, pointing out weaknesses and tendencies in their opponents' game that they might be able to exploit. On the ice, he called out adjustments to his teammates.

They strung together two or three good shifts, but all it took was a dark-haired woman walking through the stands to distract Jack. His head swung around to follow her, while his heart hammered with its hope of catching a glimpse of her.

A split-second distraction that proved disastrous when the ref dropped the puck in the face-off circle and

Jack's man sent a one-timer hurtling toward the Renegades' net. The disc leaked through the goalie's five-hole.

Jack struck the ice with his stick. What the hell was the matter with him? He was stronger than this, more disciplined. Years of meditation and work with a sports psychologist had made him mentally tough. The toughest. He should've been able to drive her from his thoughts with ease.

Why would she even be at their game when she didn't know the team was traveling? Why did it piss him off so much that she didn't know? And why, for all that was good and holy, couldn't he get her out of his head?

She'd distracted him from the pills. Made sense she'd distract him from the game, too.

His mind in chaos, he watched from his position near the blue line as Los Angeles scored a fourth goal less than three minutes later.

A highly touted first-round draft pick, Milo Bishop hadn't lived up to expectations in his first season.

Jack skated by the rookie goaltender as a string of expletives fell from the kid's lips. He skated in a tight circle in front of the net, carefully lifting each foot to avoid touching the blue line marking the crease.

"You all right?" Jack asked.

"I'm fucking fine." Milo's head jerked with sharp repetitive up and down movements.

Hands on his knees, Jack dropped his head. Great, the goalie was a head case.

The Renegades' play didn't improve in the third period and the game wound up being a 6-0 blowout.

That night, Jack lay on the bed in his hotel room, throwing a rubbery stress ball against the wall while his teammates went out to a nearby club. He didn't want to go out. He didn't want to have drinks, and laugh, and chase after pretty girls.

He wanted to win hockey games.

On the night table, his cell phone vibrated. He scooped it up, but frowned at the unfamiliar number.

"How are things with the new team?" Sutton's cheery tone chafed his eardrum.

Or maybe it was her question that grated. "Things are great." He hurled the ball at the wall. "Just great."

"So, you promised me a makeup date."

Had he promised such a stupid-ass thing?

Shit. Maybe. Who knows? After he got off the phone with Graham, he'd deposited Sutton at her apartment and turned to the logistical nightmare of relocating to a new city within a twenty-four-hour period.

"What did you have in mind?" he asked.

"I have to be in Chicago in a couple of weeks." A distinct ring of uncertainty touched her voice. "I thought maybe we could get together. Go out to a club or something."

Jack repressed a sigh. He hated clubs, but he was too numb and distracted to work up a good lie.

"See you in a couple of weeks," he said.

In Vancouver, the monotonous travel routine repeated itself, but so did the shitty play.

The debacle in Los Angeles left Milo wound too tight, and an early neutral zone turnover had him backpedaling as the Vancouver forward advanced for an easy put away. With the early goal, the team's mental errors increased.

Coach Chambers barked orders and tried making adjustments, but nothing worked. At one point, late in the third and down three goals, some guys at the end of the bench found something funny in their shutout loss.

Their laughter abraded Jack's competitive sensibilities. Anger and helpless humiliation churned in his gut.

By the time the team arrived in Edmonton, Jack understood his fate.

He'd not be winning a Stanley Cup this season.

As he made his way through the tunnel to take the ice, the piss and vinegar normally hammering through his veins at puck drop was barely a salty mix.

In fact, the predominant sentiment he felt just then was a pure, overwhelming dread. He didn't like losing, and he especially didn't like losing without, at the very least, putting up a respectable fight.

He hadn't dreaded his time on the ice so much in a very long time. Not since his dad showed up at one of his junior league games, drunk and looking for a fight. Throughout the game, Daniel had continued to drink, and when, early in the third period, a call went against Jack, he'd staggered out onto the ice and charged at the referee with clenched fists.

Jack's coaches had tried to intercede, but Daniel turned on them, too. Swinging wildly, and thoroughly inebriated, he lost his balance and went down hard. Refs and coaches had pounced on him, restraining him until the police arrived to remove him from the arena grounds.

After that, they barred Daniel from attending any of Jack's games. When coach told him, Jack was relieved.

Relieved, but destroyed.

He'd watched his dad's display with a pit of mortification churning away in his stomach, a pit that'd never fully dissolved since then. That day, Daniel had cast a taint over Jack's sacred ground. Stained his success and contaminated his joy in playing.

Worse, he'd exposed Jack to his teammates. After that, they all knew what he was. The son of a piece-of-shit father.

Not like their dads. The children of wealth and privilege—because only rich kids could afford to play hockey—they'd realized Jack was nothing like them. He'd only found his way into their midst because Shea had worked two jobs and Leo had a knack for "finding" money. That's the only way they paid for the gear, the travel, the ice time, and the tournament fees.

Now, the Renegades' starting lineup gathered at center ice for the puck drop, including the team captain in his first game back from injury. A determined scowl settled over Mathieu's angular features and sent a chord of electricity reverberating along the bench.

Coach put Jack and Mathieu together on the second line. Early in their shift, Mathieu spotted Jack racing up ice and hit him in stride with the puck, which Jack sent hurtling at the net. He picked his spot over the Edmonton goalie's left shoulder, and the puck made it home.

As the clock wound down on the first period, it appeared the suddenly engaged and fiery Renegades would take a one-goal lead into the first intermission.

Then, with under a minute to go in the period, an Edmonton player put a brutal hit on Mathieu that dropped the Renegades captain to the ice.

Instinct sent Jack flying at the Edmonton player. He landed a solid fist on the other man's jaw. A potent mix of anger and adrenaline fed Jack's wrath, and he continued throwing punches until the refs pulled them apart.

At intermission, he charged through the tunnel, ready to tweak the game plan to take down those assholes and get back out on the ice, but a somber pall hung in the air inside the locker room when he entered.

Jack searched out the source, only to find Mathieu lying on his back on a trainer's table, an arm flung over his face and a bag of ice taped to his knee. Around him, the trainers spoke with grim, hushed voices.

Jack's stomach dropped. The captain was done for.

Mathieu was thirty-seven years old. He'd probably been in the league seventeen or eighteen years. He'd missed the last eight-plus weeks rehabbing the knee, only to reinjure it within a few minutes of returning to game action.

Everyone in that locker room knew what was going through Mathieu's mind as he lay on that table. His playing days were numbered. Possibly, they were already over.

Jack turned away from Mathieu, trying not to think about the fact that, at thirty-two, he could already feel the changes in his body. No longer the fastest player in the league—the rookie in Tampa had him beat—he'd only get slower with each next season.

If he were lucky, he'd make it another four or five seasons without losing a significant amount of playing time to injury. But once the injuries started, the end would come quick.

Without hockey, and without the accolades of a champion, Jack would have nothing, except a broken body and a defective brain.

Back on the ice, the Renegades played with short bursts of focused, disciplined hockey through two periods. But they also made some boneheaded decisions and committed a rash of stupid penalties.

Still, with two minutes remaining in the game, they held on to a one-goal lead. Excitement began to buzz between the players. Might they actually win one? On the road?

Edmonton pulled their goalie, giving them the man advantage for the final minute. Their offense set up in Milwaukee's territory and Jack positioned his body in front of the net to help block shots.

The winger slapped the puck and the bullet struck Jack in the arm with a vicious sting before dropping harmlessly to the ground. There was a ruckus, with sticks and feet jabbing frantically at the black disc.

Milo knocked down the first and second shots on goal. In the chaotic scramble for the loose puck, Jack lost sight of it. He twisted and spun, searching.

Only to watch the puck float between his legs, deflect

off his back skate, and slip through Milo's pads to land in the back of the net.

Horns blared and the crowd went wild.

He'd just scored on his own team.

It was the last thing they needed. The crushing weight of lost hope did them in and they came out flat in overtime, going down on a sloppy turnover that led to a breakaway goal.

With the misery of yet another defeat hanging heavy around their necks, no one spoke in the locker room. Guys showered and packed in silence. They checked their cell phones and crammed earbuds in their ears, distracting themselves from the gloom. Or maybe they didn't care.

That dark suspicion bore out a few moments later when Jack overheard two of his teammates planning to hook up with a couple of puck bunnies later.

Jack battled the slither of apathy wriggling under his skin, trying to burrow inside him and kill his will. A few months, maybe weeks from now and he might be exactly like them. Playing without passion or hunger. Only there to collect the paycheck and take his enjoyment in parties and available women.

With a hard shove, he stuffed his pads into his hockey bag. He latched on to the anger, for just then, it was the only thing standing between him and the repulsive squirm of apathy.

He wasn't ready for the passionless life.

Yet.

That's what retirement was for.

He kicked the empty locker shut. Standing, he slung the bag over his shoulder and headed for the exit.

There was only one way out of this mess. He had to get off this team before it destroyed not only his career, but his soul as well.

Only one person had the power to make it happen for

him.

Haven.

☙

On Friday, the sting of Jack's disappointment with her and the mocking laughter of those TV jerks still throbbed in Haven's chest.

It made zero sense. She'd given up trying to please people years before, once she realized she was incapable of pleasing anyone ever.

Unless she was naked, of course.

She'd spent the week working in her dad's office, trying to learn the massive organization's structure while pouring over the stats and numbers in Mel's folder.

On her way out for the night, she stopped off at Mel's desk, which sat as a barricade to her dad's office.

Haven pushed a strand of hair back and tucked it behind her ear. "So, um, if I wanted to use the owner's box tomorrow night, who do I ask about that?"

If she was going to turn this thing around, she was going to have to figure out what was wrong with this team. Which meant she was going to have to watch them play.

Mel's sharp gaze found Haven over the rim of her cat's-eye reading glasses. "I'll let security know you'll be in attendance."

"Great. Thank you." She hovered in front of Mel's desk.

Mel waited for her.

"Do you like hockey?"

Mel's mouth turned down at the corners with her thoughtful frown. "I suppose—"

"Will you come with me?" The words burst from Haven.

Mel blinked at her. "To the game?"

"I know it's not part of your duties, and you probably have a hundred other things you'd rather be doing on a Saturday night besides watching a hockey game from the owner's box, but... would you mind? Just this once?"

"Well, I don't—"

"You can bring your family. Any of them. All of them."

"My kids are all grown and out of the house. It's just me and my husband."

"Any chance he likes hockey?"

A bemused smile flitted across Mel's face. "He's more of a football guy."

Haven's shoulders slumped. "I understand. If you can convince him to come, I hope you will."

As she'd done twice that week already, she stopped at the brewpub across the street from the arena on her way home from work. Bodies packed the bar and loud blues music flowed from the speakers overhead.

The bartender, a college student named Austin, smiled when he spotted her at the bar. "The usual?"

Haven returned his smile and climbed onto a barstool. "You talked me into it. To-go, please."

Austin slid a pint of the brewery's light beer across the bar to her and shouted her food order over the music to the guys in the kitchen.

She took a sip from the pint and then slipped off her winter coat. With a break in the music, she became aware of a commotion and turned to see three men each chugging a beer while a throng of onlookers chanted and cheered.

Their throats worked as they gulped. Liquid leaked out the sides of their mouths to trickle down their chins and onto their shirtfronts. One by one, their pint glasses struck the table. The winner bounded to his feet and pumped his fists in the air.

But Haven paid the blowhard no mind as her gaze latched on to the dark-haired man with the most incredible smile who sat watching from one end of the table, looking reluctantly amused.

Jack.

She realized then that the men, including the beer chuggers, were Renegade hockey players. Did they think she was a frivolous puck princess the same way Jack did? Were they even aware of her existence? She slipped off her stool and picked her path through the crowd.

Jack was the first of the men to notice her approach. The humor left his face, replaced by a dark simmering resentment. He leaned back in his chair and folded his arms over his broad chest.

Awareness of her presence trickled slowly around the table, until one of the beer chuggers elbowed the still-celebrating champion in the ribs. Finally, the gazes of all ten or more men focused on her.

"Hello, boys. Back from your road trip?"

Someone belched.

She arranged her features into a serene smile. "Good to see you're working on your defensive lapses."

A few expressions turned hangdog.

"I'm not sure you've earned the right to judge our play yet." Bitterness sliced through Jack's deep baritone.

Standing so near to him, she could see lines of weariness bracketed his eyes.

"That's the beauty of being a puck princess," she said. "I don't actually have to earn anything."

He held her gaze. "It's a long season. They're entitled to a little downtime."

"You may be right about that. The problem is they're doing it wrong." She plucked an empty pint glass off the short stack and reached for the pitcher of beer. She *tsked*. "You're chugging the brewed beer? That's so disrespectful."

"Yeah, but it tastes the best," said the man to her right.

"I know it does, but a beer this good should be

savored." Her glass full, she returned the pitcher to the table. "Cheap American beer is for chugging."

"Nothing wrong with American beer." This man, standing beside another man who looked exactly like him, dared to give her a flirtatious wink. "I happen to like cheap and easy."

She bit the insides of her cheeks to keep from smiling. "There is, however, something very wrong with that slop on your shirt."

The charmer ran a hand down his chest. "It shows my dedication."

"It's the mark of an amateur." She poised the glass before her. "You have to relax your throat, and if you're a purist, no spillage or you're disqualified."

Aware of Jack's eyes on her, she arched a brow at the beer-chugging champ, a burly blond with a missing incisor. "You ready?"

With a wide smile, the man scrambled to refill his glass and scurried around to stand beside her. "Set."

"Go."

The last thing she saw before she tilted her head back and drank was the nasty scowl on Jack's face. Haven regretted that she disappointed him so much, but she didn't know any other way to get the upper hand with these men. For once, they were on her turf. It might be her only chance to get their attention and, maybe, a teeny tiny smidgeon of their respect.

Calling upon her undergraduate education, she relaxed her throat and let the liquid slide down. She drank as quickly as she could, eager to be out from under Jack's displeased scrutiny. Her movements optimized for efficiency and speed, she plunked the glass onto the table with a thud a fraction of a second before her competitor.

The men's reaction was predictably loud and overblown, with plenty of taunts for their teammate for getting beat by a girl.

No amusement appeared on Jack's face that time.

Austin appeared at her elbow carrying a plastic bag with her takeout tucked inside.

"Thanks for the drink, guys." She backed away. "I hope you all get a good night's sleep and are ready to play tomorrow night."

She turned and fled, with the feel of Jack's dark scowl spearing her between the shoulder blades.

Chapter Twelve

In a Renegades jersey and baseball hat she'd swiped from the pile of promotional freebies, Haven slipped inside the arena through the employee entrance more than an hour before the game was set to begin.

People milled about in the halls beneath the arena floor, mostly Renegades staff members and a few beat writers. She pulled her ball cap lower, hoping to go undetected by the press, and rounded the corner to the bank of elevators that'd take her up to the executive suites.

She stumbled upon Wyatt and Darby huddled in the conversation.

"The press wants to talk to him," Wyatt was saying.

Darby's jowls jiggled when he shook his head. "No way."

"It might give him a chance to apologize, or show some remorse...."

"Hey, guys," Haven said. "What's going on?"

Behind his heavy glasses, Wyatt's dark eyes glittered with worry. "Bryce Lovejoy's suspension is over and he's set to play tonight. We're considering whether we should let him go before the press." Wyatt turned back to Darby. "He did express interest in repairing his image."

"It's not a bad idea," Darby conceded with a grimace. "Give him a chance to gain back the fans' trust."

"And the team's trust," Wyatt added.

Haven frowned. "What about his girlfriend's trust?"

Wyatt knuckled his glasses up the bridge of his nose. "Uh, yeah. That, too." Then he brightened. "Maybe she could take part in a quick presser. She wouldn't have to speak or anything. Just be there, you know, as a show of support."

"Stand by her man?" Haven quipped.

"Exactly," Wyatt said, missing the sarcastic taint to her words.

But Darby was shaking his head again. "Let's keep it simple."

Things moved quickly and within a few minutes, Darby chatted with a pool of press reporters at the other end of the hall while Haven hung back. A moment later Wyatt emerged from the locker room, a tall, broad man with light brown hair and eyes at his side.

Bryce Lovejoy, she presumed. Not an unattractive man, but he had an aura of conceit that cast an ugly shadow over his well-formed features. With their appearance, Haven noticed a pretty woman hovering in the hallway. A faded bruise marred her left eye.

Haven watched the way the woman watched Bryce and concluded she must be the girlfriend. And the bruise must be the reason why Darby didn't want her in front of the cameras.

Wyatt held out a loose-leaf sheet of paper to Bryce. Frowning, Bryce looked down at the paper and shook his head. Wyatt shoved the paper at him again, and with a curt remark, Bryce snatched it from Wyatt's hand, but the moment Wyatt turned away, Bryce wadded up the paper and tossed it onto the floor.

Then Wyatt gave the press the go-ahead and they surged forward to surround Bryce.

"Bryce, this is your first game back. How are you feeling?"

"Feels great," Bryce said.

"Is there anything you want to tell fans?"

"Uh, yeah. I want to apologize to my coaches and my teammates. I'm sorry I couldn't be there for them, but now I'm back, and I'm ready to get out there and hit some guys."

Haven cringed. Did he seriously just apologize for hitting his girlfriend by vowing to hit more people?

She looked to Darby and Wyatt, who appeared unperturbed.

"Bryce, how is Monica? Is it true you two have gotten engaged?"

"Monica's great. We're great, but, uh, I'm here to talk about hockey."

A reporter asked him about the Renegades' opponent, and Bryce complimented the visiting team's star player.

"Bryce, there've been some changes with the team while you were away. Have you met the new owner?"

"No, we haven't met." A smile worked its way across his face. "I've seen her though. Man, I hope she comes to the games. I wouldn't mind looking at her some more." He dropped his head in a miserable attempt to hide a snigger while uncomfortable laughter arose from the cluster of reporters.

Haven's stomach lurched.

With a look from Darby, Wyatt plunged forward and broke up the gathering. Bryce returned to the locker room and the reporters dispersed.

In the quieting hall, Haven glowered at Wyatt and Darby. "What the hell, guys?"

"It wasn't that bad," Darby said.

She gaped at him. "He had one job. All he had to do was pretend to respect women for, like, two minutes. *Two minutes*, and he couldn't do it."

Wyatt placed his eyeglasses on top of his head and scrubbed a hand over his face. "This should play really well for the next few days."

"Relax." Darby was already moving away. "Morality has no place in sports journalism. It'd interrupt their time allotted for criticism and mockery."

Haven and Wyatt watched him stride down the long hall.

"Any chance he's right?" Wyatt asked.

"Probably, but there is something worse than being criticized and mocked."

"Oh yeah, what's that?"

"Being a despicable human being."

Her first game in years off to a shaky start, Haven retreated to the sanctuary of the owner's box. The luxurious suite had a fully stocked bar and a row of plush leather seats with a bird's-eye view of the arena.

She poured herself a fountain pop behind the bar and wandered over to the cushy chairs.

Since the time she and Ryan were little kids, her dad, a season ticket holder, had taken them to hockey games. While her dad and Ryan analyzed the guys who played the same position Ryan did, Haven would take in the atmosphere.

She'd loved everything about it. The competitive fire of the players, their incredible talent, the strength of their will, the coach's ever-shifting strategies, the crowd's energy, the music and food and smells of an arena. Game days were her favorite days.

But that was a lifetime ago. A different life, of a

different girl. A girl she hadn't glimpsed in years and one she didn't particularly want to glimpse now.

She was watching the arena slowly fill with spectators and drowning in the sudden tidal wave of memories when a commotion sounded behind her.

She turned as the door to the suite pushed open and a little girl in a purple tutu bounded into the room.

Behind her, Mel emerged, her cheeks flushed pink. "I told you to wait for me, Clara Bell."

"Grandma, look!" The little girl pressed her nose to the glass.

Haven surged to her feet. "You made it."

Behind Mel, a large black man in a Packers baseball hat and puffer jacket filled the doorway.

Mel took a deep breath. "We made it." She placed a hand the man's arm. "This is my husband, Harlon, and that little blur you saw is our grandbaby, Clara Bell."

At the sound of her name, Clara Bell returned to Mel's side. She was a beautiful little girl, with warm brown skin and light blue eyes.

"Hi, sweetie," Haven said. "How old are you?"

"Six," Clara Bell announced, holding up five fingers.

Just then, the arena lights went dark and a booming voice crackled over the speakers inside the owner's box. *"Ladies and gentleman, introducing the visitors from Toronto."*

The measly crowd booed while Mel's brood settled in the front row seats and Haven fetched snacks and drinks from the bar. By the time she sank into her seat, players skated in circles on the ice, flinging pucks at the net while the goalies put up cursory attempts to block their shots.

Strobe lights flashed and flickered, and loud music pumped through the cavernous building.

Soon, the game started, and Haven found herself noticing things unrelated to the play on the ice. Beneath the arena lighting, the building appeared old and run-down. At best, the seats were half-filled with fans, and the majority of them were engrossed in conversations or busy playing on their phones.

"Is this attendance normal?" she wondered out loud.

"This is my first game, so I'm not sure what normal looks like," Mel said. "But I believe we hover around 65 percent capacity."

Haven wrinkled her nose. "That's not very good, is it?"

Mel's gaze swept over the arena below. "I wouldn't think so."

His cell phone cradled in his big hand, Harlon stared down at the device. "Dead last in attendance in the league, as a matter of fact."

Haven frowned at the glass.

Even the Renegade's jerseys looked old. The vivid royal blue on the players' torsos seemed faded, and the vibrant green accents dulled and muted. Even the white trim appeared gray and dingy.

She watched their opponents steal the puck from a Renegades player and take off for the other end of the ice. The Renegades gave chase, but they appeared slow and sluggish by comparison. When Toronto settled in on offense, she noted a surprising size difference. Unless Toronto had a roster of abnormally tall players, the Renegades were greatly undersized.

"Is Toronto good?"

Mel and Haven looked to Harlon.

His forehead creased as he took several swipes across the cell phone's screen. "They're sitting in eleventh place in the eastern conference." He settled back in his chair with a sour expression. "Out of sixteen teams."

Haven frowned down at the arena floor once more.

Only to realize Jack had come onto the ice with the last line change. He wore number seventeen.

When a Toronto player sent the puck flying toward

the net like a laser, Jack went down, throwing his body in front of the hard black disc. It struck him in the hip and bounced out into open space. Regaining his feet with one fluid motion, he took possession of the puck and headed up the ice.

His speed pushed him ahead of the others and soon only two defenders stood between him and the goalie. He shook off the first guy and juked the second to continue his reckless charge at the net. Toronto's goalie was backsliding into position as Jack, teetering on one foot, sent the puck careening toward the open net.

A collective gasp sprang from the crowd as the puck struck the crossbar with a loud clank, dropped straight down, and settled in the crease.

Jack lunged for it, but the goalie pounced on the loose puck and the referee whistled the play dead.

A beat of silence filled the arena, and then a smattering of applause arose from the stands. The clapping grew steadily, until the few thousand or so fans cheered and whistled, showing their appreciation for the new player's effort.

Time expired on the goalless first period. The players disappeared through the tunnel and fans trickled out into the concourse in search of restrooms and the concessions.

Haven smiled down at Clara Bell, sitting in the seat next to her. "Did you like the game?"

"It was awesome." She leaned forward to look past Haven. "Grandma, can I play hockey?"

Haven laughed and turned back as a group of women with small shovels skated onto the ice. Dressed in green hot pants and tiny blue jerseys that accentuated their bare midriffs and ample cleavage, they cleared slush and shavings from the surface of the ice.

From the stands, men leered and catcalled. One jiggled her breasts to a raucous gang of men plastered to the glass near center ice.

Haven looked down to find Clara Bell watching the display with huge round eyes.

At one time, Haven had thought her only worth lay in her physical assets. Men liked her body and she thought that meant they liked her. But that wasn't at all what their attentions meant. In fact, the more she packaged her body with the intent of gaining their notice, the less they seemed to think of her as an actual human being worthy of anything more than an object for their entertainment.

The second period began right where the first ended. Less than a minute in, Jack poked the puck away from a Toronto forward and sent it floating toward open ice. It was a foot race, and Jack handily beat the other players to the disc. The crowd, sparse though it was, surged to their feet to cheer Jack on his wild drive toward the net.

A foghorn blared and red lights flashed. He scored!

The Renegades held on to their lead as the second period neared an end, but with three minutes remaining, the refs charged a Renegades player with a penalty. On the power play, Toronto set up in front of the Renegades' net. A scrum broke out in one corner and when the puck squirted out, Haven followed it across the ice.

So she missed what happened to cause one of the Renegades players to suddenly drop his stick and skate toward the bench. The ref's whistle blew, calling play to a halt.

Haven shot to her feet, tracking the player. "What happened? What's he doing?"

A trail of red droplets dotted the ice in his wake, and a hushed pall fell over the crowd.

Aside from an icing or offside infraction or a player penalty, the refs didn't stop the clock in hockey. Teams made line changes on the fly and once in a great while, late in a game, a coach might use a time-out. But not often, and definitely not in the middle of an offensive strike.

"That player's hurt," Harlon said.

They all stood, trying to see what was happening. Players from both teams stood around Milwaukee's bench, talking some but mostly just standing together.

Above the arena floor, a replay of the game's last moments displayed on the jumbotron.

All the air sucked from the arena when the shot showed a Toronto player falling and his skate slashing across number fourteen's face.

Harlon cringed. "Oh man, I think that kid took a skate blade to the eye."

Mel gasped and Clara Bell climbed onto her lap. Mel distracted Clara Bell as they replayed the scene once again.

Harlon shook his head. "Oooh, that looks bad."

Haven's feet moved under her. "Will they take him to the locker room?"

"I'd expect so...."

The door fell shut on Harlon's words. Haven charged down the hall and plunged into the stairwell. In the concourse, she started to run, but soon, bodies poured out from the seats. The second intermission had arrived.

At security, Haven flashed her badge and burst into the bowels underneath the arena. She sprinted toward the locker room and shoved her way through the crowd blocking the door.

Inside, a thick, heavy silence hung over the room. Players milled around, looking lost. Her gaze scanned the area until she spotted the huddle of people in an alcove off the main area.

From outside of the group, Coach looked on, a grim set to his features.

In the chaos, no one noticed her approach.

The player lay on an oversized doctor's table while around him, men uttered medical terms and phrases

Haven didn't understand.

"How is he?" she heard herself ask.

"They're trying to stop the bleeding so they can assess the eye," Coach said.

Blood soaked through white towels pressed to the player's face and lying in a heap on the floor.

A woozy dip buckled her knees, but she managed to stay upright by gripping the edge of the table. The sharp metallic smell rushed over her, and with it, flashes of memory flitted through her mind.

She remembered coming to in the passenger seat and looking over to see Ryan. Blood had gushed from his nose in an unrelenting river.

It wasn't right, all that blood. She knew it wasn't right, but still, she'd released her seat belt latch and climbed over the center console, screaming with the wrench of pain in her shoulder. Cupping her hands, she'd tried to catch the blood that poured from Ryan's nose so that they might return the life to his body. Even though she knew.

It was too late to save him.

He was already dead.

Blood had filled her hands and soaked her T-shirt. The shirt would be ruined. She remembered thinking what a stupid thought that was to have just then.

Blindly, she'd turned away and stumbled from the car. Her knees pummeled the pavement when she went down. She was vomiting and sobbing.

He was dead.

He was dead.

He. Was. Dead.

In the locker room, someone pulled the towel away from the wounded player's face. Red stained his skin. Beneath the red-tainted wetness, a large gash ran diagonally from the center of his forehead, over his eye, and across his right cheekbone.

Her world went black.

⁊

Jack bit out a sharp curse as the locker room descended into chaos.

A teammate taking an ice blade to the eyeball hadn't sent his teammates into hysterics, but a wilting female had.

Un-fucking-believable.

Riley, the third line grinder, danced over her. "Should we pick her up?"

"Leave her." The team doctor barked the order while still tending to the wounded player, Gus. "Did she hit her head?"

"Oh, yeah. She went down like a limp—"

"Get an inhalant."

Soon, a tiny white packet passed down the line of men huddled around the table.

"Hold it under her nose."

Riley backed away. "Uh-uh. I'm not touching her."

With a sigh, Jack shoved to his feet. In skates, he crossed to Riley and snatched the tiny pouch from his hand. He cracked it to release the ammonia and crouched over Haven to press the packet under her nose.

She roused immediately.

Her eyelids fluttered and then blinked opened. Confusion puckered her forehead as she gazed up at him, and for one brief moment, he glimpsed in their brown depths a sadness so dark and so deep it knocked him back.

Then her gaze clamped on to his face and a soft smile teased her mouth. "Jack."

The way she whispered his name grabbed at his insides. "Hey, boss."

It all seemed to come back to her then. Her head moved from side to side, taking in the many men in skates and hockey garb staring down at her.

She cursed and started to sit.

"Take it easy," Jack murmured. "You bumped your head pretty hard."

Even as he said it, she cringed. He slipped his fingers into her hair and felt the lump forming on the back of her noggin.

"Send her to the quiet room?" Avery asked, referencing the trainer's room used by team doctors to assess players for symptoms of concussion.

One of the doctors crouched beside Jack. He shined a penlight on Haven's face and peered into her eyes.

She pointed to Gus, still laid out on the table. "How is he?"

"He gets to keep his eye." Relief, and a touch of befuddled amusement, tinged the doctor's voice. "I don't know how the skate missed it, but it did."

He killed the light and stood. "I don't think the quiet room is a bad idea. Let's get you an ice pack and let you rest in there for a few minutes."

"All right, guys." Coach stepped over Haven's legs. "Let's gather round."

Men shifted away, closing around Coach.

Haven climbed to her feet, but when she swayed slightly, Jack caught her by the arm.

"I'm okay," she murmured.

As she shuffled off in the direction the team doctor had disappeared, he clenched his scalding hand into a tight fist.

Back on the ice, thoughts of her kissable mouth and sad doe eyes dominated his mind. So much so that he didn't see the defender flying at him and wasn't ready for the jarring check into the boards. The hit rocked him, and he was slow to get up, but managed to get to the other end of the ice in time to deflect a wrist shot.

Problem was, the redirected puck slid toward Toronto's best shooter, left wide open by an out-of-position Renegade. The shooter wound up and let it rip. The puck wobbled through the air. Milo flailed in an attempt to make the save, but he was too late.

Tied game.

After that, the floodgates seemed to open. A Toronto player picked the pocket of the Renegades alternate captain, Bryce, and scored off the breakaway. They then put the game out of reach with a power play goal at the two-minute mark.

It was the team's eighth loss in a row.

While he watched the other team celebrate, fury whipped through him. He didn't know who pissed him off more: Bryce for playing soft and letting Toronto back in the game, Haven for taking up prime real estate in his head, or himself for being too weak to evict her.

At this level, every team had talent. Enough talent that they should be able to compete. To steal a game here or there. This team wasn't stealing anything that wasn't gift-wrapped and handed to them on a silver platter.

They were pathetic.

Disappointment and humiliation ate at him.

In the locker room, Bryce threw his helmet into the row of metal lockers with a thunderous rattle.

Then he whirled on Milo. "You've got to snap out of this slump, man. You're killing us out there."

Milo sat with his head hanging down.

"Did you hear me, Bishop? You suck."

Jack snapped. "Lay off him."

Bryce whipped around, his face red with anger. "I won't lay off him. I'm tired of losing games, and I'll say whatever needs to be said until this team stops rolling over like a goddamned dog."

"You're tired of losing games?" Jack threw his gloves

into the back of his locker. "Then why don't you take care of the puck? Or play some fucking defense?"

Someone behind him snickered.

Jack twisted toward the sound. "You think this is funny?"

"Fuck you," Bryce said.

Twisting back around, Jack locked gazes with Bryce. "You know what? You're right. Fuck me. You wanna be last in the league? You wanna be remembered as that team that couldn't compete? You wanna be laughed at in every arena in every city in two countries? Then fuck me." He turned toward the snickers. "Newsflash, fellas. We're the joke."

"You don't know what you're talking about."

Jack ignored their gutless alternate captain, Bryce.

"This isn't the NBA, boys. This is hockey. This is war. When you step out on that ice, if you haven't put in the work, if you lack the focus, or the drive, or the killer instinct, you will be shredded. They will rip out your guts and leave you empty." Jack faced Bryce. "This is a man's game. Act like one, or get the fuck out of here."

"You're way out of line," Bryce informed him.

Jack approached the smug asshole. "It was your man."

"Excuse me?"

"The score to tie it, that was your man left wide open. No one else's. And the breakaway was on you as well. Until you take care of your business, you've got no right to call out anyone else in this locker room."

"Who the fuck do you think you are?" Two veins popped out on Bryce's forehead. "You walk in here on the first day and think you know everything? Well, you don't know shit."

"I know hockey, and I know why we lost this game. Because you didn't pick up your man. You didn't take care of the puck."

Jack thought Bryce would charge him, or hit him, and

he was ready for it. Invited it, actually.

But just then, movement out of the corner of his eye caught his notice. He turned his head as Haven emerged from the trainer's room. She appeared pale, but well-balanced—

Bryce's fist crashed into his jaw.

Pain exploded in Jack's head. Unprepared for the blow, he lost his balance and tumbled to the concrete floor. He lay there a moment, embracing the pain.

With a groan, he rolled to his side and two sneaker-clad feet appeared in his line of sight. She crouched down beside him and, without saying a word, held out her ice pack to him.

Jack pressed the lukewarm bag to his sore jaw and glared at her.

She was worse than a distraction.

She was a disaster.

And damn it all if the fire and fervor pumping through his body didn't surge to his groin when he caught the slightest hint of her shampoo, whatever the hell brand she'd used that day.

Lust crashed into him with the force of an illegal crosscheck, and the need to return to that hot, secret place between her thighs consumed him.

One more night. That's what she owed him.

One more night was all he needed to slake his lust and get her out of his system.

Hey, asshole, she's your boss. Touch her and you will regret it. You could lose everything.

While his mind pleaded reason, his body snarled, *She's mine.*

One. More. Night.

Chapter Thirteen

By the time Haven returned to the owner's suite, it neared eleven o'clock, and Mel and her family had gone. She collected her coat and purse, and on her way out flipped off the lights.

The arena had nearly emptied when she made her way to the south entrance, but as she approached the doors to the employee parking ramp, she was startled to find Jack leaning against the wall near the exit, his bag on the floor at his feet.

She slowed her steps.

Spotting her, he straightened away from the wall. "Headed out?"

His dark hair still wet from the shower, he wore a black suit beneath a charcoal-gray wool coat.

"I'm going to grab a cab."

"No, you're not." He plucked his bag off the floor and, tossing it over his shoulder, pushed open the exterior door. He held it for her. "I'll drive you."

With the cold air sweeping in, her heart froze. The only thing she disliked more than driving was riding in a car with someone else. Though she supposed if given the choice of putting her life in Jack's hands or those of a random cabbie, she'd probably take her chances with Jack.

He assumed a different reason for her hesitation.

"Haven, please. We need to talk."

"What do we need to talk about?"

His gaze swept the area behind her. "Not here."

Among her many flaws, Haven couldn't control the wounded, angry-at-the-world teenage girl inside her.

"Are we going to talk about all the ways I've ruined your life?" She saw her blow hit its mark. "Or would you rather talk about the next hockey player I've decided to seduce? I think I might acquire an entire team full of men I've fucked. That way—"

The door fell shut and in a flash of movement, he snatched her to him. "Stop it." He buried his hands in her hair. "Please, just stop. I was angry, and I lashed out at you." Nuzzling her ear, he inhaled deeply and then pulled back. "It was wrong. Please forgive me. I'm so sorry." Regret, real regret, tugged at his smooth features.

His face, his words, his touch, all acted as a balm to her battered heart. She choked back sudden, silly tears.

"Where are you staying?" His fingers toyed with her hair.

"At Hamilton Place."

She felt him stiffen and she drew back so that she might see his face, but he turned away before she had a chance to read his expression.

Lacing his fingers through hers, he pulled her out into the cold night. With his other hand, he slid a set of car keys from the pocket of his wool coat as they moved through the ramp toward a sleek black utility vehicle.

They ducked inside and shut out the chill. He exited the ramp and eased onto the dark street. At his driving, slow and smooth, without any of the aggression she saw in so many others, she relaxed in her seat.

In the dark confines of the car, his scent, fresh like clean earth, filled her senses. She laid her head on the headrest and studied his profile, the subtle perfection of his features and the shadowy whiskers along his jawline. A shiver passed through her when she recalled the feel of his scruff on her inner thighs.

Heat warmed her skin and she turned her face to the window. It was New Year's Eve and people packed the sidewalks and spilled out of bars.

"How's your head? Any headache or nausea?"

"A little." Though she wondered if the nausea was a product of her slight headache or the heartsickness brought on by the memories. "How about your face?"

"All in a day's work." His tone remained light while his smile struggled to form. "I suppose Gus should get all your sympathy. He deserves it more than I do."

A ripple of nausea hit her.

Jack reached over and grasped her hand. "Hey, it's all right. He's going to be all right, and he'll have a badass scar to show for it." He stole another glance at her. "It really upset you, didn't it?"

"I'm okay." She watched the streetlights roll past. "It's just... all that blood. It caught me off guard, I guess."

"Because of your car accident?"

She nodded.

He didn't let go of her hand until he turned the SUV into her lot.

Leaning forward in his seat, he peered up at the twenty-story stone structure. "You on the top floor?"

"It's my dad's place. I'm just staying here... for now."

She didn't know why she told him that, except she didn't like him painting her with the broad brushstrokes of spoiled rich girl.

They moved through the elegant lobby and at the elevator, he stepped into the car behind her. On a keypad, she punched in the four-digit code that granted them access to the top floor. They rode in silence, and the higher they ascended, the more remote he began to feel to her.

He stood a little straighter, a little farther away from her, and by the time the elevator door dinged, the intimacy of his car seemed like nothing more than a distant, delicious dream.

The doors slid open on a spacious landing with the apartment's security door and Jack waited while she worked the lock, her fingers made clumsy by both his nearness and his sudden remoteness.

Finally, she managed to turn over the lock, and he followed her inside the luxury apartment. The home's sleek lines, high-end finishes, and monochromatic color scheme did little to please her tastes, and it appeared to be that way with Jack as well.

Like her, he ignored all of it and strode across the oversized living room to the floor-to-ceiling windows overlooking the lake. He gazed out at the soft lights along the lakeshore's pedestrian walkway and beyond, the vast blackness of Lake Michigan. In the distance, tiny lights winked from the dark. One belonged to the lighthouse, the others she assumed were ships passing by.

"Now that's a view." He turned, and his gaze swept around the open-concept penthouse.

Over the random articles of her clothing, strewn across the black leather sofa and armchairs, and the pedicure set, still spread out on the coffee table. At the empty cartons of takeout food littering the end table and the kitchen island, his smile cracked wide open.

"You're a slob." It was a statement.

"I, uh... I'm still unpacking."

She spotted a pair of leopard-print panties on the chair in front of her. Her gaze snapped back to his face, but he'd already discovered the panties for himself.

Slipping out of her coat, she tossed it over the chair to hide her intimates.

But that didn't veil the heat and hunger simmering in his changeable hazel eyes. An electrical current arced between them, linking them, passing shared memories of the two nights they'd spent together on the island across the sea.

Just then, fireworks exploded in the night sky through the window behind him.

The remoteness from the elevator returned to his eyes, and their connection fizzled and died, like the streams of green and blue that dissolved into nothingness on the other side of that window.

Sharp sorrow struck her beneath the breastbone. Why did he do that, run so hot one moment only to turn cold the next?

Her heart sank, as though she'd lost a friend.

His mouth moved, as though he might say something.

She waited, her heart in her throat.

But he didn't speak. Emotions rushed across his features—desire and frustration, a touch of anger—before a determined scowl finally settled in.

"You owe me."

A bloom of white and gold blanketed the sky.

At his cool tone, a chill seeped over her. "What do I owe you?"

"I can't focus. Can't concentrate, not on hockey or anything else. You're all I can think about."

"I'm sorry," she said, because he sounded mad.

Gooseflesh prickled over her skin at the way he watched her from behind hooded eyes as he slowly walked toward her.

"Two nights wasn't enough. I knew it when I met you.

I need more, Haven. I need one more night."

A delicious tingle of arousal licked low in her belly. "Do you think that's a good idea?"

"Right now, I don't give a fuck if it's a good idea or not." He stood before her. "I want you."

Then take me. I'm yours.

She bit down ruthlessly on the reckless words. "What if the media finds out? Or your teammates?"

"It'd turn into a circus around here." His fingers danced along her collarbone, over the uneven bone. "But I think we can be discreet, and you're worth the risk."

Her body thrummed with consent.

Still, she hesitated.

And in that moment of hesitation, he broke her heart.

"I'm not asking for forever, Haven. Just one more night." A cool practicality chased some of the heat from his eyes. "We don't even have to like each other."

She nearly gasped with the pain. On a night when the memories hounded her, his cool calculation sliced like a thousand tiny paper cuts. Memories of a time when she wanted attention, affection, more than she wanted to protect her self-worth.

She pushed the dark memories aside. "I don't want to say no."

He watched her closely. "But you're going to anyway."

"Maybe when all of this is over...?"

Another firework burst across the night sky. Shades of red and blue danced over his face while she searched for proof of his anger or resentment.

She saw none.

A shaky breath eased from her. "I want one more night, too, Jack. When I'm no longer your boss."

His eyes narrowed. "When will that be, exactly?"

She couldn't resist the light in his eyes, and a smile found its way to her lips. "In fifty-five days, I think."

"In fifty-five days, you'll come back to my bed?"

She shuddered at the possibility. "Unless we've changed our minds."

"I won't change my mind."

Fireworks continued to paint the sky with breathtaking brilliance.

"Jack, I'm sorry that I ruined your life."

He started to protest, but she rushed ahead of him. "We were talking about a lot of different players that day, and I don't remember ever hearing your name. If I had, I never would've pushed to get you here. I never meant to ruin your life, or your career."

"I know that," he said softly.

Relief tasted sweet on her tongue. "For the record, I completely understand why you don't want to be here. This city can be...." She shuddered.

"You grew up here?"

She shoved her hands into the back pockets of her blue jeans. "Yeah." She didn't say more.

"The town's not so bad, actually." He lifted one shoulder and a cock-eyed smile turned up one corner of his mouth. "It beats playing hockey in the desert or someplace where it snows less than ten inches a year."

A thought niggled in the back of her mind and she frowned, chasing after it. Something Mel had said about the upcoming trade deadline....

Her gaze swung to Jack's face. "What if I can fix it?"

His eyebrows inched upward. "What do you mean? You're going to let me go to Detroit?"

She bit her bottom lip. "How about a deal?"

Wary dread clouded his features. "What kind of deal?"

"You help me get this team's collective head out of their collective ass, and I'll find a way to get you to Detroit."

"Define 'head out of ass.'"

"Get us into the playoffs."

His low chuckle rumbled in his chest. "Just snap my

fingers and it's done? I appreciate your vote of confidence, I really do, but it's not that easy."

She frowned. "Well, what do you need to make it possible?"

"What, like, personnel-wise?"

She bobbed her head. "Do you need more speed? Size? Guys who like to fight? Finesse players? What?"

"Yeah, all that would be nice. Add in an all-star goaltender, a packed arena, and some home cooking by the refs, and you got yourself a deal."

She nodded some more. "Anything else?"

He gaped at her. "You're serious."

"As a heart attack."

"All right, hold on." He showed her his palms. "Let's sprinkle a little reality salt on this meal."

She laughed at his choice of words, then bit back a smile when his scowl deepened.

"Even if you could give me all of that, which you can't because it's impossible, there's no guarantee we'd make it into the playoffs. There're too many other factors at play. Things that can't be coached or acquired in a trade."

"What kinds of things?"

"Chemistry. Endurance. Momentum. Willpower. Luck." His voice rose with each intangible he named. "No matter how much of all the other stuff you have, luck still plays a bigger part in all of this than any of us likes to admit. Everything from injuries to bad bounces and blown calls. Any one of them can derail a game, or even a season."

She gnawed on her bottom lip.

"Haven, look, I appreciate the offer, but what you're talking about can't be done in the three months between now and the playoffs."

"Fifty-five days."

A flash of yearning pulled at his features. "Right. I rest my case. It's impossible."

"All I need you to do is give us a chance, Jack. Get us into *position* to make the playoffs, and I'll send you to Detroit before the trade deadline."

He eyed her for a moment. "Why?"

"Because that's where you want to be. Isn't it?"

He gave his head a small shake. "Not that. Last I knew, you didn't want anything to do with this team. Now you're determined to turn them into a playoff contender? Why? What changed?"

Her face heated with the memory of Dave and Jerry laughing at her dad, and her, but honestly, Jack's biting disapproval hurt more than she could understand or explain. All her life, all she'd ever done was let people down, to the point that they no longer expected anything of her.

Just this once, she wanted to prove them wrong, and maybe gain a scrap of Jack's approval.

He studied her for a long moment, waiting, but emotion welled up to close the back of her throat. His face blurred.

"I'm not saying no." His voice possessed a gentleness that squeezed her heart. "I'm just trying to understand."

"My dad.... I want to help him."

And I want you to respect me.

She swallowed back the words that tried to leap to her tongue.

"I can't promise you the playoffs. From last place in the league to third place in the division will be... difficult, to say the least."

"Then just make it so we're not a laughingstock."

A flash sparked in his eyes, which he quickly concealed.

"I know," she said. "It's silly, but–"

"Okay," he said quietly.

She blinked at him. "Okay, yes? You'll help me?"

"All I'm saying is that I'll try. I'm not making any

promises."

Her heart soared. "I understand."

"But I can't do it alone."

"You won't have to. I'm all-in." Just this once, she thought, to stop herself gagging on the words.

A reluctant smile played over his lips. "I think you might be crazy."

She waved off his words. "Oh, for sure." Then she stuck out her arm. "We have a deal?"

He stared down at her hand. "If you don't mind, I'm going to refrain from touching you for the next fifty-five days."

Fifty-five days. It sounded like an eternity.

He stepped around her and moved toward the front door. At the armchair, he drew up. His head bent, he reached out and lifted something off the armrest.

He twisted around to look at her with accusation in his eyes. "You stole my lucky T-shirt?"

"Wh-What?"

His hand came up and a white undershirt dangled from his fingertips. The one she'd taken from the inn in her fit of kleptomania. Though mostly faded now, the faintest hint of his earthy scent still lingered on the soft fabric.

"This is mine. It went missing the weekend of my brother's wedding." Heat but no anger simmered in his green-gold eyes. "You stole it."

"I-I-I was in a hurry, and-and it was still half-dark. I must've grabbed it by mistake." She swallowed her rambling lies.

He studied her, a calculating glint in his eyes.

"Take it." She feigned disinterest. "Though you don't strike me as the superstitious type. How many games has it won you?"

He scoffed. "I don't need luck to win hockey games."

She laughed at his audacity.

"That's not why it's my lucky T-shirt."

"Why is it lucky, then?"

His hot gaze sent a spark sizzling through her. "I was wearing it the night I met you."

The laughter died in her throat. "Oh."

He moved close. His scent assailing her senses, he peered down into her face. His gaze lingered on her mouth.

"Fifty-five days," he murmured, while the backs of his fingers caressed her cheek. Then his hand dropped away and he eased back. "If we make it that long."

Turning, he crossed the foyer, and just before he disappeared through the heavy wood door, she glimpsed his delicious-smelling lucky T-shirt still clutched in his paw.

Chapter Fourteen

On New Year's Day, the team was given a rare day off.

Except Jack never took a day off.

He climbed out of bed at 6:00 a.m. and went for a short five-mile run along the lakeshore. Back at his apartment, he drank a protein shake and watched some film on the Renegades' division opponents. He meditated, and then he hit the apartment complex's fifth-floor gym for a core workout. With his extra time, he ran through the sets to work out his chest and back muscles as well.

Before heading back upstairs to shower and watch more film, he rode the elevator down to the lobby. The doors pulled open and he stepped from the car as a soft ding sounded and another of the three pairs of elevator doors slid apart to reveal Haven.

She wore a brown leather coat with a fuzzy collar and tight blue jeans that showed off her shapely legs. He wondered what they did for her round ass.

She drew up when she saw him. "Jack, what are you doing here?"

He raised the key in his hand. "Checking my mail."

Her huge brown eyes widened. "You live here? In this building?"

He smiled. "Yep."

"Where?"

"Eighteenth floor."

"Eighteenth...." She gave her head a small shake. "Were you going to tell me?"

He shrugged. "Why would I?"

"Because... because...." Her pink tongue darted out to lick her bottom lip. "If I'd known you were sleeping downstairs...."

His smile fell.

"I would've...."

He probably should warn her half the team lived in the building, which was owned by her father, but he didn't want to be reminded of who her dad was just as the punch of lust knocked the breath from his body.

"What? What if you'd known?" he asked, desperate now to know.

"I would've...." She blinked slowly. "I would've asked you what you look for in a goalie."

Disappointment slashed through him. "What do I look for in a goalie?" He repeated her question while his mind struggled to think clearly about anything other than her naked body. "Quick reflexes. Reaction time. Flexibility. Size doesn't hurt."

She fumbled for the bag hanging from her shoulder and dragged out a manila file folder. Flipping through it, her gaze scanned down one of the pages. "Is six-six good size for a goalie?"

"Very."

"And for a defenseman? Is height important?"

Jack folded his arms over his chest. "What are you

doing?"

"This is the Mayhem's roster." She pulled a paper from the folder and he glimpsed the logo of the Madison Mayhem, the minor league feeder team for the Renegades, at the top of the page. "I'm going to drive over and catch their game today." Her dark eyes shone when she smiled up at him. "I guess we can take any of their players whenever we want to."

"You're going on a scouting trip?"

"Yeah, well, I wanted to see them play before I say anything to Darby."

He shot her a side-eyed glance. "You know how to assess hockey players?"

"Not at all." She laughed. "I'm hoping someone will score a ton of goals or something and make it really obvious for me."

His soft laughter mingled with hers. "Let me know how that works out for you."

"Do you, uh, want to come with me?"

His first thought in response to her question had nothing to do with hockey and everything to do with her hot little body under his, but then he replayed her words in his mind to grasp that she was talking about attending a hockey game and not getting naked.

He hadn't been to a hockey game as a pure spectator in, well, ever.

"Give me twenty minutes to shower and change?"

Her smile knocked him back a step. "Sure. I'll wait for you."

Twenty minutes later, Jack had dressed in a pair of blue jeans and an army green crew neck sweater. He finger combed his still-wet hair and snatched his coat off a dining chair. Sticking his arms in the sleeves, he crossed to the refrigerator and stuffed his pockets with a quart of chocolate milk, the other half of a sub sandwich left over from the previous night's dinner, and a banana.

Back downstairs, he found Haven on a couch with the folder spread open on her lap. He followed her outside to an economical sedan.

The drive from Milwaukee to Madison should've taken an hour, but an hour into the trip they remained well outside the city. In the passenger seat, he stretched to get another glimpse at the speedometer.

The needle hovered below fifty.

"What time does the game start?" he asked casually.

"Four o'clock."

"It's four now."

A white Cadillac flew by them, and Jack thought he glimpsed the white-haired driver flipping them the middle finger.

Her knuckles white on the steering wheel, Haven's concentration was singular and intense. A bead of moisture broke out on her forehead.

"You okay?" Jack asked.

She nodded, her gaze darting between the road and the rearview mirror.

In the side mirror, he watched a semi ride up on them before whipping out and around them.

"You know, the speed limit on the interstate is seventy. If you wanted to pick it up—"

She shushed him. "Don't distract me. I'm driving."

"Is that what you call it?"

Thirty minutes later, they finally arrived at the arena. They'd missed the puck drop and by the time they found their seats behind one of the goals, five rows up from the glass, the game was well underway.

Jack let out a low whistle. "Nice seats. These come with the job?"

"I don't know. Mel got them for me."

She removed her coat and started down the row ahead of him. The blue jeans did everything and more that he'd imagined to accentuate her sweet ass, and for the first time, he questioned his judgement in agreeing to attend the game with her. How in the hell was he going to keep his hands off her for so long?

The teams played fast and physical, and he watched several shifts before one player jumped out at him.

"Who's number thirty-five?"

She squinted at the roster. "Kai Okalik."

"He's shifty. Elusive," Jack noted. "You can't coach that."

Her brow puckered while she scrawled notes in the margin of the paper. She was kind of adorable, actually.

Smiling, he turned his attention back to the game.

They shared a few observations about the other players, but then the Mayhem made a line change and a massive player staggered out onto the ice. With the finesse of a drunken sailor, number eight mauled his way to the net at will.

"Whoa."

Haven was already looking him up on the roster. "Number eight... Gabriel Killorn. Six eight, two forty. He plays Bryce's position?"

Killorn knocked his man off the puck, took possession of the disc, and skated up ice.

"Yeah, except this guy plays defense."

At intermission, Jack stood. "I'm going to grab a hot dog. You want anything?"

"A hot dog sounds good, and a beer." She reached for her bag at her feet. "I've got money."

"Stop it."

Long lines delayed him, and by the time he returned to their seats, the players were back on the ice going through warmups.

She thanked him when she accepted a hot dog and beer from him.

Placing her drink in the cup holder, she poised the hot dog before her mouth and removed the paper wrapper.

"What do you think of Coach Chambers?"

"I think he's a good coach."

The players gathered at center ice and the ref dropped the puck.

"You think he's a good coach, but...?"

Jack selected his words carefully. "He's a little young yet. What is he, thirty-eight?"

She nodded. "That's a theme with this team. Youngest coach in the league *and* the youngest roster."

And all the pitfalls that came with youth, Jack thought. Immaturity. Inconsistency. The tendency to get too high and too low too quickly, and commit stupid penalties.

The smooth shooter, Okalik, wound up and slapped a one-timer at the net. The goalie knocked it down and the Mayhem recovered the rebound.

"But when Coach decides to take control of this team, look out."

"You don't think he's in control?"

He shook his head. "Forget it. You're not going to bait me into ratting out my coach."

She rolled her eyes. "Has anyone ever baited you into anything?"

"Not once," he admitted.

"And don't worry. Cal's job is safe. I was just curious." She frowned at her hot dog. "It is odd though. He's a defense-minded coach, but Darby can't seem to get enough offensive skill players. I wonder what Cal could do if he had a few more players that fit into his scheme better."

Jack shot her an incredulous look.

Her hand came up to touch her mouth. "What?"

"For someone who hates sports, you sure know an awful lot about hockey."

A soft smile touched her lips. "My dad was a super fan. He was a season ticket holder and he used to take my brother and me to games—*every* game—when we were kids. Also, my brother played."

Jack didn't know she had a brother. He was about to ask her about him when her mouth opened and she wrapped her lips around the long shaft of her hot dog.

A moan of ecstasy sounded in her throat.

All the heat eddying through his body coalesced in his cock, and he knew with a certainty that no amount of guided meditation would ever erase the memory of Haven Callahan eating that hot dog.

Her tongue peeked out from between her lips to lick a splotch of ketchup from the corner of her mouth. "This is so good."

The horns blared and he whipped his head around to see that the Mayhem had scored.

He shifted in his seat, trying to ease the pressure on his hard cock while they showed the replay on the jumbotron. Number eight, camped out in front of the net, had deflected the winger's slap shot and the wobbling puck hit the hole over the goalie's right shoulder.

Haven scribbled notes on her paper. The long sweep of her eyelashes rested on the soft curve of her cheek, and when he glimpsed her small, neat handwriting, a tiny pinch nipped him in the center of his chest.

"I'll say one more thing about Coach, and then my lips are sealed on the topic."

"What's that?" She sipped her beer.

"The players are confused. Coach tells them one thing and then Poitiers swoops in and the whole plan changes."

A crease formed between her brows while she chewed on his words.

"The guys, especially the young guys, they don't know their roles. If they knew who to trust and could figure out their place on this team, I think you'd see a big improvement on the ice."

Number eight checked his defender against the board. Jack surged to his feet as the crowd erupted with the resounding hit. The prone player climbed to his feet and caught up with Killorn at the other end. The men circled each other, heedless to the game being played around them.

Both men dropped their gloves and it was on. With Killorn's long reach, the fight ended quickly.

At his side, Haven's heat reached out to him.

He smiled down at her. "I think that's a Gordie Howe hat trick for number eight."

Her mouth dropped open in an O. "I've never seen one live."

That he didn't have to explain to her the term used for a player with a goal, an assist, and a fight all in one game sent Jack's pulse pounding.

As the game played on, his gaze continued to stray to her. His first game as a spectator, a thrilling game before an unruly crowd, and unbelievably, the action didn't hold his attention. Instead, she drew him to her like a magnetic force, and by the time the final buzzer sounded, he was repeating one phrase over and over again in his undisciplined mind.

Fifty-four days.

As they filed out of the arena, Haven read something on her cell phone and then dropped the device back inside her bag.

"Do you mind if we make a quick stop on the way back to town?" she asked.

He bared his teeth. "I'm just along for the ride."

The slow, painful ride.

Though if it meant he got to sit beside her and breathe in her intoxicating scent for a little while longer, he may not complain too loudly.

Darkness had settled in when they pulled up to a wrought iron gate. In a neighborhood that kindled the fire of resentment in Jack's gut. Haven punched in a code on the intercom and the ornate bars slid open. She eased the car up the curved cobblestone driveway and parked in front of a sprawling mansion so opulent and overdone it appeared garish to his lower-middle-class eye.

Fine, he probably couldn't be considered middle class now. He made plenty of money. It didn't mean he understood these people or their lifestyle. Or that he wanted much of anything to do with their world. He barely concealed a bitter sneer.

It just figured the woman he wanted more than any other had grown up in a place like this.

A leggy blonde let them into the lavish foyer, and Haven introduced the woman, who had to be close to him in age, as her stepmom, Kristen.

"I'll go grab the envelope." Kristen disappeared into a room beneath a grand staircase.

He could feel Haven's eyes on him, watching him, so he wandered over to a wall of framed photographs.

Two little boys featured prominently, along with a number of photos of Hank Callahan, his trophy wife, Kristen, and an assortment of famous hockey players from the past several decades.

Before one photo, Jack leaned closer, squinting at the two teenage girls.

He pulled up, and then whipped his head around to gape at Haven. "You were a punk rock girl?"

She cringed. "The purple hair didn't do anything for my complexion."

He peered more closely at the picture. "Wait. Is that...?"

"Kristen."

His unspoken questions hung in the air.

Soft pink stained Haven's cheeks. "She and I were best friends since the time we were in preschool together. Our senior year in high school, she and my dad...."

Jack recoiled. With a glance around to make sure the stepmom wasn't nearby, he whispered, "That's disgusting. Was she even legal?"

She gave him a pointed look. "Just barely."

Twisting back around, he stared into Haven's younger face and shook his head. "Damn," he muttered. "You deserved better than that."

A moment later, he turned away from the wall of memories.

"Thank you," she said softly.

"For what?"

She spoke to his shirtfront. "For taking my side, even though you hardly know me."

"I know you," he said.

The pink color on her cheeks deepened.

A commotion at the top of the stairs sounded a beat before two boys burst out onto the landing. They plunged down the wide staircase.

"Mom's on the phone." The taller and, presumably, older boy told Haven while his bright eyes sized up Jack. "She said to tell you she'll be down in a minute."

"Have you guys met Jack Nolan yet?" Haven asked.

Two blond heads shook.

"Jack, this is Chance and Braden. They're hockey players, like you."

Two narrow chests puffed up.

One of Jack's favorite things about being a semicelebrity was meeting a wide-eyed kid and shooting the shit with them for a bit.

"Hockey players, eh?"

Two heads bobbed.

"What positions do you play?"

"I'm the goalie," the little guy said.

"A goalie? Wow. That's big time. How about you?"

"I play forward. You wanna see my new stick?"

"I'd love to see your new stick." Jack smiled with Haven as they followed the boys to a kitchen at the back of the house.

Chance darted toward the pile of hockey gear in the corner behind the kitchen table while Braden climbed onto a barstool at the island and plucked a grape from the stainless steel colander.

While Jack and Chance discussed the curve and angle he'd chosen for his stick, Haven chatted with Braden at the island.

She tossed a grape in the air and caught it with her mouth.

A smile broke across Jack's face.

The little boy lunged at the colander. His first attempt sailed over his head.

"Like this." Haven flicked another grape in the air and it bounced off Braden's tiny nose. "Ooh, so close. Try again."

She sent another grape flying and that time the kid reeled it in.

Haven's face lit up with the prettiest smile Jack had ever seen and her throaty laughter rang out. Was it the first full-blown smile he'd ever seen on her?

Two more grapes disappeared into the boy's mouth before Kristen reappeared.

"I'm so sorry about that," she said, her cheeks flushed. "Here's your paycheck."

"It's no problem." Haven tossed up another grape and Braden ducked under it to make the catch. She turned her smile on Kristen. "He's a natural. I think he's even better than Ryan."

Braden chewed happily. "Who's Ryan?"

Haven froze. She blinked at the little boy several times before turning to her stepmom.

Kristen appeared stricken.

Haven's arms dropped to her sides. "You never told them about Ryan?"

Jack would never forget the anguish in Haven's voice when she asked that question, or the vicious slash of pain that sliced across her face when Kristen's guilty expression provided the answer. It knocked him in the chest with such force it nearly felled him.

"There hasn't been a good time...." Kristen's voice trailed off.

Haven stood motionless while she stared. He thought she might crumble to dust right there before their eyes, and he was about to go to her when she suddenly drew herself up.

She set down a handful of grapes on the island counter, which rolled and settled as she strode to the kitchen door.

Kristen turned, following Haven's retreat. "When they're older, I'm sure—"

But Haven didn't slow down long enough to hear Kristen's explanations.

A heavy silence hung in the room.

"Mom, watch this." Braden tossed a grape in the air and snatched it.

"Good job, buddy," Kristen said weakly.

Jack said a quick good-bye to the boys and took the envelope Kristen handed him.

In the car, he found Haven in the passenger seat, staring straight ahead.

He settled behind the steering wheel.

For many long moments, they sat in silence.

Until, finally, he asked, "Will you tell me who Ryan is?"

"He was my brother. My twin brother, actually." Her features crumpled and she turned her face away.

"What happened to him?"

Her fingers flitted over her collarbone. "There was an accident...."

"The car accident you were in?"

She nodded.

Sickened, he closed his eyes.

"We were arguing." Her voice trembled. "I can't even

remember what about, but I'm pretty sure I was being a bitch. Another car ran a stop sign."

He could think of no words that might stop the bleeding, so he didn't try. "How old was he?"

"Sixteen."

"Damn. That's so young. He played hockey?"

"Same position as you." A ghost of a smile touched her lips. "He used to have a knack for spotting the gaps, you know? He could slip around and between defenders better than anyone else his age."

There was a long silence while she folded and unfolded the hem of her coat.

"What happened after he died?"

She stared down at her hands. "Everything changed. My parents became... different people. My mom was... so sad. All the time. Then my dad and Kristen...."

He swallowed the lump in his throat. "What about you?"

"Someone had to take out the trash. Buy the milk. Make sure my mom didn't mix up her meds and accidentally overdose again."

His throat closed and he couldn't get any more words out. Not that he had any words which might alleviate, even a little, the aching tear inside her.

She stared into the darkness through the windshield. "And I..."

"What?"

She shook her head. "Nothing. It doesn't matter." She inhaled a sharp breath and pushed it out between her lips. "I'm sorry. It's late. We should go."

He wanted to argue, to demand she talk to him and tell him everything that was in her heart. But when he glimpsed the defeated, despaired expression on her precious face, he just couldn't bring himself to push her.

The drive back to Hamilton Place was more excruciating than any ride he'd ever taken. Though it paled in comparison to the pain he felt when he delivered her to the penthouse door and watched her disappear into its dark interior alone.

Chapter Fifteen

Jack skated up ice and drove toward the net.

From his position near the bench, Coach blew his whistle. "Where the hell you going, Lovejoy?" His voice cracked hoarsely. "Your man's way the hell over here!"

Hands on his knees, Bryce skated in circles and dragged air into his lungs.

Jack felt little sympathy for the alternate captain, who'd shown up to practice hungover.

"Do it again," Coach barked.

Poitiers sat in the arena seats a few rows behind the bench, hovering like a devil over Coach's right shoulder.

They ran the drill again, and again Bryce missed his assignment. The tediousness began to wear on Jack.

Then he caught sight of her on the mezzanine, talking with the facilities manager. Haven pointed up at the rafters while the facilities manager nodded. Then he said something that made her laugh.

With that one simple laugh, the tension that'd been rattling through him since he'd last seen her two days before eased suddenly. In those two days, he'd thought of her often. Constantly. Strangely enough, when his mind played with his memories of her, more often than not, she was wearing clothes.

The team ran through the drill again, that time without provoking Coach's ire. They repeated the exercise, and when Jack found a seam, he squeaked the puck through with a slap shot, but Milo reacted with a flash of speed to make the backbreaking save.

A swell of appreciation rippled around the team and coaches, putting a wide, unrestrained smile on Milo's youthful face.

After setting up the next drill, Coach waved Jack over. "Give the kid a few more looks like that, would ya? Let's see if we can build his confidence back up."

"Yes, sir."

The next set began, and he and Coach turned to watch the action on the ice.

Behind them, Haven had moved down into the lower bowl and now sat beside Darby. Her words garbled when she said something to him, but the general manager's booming laugh rang out.

"You've got to be joking." Poitiers coughed and laughed at the same time. "Oh God, you're serious, aren't you?"

"Yes, I'm serious," she bit out.

"Then no, they're staying in Madison. They need more time to season. Both of them."

Coach pretended great interest in the action on the ice, but Jack could tell he was keeping track of the conversation going on behind them.

"I think they can contribute to this team now," Haven was saying.

"You think so, do you? And tell me, what do you think

they can contribute?"

Jack risked a glance at her. Her mouth twisted in a determined frown, she snatched Coach's whiteboard and marker off the seat in front of her.

Head down, she started to draw. "Put Kai on the wing opposite Jack. They'll be one of the fastest lines in the league. Or put them on different lines and have two lines with above-average speed. We'll be able to tire teams out early, and then grind them down late."

Poitiers didn't spare a glance at her sketches. "You need more than speed to play at this level." He leaned forward in his seat and pointed at something on the ice. "You see that?" he asked Coach. "Donovan needs to come in on those routes so Lovejoy can take the shot."

With a swipe to wipe the board clean, Haven sketched out a new formation. "Killorn is a tree. Plant him in front of the net and the goalie won't be able to see the puck coming. That's if anyone manages to get one past him in the first place, which they'll struggle to do because he has eyes in the back of his head and anticipates better than most guys I've seen."

"And how many guys have you seen?" Poitiers asked.

She fell quiet.

"That's what I thought." He leaned back and spread his arms wide over the chair backs. "He's got tight hips. He needs more work."

"Tight hips? Is that a joke?"

"He has trouble making the switch to offense."

"Then put him on Bryce's line and let him be a defensive specialist."

Coach chewed the inside of his cheek, the way he did when deep in thought.

"Look, sweetheart, we're busy here," Poitiers said. "Why don't you go check on that uniform order, would ya?"

A fiery blush bloomed on her chest and rushed into

her face. "Will you at least think about it?"

"No. Now I'm done talking about this."

She drew back at his rebuke.

A pang struck Jack in the center of his chest. "You know, I've seen those guys play," he said casually. "They're pretty good."

Surprise beat a swift path across Haven's features, while Poitiers groaned and Coach turned his head to look fully at Jack.

"She's right," Jack told Coach. "Killorn has incredible vision, and Okalik's speed is elite."

Coach chewed on his cheek some more. "I've seen them in camp. Good, coachable players. Was close to grabbing them both earlier this year." A light danced in his gray eyes as he looked out over the ice. "We could probably get Killorn stretching to work on those tight hips."

Jack bit back a smile and rested his arms on the blunt end of his stick. "Both guys give us a lot of options."

Poitiers shoved abruptly to his feet. "They've got until Nashville to prove themselves or I'm sending them back to Madison."

As Poitiers stalked away, Jack's gaze found Haven's warm brown eyes. At the unmistakable glimmer of gratitude brimming in them, a sliver of softness sloped through him.

Until he caught Coach watching them.

⁊

On Tuesday, the team left on a three-day road trip, and Haven assumed Darby must have traveled with them because he wasn't in the building to pester her. The Renegades dropped both games before returning to Milwaukee Friday, and around noon that day, Darby swept into her office, an ugly glower on his round face.

"You fired the ice girls?"

She sat back in her chair. "Yes."

"You can't fire the ice girls."

"I can do whatever I want." The line, borrowed from her dad, was fast becoming her favorite. "I'm the owner of this team."

"Your dad—"

"My dad isn't here, and those girls are ridiculous. This is hockey, not football."

"The fans love those girls."

Haven snorted. "The old horndogs love them. If they want to ogle half-naked women, they can stay home and do what one does on the Internet when they want to ogle half-naked women."

A lethal iciness came into his eyes. "They sell tickets."

"Can you prove that?"

His thin lips disappeared behind a tight line.

"I didn't think so." She folded her arms over her abdomen. "Our ticket sales are dead last in the league. You know what sells tickets? Winning. Not pretty girls. Not T-shirt cannons or dollar beers. Okay, the beers might, but we're going to get some data on that before we give away all our alcohol."

"Look, doll, I know you think you're helping, but you're taking this whole thing way too seriously."

She couldn't help it, she laughed. "You do realize men stopped talking to women like that in the workplace about three decades ago, don't you?"

"You don't have a clue about how to run a professional sports organization. Those girls do more than clean up ice shavings."

"What are you talking about? What else do they do?"

Did they peddle beer and hot dogs in the stands during the game? Perform maintenance on the Zamboni? Keep the water coolers filled for the players?

In the uncomfortable silence that greeted her questions, a splotchy redness crept up Darby's neck to flood his face.

Her mouth dropped open. "You're sleeping with one of those girls, aren't you?"

His mouth remained clamped tight.

"Are we talking one girl or more than one?"

"It's not only me—"

Haven lifted a hand. "Don't say another word. I might puke."

"Oh, c'mon. There's nothing wrong with it. We're all consenting adults here."

Her anger bubbled just under the surface.

"There's a lot wrong with it, and if you can't see that, I can't help you." She cut him off when he began to argue with her. "I don't care who you're sleeping with, Darby. You say I'm taking this job too seriously. Well, if you ask me, you're not taking it seriously enough. You should be figuring out what players we can pick up or deal away before the trade deadline next month, but instead, you're in my office scolding me for firing your mistress."

"This is important. We need to stay competitive with the other teams in the league, and that includes in the PR department."

She snapped. "Detroit doesn't have ice girls. San Jose doesn't have ice girls. Montreal doesn't have ice girls. We want to be one of the best teams in this league, we might as well start acting like them, because we sure as hell don't play like one."

"If you think—"

She held up her hand. "The ice girls are gone. If you want, you can bring them back in forty-nine days."

Darby made a noise in his throat.

With a scowl, she filched a spreadsheet from the wreckage on her desk.

Running her finger along the column, she located the

number she'd factored in the margin. "Now, can you tell me why we're paying 70 percent of our salary cap to eleven players who have never gotten us into the postseason?"

☙

Later that day, Haven poked her head into the arena sound booth.

"Hi, Bob, do you have a minute?"

The elderly gentleman who worked as the emcee for the Renegades' home games peered at her through thick bifocals. "What can I do for you, young lady?"

"I wanted to talk to you about the music."

Frown lines appeared alongside the deep creases of his craggy skin. "Is something wrong?"

"No, no, nothing's wrong." She moved farther into the booth. "It's just that I've given away a crap-ton of tickets to a bunch of kids for tomorrow night's game, and I wondered if you might, you know, maybe consider playing a few songs they might like." With an eye roll, she shook her head. "You know how kids are these days. I mean, who knows what they're even listening to."

Bob grew uneasy. "Oh. Well, Mr. Poitiers already gave me the song list. I'm pretty sure he wants me to stick to it."

Haven pointed at something on Bob's desk. "This list right here?" She snatched the sheet, crumpled it into a tight ball inside her fist, and crammed her hand deep into the front pocket of her coat.

Oversized eyeballs blinked at her.

She smiled. "Oops."

Bob's chair creaked as he scratched the back of his head.

Worried he might freak out on her, Haven pressed

forward. "Do you think you can you play something that isn't teenage pop music from the eighties? Don't get me wrong, I love eighties music, but these kids are so young I doubt they can appreciate the genius of the genre. Would you like me to put together a new list for you? I don't mind."

Haven held her breath while Bob considered her words.

Then he gave his head a firm shake, which rattled his loose jowls. "No need for that." A glint entered his ginormous eyes. "I have thirteen grandkids under the age of twenty. I think I got this covered."

A startled laugh burst from her. "You're the best, Bob. See you at the game."

"Go Renegades."

Haven left the sound booth and started for the exits. Voices carried up to her from the ice rink and she looked down to see Jack and another player shooting pucks at an empty net. The other man breezed by and Jack laughed at something he said.

An answering smile teased its way to Haven's face, and she couldn't resist moving closer. Near the glass partition, she perched on the armrests between two seats to watch them practice.

At one point, Jack caught sight of her. His gaze lingered on her face and he inclined his head, an infinitesimal nod that in no way betrayed the heat in his eyes.

She was about to head out when Coach settled into a nearby seat.

Other players joined the two men already on the ice, and they started to run through warmup drills.

"I like the new guys," Coach said.

A wave of relief washed over Haven. The Mayhem players had joined the team two days before, and she'd been worrying about their development since then. She'd won the battle with Darby to get them there, and now she wanted to prove she'd been right.

Did that make her a bad person? Maybe, but Haven never claimed to be above a little vindication.

Coach turned to her. "I was thinking we could put Killorn on the third line and bump Avery to the fourth line with the twins."

The twins. Haven recalled two identical men from the bar and searched her memory of the team roster. There were two Donovans, Eli and Ezra, maybe?

Coach must've taken her silence to mean she required more information. "Or we could flip Nolan and Tierney around and put Killorn with Nolan's line. If you think that'd work. I'll talk to Darby about it, of course."

Haven leaned back and propped her elbows on the chairs' backrests. "Coach, can I ask you something?"

"Uh, sure."

"Do you think my hair needs more highlights?"

A beat of stunned silence greeted her question. "Um...."

"Because I had a girl give me some caramel highlights a few months ago, but I don't know, I'm feeling like I need a little something more. Like, maybe I should add some honey tones? Or would that be too much? Too out there? I am a brunette, after all." She bit her bottom lip. "I'm just so torn. What do you think?"

"I think... you should... do... whatever you want."

"Do you? That's good to hear." She sat forward. "Because the thing is, I know as much about coaching hockey players as you know about adding highlights to dark hair. That's diddly squat, isn't it, Coach?"

Coach managed a nod.

"Why don't you do your job and we'll let my hairdresser do hers, shall we?" She stood, but then another thought struck her. "Oh, and if Darby has a problem with that, you tell him to come see me, all

right?"
Coach's smile formed slow but held steady. "Will do."

Chapter Sixteen

An hour before puck drop, Haven paced in the owner's box. She'd spent the first half of the week concocting a plan and the second half helping the marketing team carry it out on such short notice. Working with the Milwaukee area schools, they'd offered any child under the age of fifteen and one accompanying adult per child a free ticket to the game, plus free soda pop and popcorn.

Now she waited to see if anyone bothered to show up.

An hour and twenty minutes later, she had her answer.

People poured into the arena from the concourse, their arms loaded down with popcorn and fountain pops. A buzz built in the building, and when the team took the ice, a huge roar carried up to the rafters. Haven made a mental note to thank Jennifer in marketing for her brilliant idea to give away sugary beverages.

Music Man Bob made sure the enthusiasm remained

high throughout the game. Rock songs with driving beats blasted from the loud speakers, and for penalties, he played catchy old tunes with singers crooning about hooking and holding and fighting the law.

The crowd's energy seemed to extend to the team. They played faster and hit harder than their opponents did. With a one-goal lead in the third period, they even looked for a minute as though they were having fun.

As the clock ticked down and the Renegades closed in on the win, Haven's heart raced. She wanted this win for them. When the horns blared at the end of regulation, she let out a yelp in the empty owner's box.

She flipped off the lights when she left the suite and worked her way through the arena. When she arrived outside the locker room, a crush of bodies blocked the door and she hung back to wait for them to clear.

Instead, one of the reporters recognized her. "Ms. Callahan, do you have a few moments to talk?"

As one, the crowd surged toward her. She shrunk back against the wall while they all began talking at once.

Finally, one question rose above the din and the other voices quieted. "Ms. Callahan, where were the ice girls tonight?"

Haven ground her teeth. "Going forward, rink management staff will be responsible for maintaining the condition of the ice."

The barrage of questions swelled once more. "But why?"

"What about fan engagement? Who's going to do that?"

"It's my hope the hockey game being played on the ice engages the fans," she bit out.

"Will you reconsider in the future?"

She rolled her eyes. "Seriously? The Renegades win for the first time in ten games and all you want to talk about is the ice girls?"

"More like the lack of ice girls," someone quipped. "Look, it's a fact the fans enjoy the girls. They'll want to know what happened to them."

Haven released a slow, steadying breath, but it was no use. The words started to pour out of her. "Here's a fact," she said. "I am a woman. I like hockey. I used to really like it. A lot. Like, as much as you do. But then the league and the teams go and do things that really piss me off, like shove half-naked women in my face and coddle players who beat up their wives and girlfriends. Or worse."

A camera flashed in her face.

"They're always talking about growing their audience and pushing into new consumer markets, but then they ignore half of the fan base they already have." Over the hum of soft murmurs, she rushed on. "This sport needs me. You need to hear what I have to say. You need to hear from other women, but I'm all you have. For now. You ought to consider inviting more women to the table, not because you want a pretty face to throw to commercial break or a gimmick to titillate intoxicated fans in between game action, but because we're fans. Real fans, who happen to have breasts, but who love the game of hockey, who have valid thoughts and opinions about it, and who have really good ideas about how to make it better."

Wyatt stepped in front of her. "All right, that's gonna do it, folks."

Oops.

⚃

Jack spent a few minutes talking with reporters while he waited for the halls to clear. Over the tops of their heads, he spotted Haven loitering by the door to the employee parking ramp.

187

Their gazes tangled, and a soft, secret smile touched her lips. She slipped through the exit.

He rushed through the next few questions, giving overly simplistic answers so he might hurry after her.

In the parking ramp, he found her waiting beside his SUV. They climbed inside and he started the engine, letting the car idle while the interior warmed.

"That crowd was great tonight," he said. "Did you do that?"

She couldn't hide her pleasure. "Just a little PR trick."

"Well, it was nicely done, Callahan."

She gifted him with a smile he'd never seen from her before. Slightly cautious, but full of unmistakable pride.

Putting the SUV in gear, he passed through the winding ramp toward the exit. He kept a watch out for teammates or reporters, despite the fact that he and Haven weren't even sleeping together.

At least, not yet.

He'd been around long enough to know the suspicion of an affair might be all it took to blow up their lives, and the team's season. Once he'd maneuvered out onto State Street and merged into traffic, he breathed a little easier.

At a stoplight two blocks from the arena, a crowd of revelers in Renegade jerseys danced through the crosswalk. Cars honked at them, taking part in the celebration.

His low laughter mingled with hers.

Her dark eyes shimmered when she smiled at him. "Okay, that has to feel good, knowing you made their night."

The light changed and he eased the SUV forward.

"I'm not gonna lie. Some days, it's the only thing that gets me to the gym or through another workout."

"Really?"

He shifted in his seat. "I know what kinds of things people are dealing with from one day to the next. A game might be their only escape from the shitty day job or a chronic illness. If what I do, if what I love to do, somehow makes their day a little less shitty, then all that work was worth it."

She was quiet, so he snuck a glance at her.

A soft curve played over her mouth as she watched him with large, round eyes. He'd grown so used to seeing a sarcastic tilt on her wide mouth that his gaze lingered a moment, appreciating the novelty.

"Wow, Jack, that's really noble."

He laughed.

"No, I'm serious. I mean, I serve beer for a living."

He slowed the vehicle as he approached a red light. "Do not underestimate the value of a bartender. In order of importance, it goes your priest, your therapist, your bartender, and if you don't have the first two, your bartender gets promoted."

Her wide smile lit up the dark interior of the car.

"And it's not noble. Hockey saved me," he said. "I owe it everything I have."

"Saved you how?" she asked, her tone suddenly serious.

"I was not a good student. I struggled in school. Hockey was my escape. The one place I exceled. When I have a stick in my hand, everything makes sense."

"School is hard for a lot of people. Most of them don't become highly successful professional athletes to compensate."

A wry smile touched her mouth. "True, but most people aren't dyslexic."

He watched closely for her reaction, but saw only a soft sorrow and not a hint of pity.

"I didn't know," she said softly.

The light changed and he eased the car forward. "I don't tell a lot of people. I'm a hockey player. It doesn't matter if I have a bad brain."

"You don't have a bad brain."

The snap in her tone warmed his insides.

"Your brain is why I picked you."

He shot her a look.

"When they were discussing which players to take, Coach said your hockey IQ was remarkable." Then her voice turned all soft and slippery when she said, "I knew then that I had to have you."

Staring through the windshield, Jack marveled at her words. "You picked me for my IQ?"

"Well, that and your big, powerful thighs."

At the next stoplight, he pondered why he'd told her all that stuff, but he couldn't come up with a reason, other than she'd asked and then listened to his response.

"I thought I read you have a degree in communication." She laid her head on the headrest. "You must've done pretty well in school."

"It took me eight years to get my bachelor's, with tutors and all kinds of extra help. When I was kid, I hid it for years, but eventually Noah figured it out and told Shea."

"Noah, the professor? And Shea?"

"Shea's the oldest. He sort of did all the stuff for us a parent is supposed to do. Anyway, by the time Shea found out, Neal had offered me a spot with his club, and Shea decided there'd be more options available to me if I went to live with him."

"You left your family? How old were you?"

"Fifteen. And it was for the best. Lord knew they had enough to deal with already." Light from the streetlamp passed through the car's dark interior. "It worked out. Neal found the tutors I needed and with the extra help, I managed to get through high school and college."

"Who's Neal?"

"Neal Thompson. He's a retired player, now the GM in Detroit."

"He's why you want to play in Detroit?"

"Partly, yeah. He's been good to me. I don't know what I would've become if he hadn't offered me a spot on his roster and a place to live."

At Hamilton Place, Jack steered the SUV into the lot.

"They must love watching you play. All of them. Especially your brothers."

He frowned as he eased into a parking spot.

"Jack? They've seen you play, haven't they?"

He killed the engine. "They don't come to my games."

She twisted in the seat. "Why not? Don't you get along?"

"We get along fine." He rolled his shoulders. "They're busy."

Her mouth fell slightly open. "You asked your brothers to come to your games and they said they're busy?"

"I don't need to ask them. I already know."

She gasped his name.

"What? Noah and Leo have lived overseas most of my career."

"But the other two live in Michigan, don't they?"

"Shea's married with three kids. Luke's a newlywed."

The sarcastic slant to her mouth reappeared. "Yeah, you know how marriage is. Like a life sentence without the scenery. Those poor guys. Wonder what will become of them?"

"So says she who can't commit to a brand of shampoo."

She poked his arm. "Don't you judge me."

"Not judging." He held up his hands. "Just happy to prove you wrong."

"You haven't proven anything, except you don't want your brothers at your games." Her dark eyes softened with gooey warmth. "Why?"

He stared through the windshield while words that didn't come close to explaining anything curled and tangled inside his head. Shame at the memory of the last time one of his blood relations had showed at one of his games. Guilt that he got out, leaving them behind to deal with their dad's black soul.

He opened his mouth and then, shaking his head, snapped it shut again. "It's just easier that way."

In the silence, he turned his face to her. Her expression, one of pure heartbreak, wrenched something inside him when she reached over and placed her hand over his heart.

"I understand, Jack. I really do."

Chapter Seventeen

Haven woke early Monday morning, eager to get to the arena and deal with the offer from Ottawa.

It'd been a week since Darby blew up at her for firing the ice girls, and she hadn't seen him since. The team traveled the first part of the week, and she'd assumed he'd joined them on the road, but when they returned Wednesday after winning won one game but losing the other and Darby still hadn't shown up, she asked Mel to look into it.

Come to find out, he wasn't ill or abducted.

"What do you mean, he's not coming in?" Haven had asked Mel.

Mel held up the pink slip of paper where she'd scribbled Darby's message. "He said, 'If she thinks she knows so much, then she can go ahead and do it all without me.'"

Haven had scrunched up her nose. "So, did he quit?"

Mel peered at her over the rim of her glasses. "I think he's pouting."

At first, Haven thought about freaking out, but frankly, things had hummed along nicely without Darby in the building distracting everyone from their work.

Now, in the elevator at Hamilton Place, she pressed the button for the first floor and leaned back against the wall as the car started its descent. But at the eighteenth floor, the elevator stopped. The doors eased open and a strikingly beautiful woman climbed into the car.

Haven gave the woman some side eye as the elevator carried them down.

She was stunning. Tall and fine-boned, with silky blonde hair, not a color obtained from a bottle but real blonde, that shimmered around her shoulders and floated down her back. Her eyes were the purest blue, and her impeccably formed features retained the softness of youth.

Haven decided she disliked her. To be that pretty, she had to be a bitch.

The beauty offered Haven a sweet smile, and Haven begrudgingly smiled back.

Then the woman gasped and whirled on Haven. "Omigosh, you're Haven Callahan, aren't you?"

With extreme reluctance, Haven admitted the truth. "Yes."

Blondie squealed. "Omigosh, I can't believe it's you. I heard what you said, about women, and hockey, and omigosh, thank you. Thank you so much for that."

"Um, you're welcome?" Haven said, unsure whether the woman was joking or not.

"I kind of want to ask for your autograph, but that's probably weird, right?"

That pulled a laugh from Haven.

Her hand shot out. "Hi, I'm Sutton. It's so great to meet you."

Haven reached for the woman's hand. "It's really great to meet you, too," she said, and she wasn't even lying.

⚃

By midmorning, the warm glow of Sutton's sweetness had deserted Haven.

"You did *what?*"

Haven held Darby's gaze. "I traded Bryce Lovejoy to Ottawa."

"You can't do that," Darby spluttered. "He's our best player."

"He's a locker room cancer, and he hasn't produced for us in eight seasons."

"He's our star. We've built this team—hell, our entire franchise—around him."

It was on the tip of her tongue to ask Darby why, if he meant to make Bryce the centerpiece of the team, he hadn't included a no-trade clause in the man's contract, but she chose to focus instead on the battle in front of her.

"We need to make a change. What we've been doing isn't working."

Darby gaped at her as though she'd sprouted a second head.

"Why are you even here? I thought you were on strike or something."

He sputtered, bristling with indignation. "I'm trying to stop you from destroying this team. Get Ottawa on the phone. I'm going to try to undo this idiotic deal."

"We gain two forwards and a defenseman, *and* we free up five million in salary cap space. I had to take their offer."

A cursory knock sounded on the office door and Mel poked her head inside. "Mr. Lovejoy is here to see you."

195

"Please, send him in," Haven said. "Oh, and Mel? Will you see if Coach Chambers is available to come see me? And Jack Nolan, too, please?"

"Nolan?" Darby asked when Mel closed the door. "What's he got to do with this?"

"Coach and I agree that Jack should take over as the alternate team captain."

"You talked to Chambers about this behind my back?" Darby seethed with fury.

"You weren't here," Haven reminded him. "I needed to consult with somebody, and Cal's the one who has to deal with any moves we make."

With another sharp rap, the office door opened and Mel ushered Bryce into the room.

Darby held up his hands. "I don't want any part of this. You want to take this team down, you're going to have to do it without me." He stalked from the office, slamming the door shut behind him.

Bryce's large body seemed to take up all the space in the roomy office. He watched her with cold eyes, his expression holding that inscrutable aspect she'd become used to seeing on his face when he looked at her.

The hairs lifted on her arms, but she ignored the splinter of fear. "I wanted to personally thank you for all you've done for the Renegades organization, but we—I—feel it's time we take the team in a new direction."

His eyes flashed. "What are you saying?"

"You've been traded to Ottawa. Congratulations."

Shock and rage warred for dominance of his features. Rage won out. "You traded me? Are you fucking serious? I'm the best player on this team."

Not even close, she thought.

"I'm sorry if it's upsetting to you, but the deal's done." She crossed to the office door and pulled it open, suppressing the urge to suck in a desperate gulp of air. "That's all I have."

A wild, reckless light came into his eyes, and she wondered if that's how he'd looked the moment before he started hitting his girlfriend. He moved toward her with slow, predatory steps, his gaze never leaving her face.

She snuck a glance at the reception area. Mel was not at her desk.

Drawing close, he pushed into her space. "You're going to regret this."

"I don't think I will." She could feel his breath on her skin.

In a sudden flare of fury, he punched the door beside her head. "You stupid bitch."

Her heart walloped against her breastbone as she steadied the door behind her. "Coming from you, I'll take that as a compliment."

In the hall, she heard a faint sound. Mel was on her way back.

"You deserve what they did to you."

She blinked at him. "What?"

His lips curled. "I hope you get raped again. It's what you deserve."

Her mind grappled with his words, but they were all out of order, and no matter how many variations she tried, she couldn't line them up in any sensible pattern.

"Get your hands off her. Now." Jack's distinctive baritone brimmed with violence.

Dumbly, she looked down at Bryce's fingertips driving white indentations into her flesh. He released her arm, but with a hard shove that knocked her back against the door.

With measured strides, he crossed the reception area, but as he neared the door, Jack refused to move from his path. The two men stood eye to eye, their muscles coiled, while a charged tension swirled around them.

The trembling in her body carried to her voice when

she spoke. "Jack. Please, come in."

She retreated into her dad's office, and a moment later, Jack appeared in the doorway.

When she found the courage to look into his eyes, his fierce green-gold gaze pierced her. Unspoken questions hung in the air, but she didn't have the answers he sought.

She hadn't seen him in two days and her mind latched on to the changes in him. The slight shadow touching his jawline. The fresh bruise darkening the corner of his right eye.

"Haven?" His throat worked when he swallowed. "What he said...?"

Oh, how she regretted this moment. "It was a long time ago."

The color leached from his face.

Coach Chambers's head poked around the doorframe.

She managed a weak smile and he stepped into the room.

"Have you told him?" he asked.

She shook her head and made a motion with her hand. "You go ahead."

Cal faced Jack. "Bryce has been traded to Ottawa."

Jack's discerning gaze swung to her. She pretended something on her desk had captured her interest, but her hands shook so badly when she shuffled through the scattered papers that she abandoned the pretense.

"We want to name you the alternate captain."

Surprise flickered across Jack's features. "I'm honored," he said carefully. "But I think you should consider one of the other guys who've been with the team longer than I have."

"We all agree it should be you," Cal said.

She made the mistake of looking him directly in the eye. "Say yes, Jack. You deserve it."

"If the guys accept it, so will I."

"They'll accept it." She didn't have to force her smile this time. "You're the leader of this team. They know that as well as Cal and I do."

Cal's bright smile dimmed. "I saw Bryce in the hall. He didn't look too happy."

Haven could feel Jack watching her. "He wasn't."

A frown pulled at Cal's features. "That's too bad. But for the record, I think this is a good thing for the team. Has the press release gone out?"

She shook her head. "Not yet."

"Can you give us twenty minutes?" He turned to Jack. "We should talk to the team before the news gets out. You ready?"

Jack's gaze drifted to her. A lifetime's worth of words played across his features.

"Go," she said. "The team needs you."

When the men left her office, the adrenaline rushed from her body and she collapsed into the leather desk chair. She went through the motions of the rest of her workday, but the whole time her mind did combat with the dark memories of that night a decade past.

The memories had never been clear or sharp, which should've been a blessing, but instead had only served to heighten the nameless demons stalking her from the shadows.

As dusk settled over the city, she gathered her things, flipped off the office light, and pulled the door closed behind her.

At the penthouse, she kicked off her shoes and went to stand before the east-facing windows. She stared out into the darkness, in the direction of a little island beyond the horizon. She longed to be there again. To be the girl who found herself enamored with a boy. A boy who thought her pretty and treated her with kindness and respect.

She wasn't aware how much time had passed when a

knock sounded at the penthouse door, though she knew who she'd find on the other side before she pulled open the heavy wood.

He held himself unnaturally still, as if keeping some raw emotion in check. His army green sweater picked out the moss-colored flecks in his troubled eyes. "Can I come in?"

She moved aside to let him in and closed the door behind him.

In the living room, she sat in one of the leather club chairs and tucked her feet under her.

Through the room's glass walls, snow had begun to fall. Large fluffy flakes floated down from the sky.

He lowered himself into the club chair next to hers. "You don't have to tell me anything, but if you can talk about what happened, I'd like to hear—" He stopped abruptly. "I'd listen."

"You showed me yours. I suppose it's only fair if I show you mine."

Pain slashed across his face. "That's not how this works."

"I know," she whispered. "My therapist says I use sarcasm as a coping mechanism."

He waited.

Knots of dread twisted in her stomach. "I was in college. I went to a party and—" That's as far as she made it before she stumbled. "I'm sorry," she whispered.

"You have nothing to be sorry for."

When she could speak, she started again. "I drank too much and blacked out, or passed out. It wasn't until I woke up in the hospital that I found out what they'd done to me."

She watched the snow falling while inside her clenched fists, her fingernails dug into her palms. "I pressed charges."

"And?"

"And...." The memories lashed at her. "After that, I was no longer a victim. I was a perpetrator. Maybe it wouldn't have happened that way, except the boys were all scholarship athletes. A football player and three hockey players."

When his hand came up to smooth over his mouth, she saw that it trembled.

"People demanded to know who I was and why I was trying to ruin those boys' lives. They kept my name out of the papers, I think maybe because they were all convicted, but everyone on campus knew it was me."

"And Bryce Lovejoy? What does he have to do with this?

"It was a difficult time...." Her throat constricted.

For a year or more after that night, she'd spent her days in a fog. She was having two to three panic attacks a day, and whenever she wasn't in class, she stayed holed up in her bedroom in the apartment she rented with a couple other girls.

"I assume he was there at the time, maybe he played on the hockey team, but I don't remember him."

"I understand," he said quietly. "And your rapists? They're in prison?"

"Not anymore. One served two years, and the others were released sometime before that."

He made a sound, like a curse, but didn't speak.

"One's married and lives on the East Coast somewhere. The others are out west."

Outside, the wind picked up and sent snowflakes swirling through the black sky.

Her throat ached with the effort to swallow back tears. What they did to her, it'd been one of those turning points in her life. There was everything up to that moment, and then everything after, and there was no way to reconcile the two halves of herself. She couldn't go back to being the person she was before, but neither was she able to move forward, becoming someone else. She was just... broken.

The leather groaned beneath him when he sat forward. "Haven, I want to touch you. Would that be okay?"

"I'm not fragile, Jack."

"No, you're not." He held out his hand, palm up. "You're one of the strongest people I know."

She placed her hand inside his.

"What about your dad?" His warm grip closed around her hand. "Was he there with you?"

"Oh... well, he'd just bought the team and was pretty busy here with everything."

Some sharp emotion sliced across her features, but he ducked his head before she could read it. Pulling her hand to his mouth, he pressed his lips to the heart of her palm.

The kiss sent a jolt up her arm to spread warmth through her cold body.

"If you want me to go, I will." His fingertips danced over her pulse point. "But I'd like to stay, if that's okay. I want to be with you."

Her pulse skittered. "You do?"

"I really do."

"You mean...?"

Heat chased some of the shadows from his eyes. "Since I've met you, there hasn't been a time when I didn't want you, but that's not what I'm after right now. Right now, I just want to be with you, in whatever way you're comfortable."

Her heart stuttered at his words. She scooted to the edge of her seat and took his hand in both of hers. Her fingers brushed over his roughened skin, touching a small cut and the blackened mark beneath the tip of one fingernail.

"Jack, I want to be with you, too."

His hand squeezed hers.

"But what if someone finds out?"

His eyes filled with unbearable tenderness. "I don't care. The only thing that matters to me is you." He brushed a strand of her hair off her forehead and his fingers traced the curve of her cheek. "I want to give you pleasure, Haven. I want to comfort you."

The words touched her like the slow lick of his tongue. "I want that, too."

He stood and helped her to her feet. "But I need a promise from you first."

Wariness stole over her. "What's that?"

"If you change your mind, or have any doubts at all about anything, just say the word and I'll go. All you have to do is say 'no' and I won't ask again."

She tilted her face up to him. "I won't say no, Jack."

Chapter Eighteen

Haven took his hand in hers and led him down the hall to the bedroom. She didn't touch the light switch, leaving the door open so the light from the hallway could reach them. Then she moved to the nightstand and used the remote control to lower the shade over the glass wall.

He came to stand behind her. Not touching, but close enough that his heat singed. She turned to him, but he didn't reach for her.

Uncertainty crept up her spine.

The shaking started in her hands, and she fumbled with the hem of his T-shirt. Jack lifted his arms and drew the shirt over his head. Her fingers rushed over his sculpted torso and traced the lines of the tattoo on his right arm. She raised up on her tiptoes to lick the black ink on the side of his neck.

His entire body vibrated with barely restrained control.

Why wouldn't he touch her?

Icy fear wrenched her heart. "Put your hands on me, Jack."

"Where?" The word shot from him. "Show me."

She took his hand in hers and, lifting it to her face, pressed her cheek against his palm. The pad of his thumb brushed over her bottom lip.

She guided him to sit on the bed. Standing before him, she worked the buttons of her blouse and the sheer fabric fell away. Her chest at his eye level, she unhooked the clasp of her bra and pulled the scrap of material away from her body.

She heard the sound of his throat working when he swallowed. Still, he hesitated to touch her, so she wriggled her skirt down over her hips. Then she reclaimed his hand and placed his palm over her breastbone.

With his fingertips, he outlined the tips of her breasts and then traced the heavy curve. A gasp of pleasure caught in her throat.

His mouth replaced his fingers, taking a slow, leisurely path over her breasts. He pressed his lips to her shoulder where the straps of her bra left indentations on her skin.

His hands moved to either side of her face as he continued dropping kisses everywhere. Light, lingering kisses at her temple. The corner beneath her eye. The tip of her nose. Her mouth. The thousand-and-one sensitive spots on her neck. Her collarbone, over the old wound.

With a gentle nudge, he eased her onto the bed. Dark moss green eyes watched her face as he discarded his jean and boxers and then moved over her.

His mouth forged a path down her body, kissing her ribcage, over her belly, on her inner thigh, and the inside of her ankle. He lingered over her, nibbling and tasting, lifting and turning her until she was sure he'd not missed any part of her body, no matter how intimate.

Scars of betrayal were melted away by his gentle, soothing touch. In his body, she found absolution.

His deep voice rumbled near her ear. "Do you have any condoms?"

She shook her head. He was clean, she knew, because they'd given her the results of the medical exam the team doctors had conducted before clearing him to play.

"I've been on the pill for years," whispered near his ear. "And I've always been careful. Except for that night... at that party...."

Jack's gasp, the sound like a broken sob, stopped her rambling.

Then he slipped inside her and she squirmed at the impossible thickness of him. His mouth moved along the side of her neck while he murmured for her to relax, and to please, let him in.

With slow, gentle force, he began to pump his hips. Every slide and stroke sent a shock of pleasure tingling through her belly and thighs.

She'd never existed in a place of such pure sensation. She thought nothing, sought nothing. Aware only of her need, and the craving.

He pulled back and looked down into her face. "Haven, look at me."

She opened her eyes to find she floated in a green-gold dream.

His fingertips danced over her cheeks. "I can't tell how you're doing. What are you thinking?"

Thoughts. She should have some.

The tension coiled within her, so exquisite and taut that tears sprang to her eyes.

She loved the way it felt to lie in his arms with him wedged inside her. But she didn't tell him that, because she never used the word "love" when she was with a man.

So she shook her head. "Don't stop, Jack. Please. Never stop."

Cঙ

Her heart lighter than she would've ever believed possible, Haven arrived at the arena the next morning before most of the staff.

With a home game on the schedule that night, she prepared for a long day. Instead, she seemed to float through the hours, and as it neared five o'clock, she realized it hadn't occurred to her, not once, to freak out about the night before. The intense intimacy between her and Jack hadn't triggered the clawing claustrophobia. No hives marred her skin.

What would be the point of running from him? After the previous night, he'd be a part of her forever anyway, residing in her heart as surely as a tattoo branded the skin.

When her stomach started to growl, she stopped work for the day and packed up to head to the penthouse for a quick dinner before coming back to the arena for the game later. She stepped from the ground-level elevator and turned in the direction of the south entrance. In the hall as she passed through the players' area, she happened upon Jack talking with Coach outside one of the team meeting rooms.

She slowed her steps, and when Jack caught sight of her over Coach's shoulder, a hot heat flared in his eyes.

Soon, Coach moved away and down the hall, and she timed her approach so that he'd rounded the corner when she reached Jack's side.

"Hey." She inhaled his incredible scent.

"Hey." His gaze fastened on her mouth and then slipped lower, to the top button of her blouse.

Liquid warmth spread low in her belly.

He drew closer but didn't touch her. His almost-touch was excruciating.

"I'm headed out. Are you?" She couldn't quell the hopeful ring in her voice.

He gave his head a small shake. "Team meeting."

At the wrench of disappointment, she bit down hard on her bottom lip. "Maybe you could stop by later?"

He pulled her into a nook and pressed his body against hers so that they touched all the way from hips to feet. "I don't think I can wait that long."

Her fingertips traced over the black ink on his neck peeking out from his collar.

His mouth crashed down over hers and she clutched at his suit coat.

He drove her deeper into the alcove even as his hands gripped fistfuls of her skirt, hauling the hem higher until cool air rushed over her naked flesh.

She gasped when he tugged her panties down, then moaned when his fingers brushed her core. Her body opened eagerly for him, wet with anticipation.

Her core clenched, and the desperate hunger took over. "Jack, please."

For the first time in her life, she wanted something more than her freedom.

With one hand, she gripped him through his pants. He glanced over his shoulder and drew down his zipper.

His proud erection bobbed free. Gripping her buttocks, he lifted her and her bare bottom pressed into the cool cinderblock wall.

She tilted her hips so that his hard length rubbed the heart of her wet heat.

The head of his cock nudged up against her swollen slit and when he slid home, a growl vibrated in the back of his throat.

He'd only just begun to pump his hips when a noise sounded from the hall. He froze with his erection inside her, stretching her.

She wriggled beneath him. "Hurry, Jack."

His hips started to move. Still fully dressed, she felt his flesh only where their bodies joined. Each thrust sent a ripple of sensation spiraling through her. With the ecstasy, her head dropped back against the wall.

He filled her vision and conquered her senses. With shaking hands, he cupped the sides of her face and kissed her while he pumped into her with long, smooth strokes. The kiss turned tender, reverent.

She kissed him with everything she had. Everything he'd awakened in her since that wedding. Everything she'd been trying to dampen, to smother, over the past lonely years.

With each delicious slide of his hardness, the waves of sensation intensified, the pressure and pleasure so exquisite she never wanted it to end.

He thrust up into her once, twice, three times and then held while his body shuddered. Soft whimpers fell from her lips as she bucked and shimmied against him, chasing the fading ripples.

He dropped a soft kiss to the heated skin of her forehead. "I have to go."

Dazedly, she unwrapped her legs from around his waist.

"You okay?"

She nodded and tugged her panties and skirt back into place.

He pulled away, but at the last minute he spun back and, in a flash of sudden movement, pinned her against the wall once more. His mouth covered hers and he shoved his hands through her hair to cradle her head in his firm grip. His soft tongue took a long, lingering nibble of her bottom lip.

"I'll come to you tonight." The honeyed warmth in his tone tasted sweet on her lips when he kissed her one more time.

Then he was gone.

Chapter Nineteen

Haven arrived in the owner's box before the arena seats had started to fill. At the bar, she poured a diet pop and dumped a bag of chips into a bowl. When she heard someone at the door, she bounded forward to greet Mel and Harlon.

Except her friends weren't on the other side of the door when she flung it open.

Instead, Wyatt hovered in the hall. He held his tablet in both hands in front of him, like a shield.

"Oh hey, Wyatt. C'mon in."

He hesitated while his gaze scanned the interior of the suite, and then he took a tentative step inside.

"Can I get you a drink?"

"No, thank you." His voice cracked and he cleared his throat.

A queasy sort of uneasiness clung to him while his throat worked, as though he searched to find difficult words.

Haven groaned. "Oh no. You're here to tell me I have to go to the post-game press conference, aren't you?"

A reluctant smile touched his face. "No. Something else has come up."

"Oh, all right." She flopped down in a leather chair. "Hit me."

He stared down at the tablet cradled in his hands for a long time, though the screen remained dark.

When he lifted his head, her stomach dropped.

"The *Gazette* sent over a story they plan to post later tonight. They've asked us for comment."

Dread slithered through her veins. "What's the story? Is it about my dad?"

His gaze didn't quite meet hers. "Not this time."

Her heart wedged in her throat. Had they found out about her and Jack already?

She swallowed with difficulty and pointed to the tablet. "Can I see it?"

Wyatt hesitated, but then the tablet winked on and he handed her the device. She started to read, but the meaning of the words on the screen lumbered to her brain.

Trade of All-Star Bryce Lovejoy Raises Questions of Motive

She skimmed past the summary of the deal that sent Bryce to Ottawa, but the next words jumped out at her like angry beasts.

In many ways, a familiar story. A college party, alcohol consumption, scholarship athletes, a girl. An incident. Accusations and allegations and, in this particular case, several convictions. But over ten years later, this story takes a dissimilar path to all those other

stories.

The reporter had done his research, down to the details of her assault and trial.

Then he went on to ponder whether Haven's decision to trade Bryce had more to do with this "unpleasant" history than it did anything else. Had she traded the Renegades' star forward away from the franchise where he'd spent the majority of his playing career as some form of retribution on him for the crimes of his former teammates? Did the fact that the trade rendered Bryce ineligible to participate in the upcoming All-Star game, potentially robbing him of the $90,000 bonus awarded to players on the winning team, lend support to this notion?

The writer concluded with "The optics appear suspicious and could prompt the players' union to investigate the matter. If they conclude Lovejoy suffered an economic loss as a result of the trade, they may have grounds for filing a grievance."

She stared wordlessly out over the arena. The fans had begun filling the seats, and a buzz of excitement started to hum throughout the building.

"We'll deny it, of course," Wyatt said. "All of it."

Haven set aside the device. "Well, some of it's true."

Behind his glasses, his warm brown eyes squeezed shut. He eased himself down into the chair beside her. "I'm sorry."

"Thank you." She pushed the words past her constricted throat.

A cheer went up when the Renegades' players shot from the tunnel and spilled out over the ice.

"I'm not carrying out a vendetta against Bryce." She hated the tremor in her voice. "I traded him because he hasn't produced in years and because I'm looking for something, anything, to get this team going in the right direction."

"Then that's what we'll say." He pushed to his feet. "I'll talk to Legal and we'll get a statement written up."

The game flew by while Haven's nerves coiled tighter and tighter around the threat of the *Gazette's* news story. She tried keeping up the conversation with Mel and Harlon, but every chance she got, she pulled out her phone and checked the newspaper's website. Dread snaked through her each time she waited for the page to refresh.

With ten minutes remaining in regulation, the story posted.

Thirty minutes later, when the Renegades won the game, she didn't feel like celebrating. She gathered her belongings and, outside the arena, hailed a cab.

She was gone before the players emerged from the locker room.

Later, Jack called her cell phone, but she didn't pick up. While his call went to voice mail, she headed down the hall to take a shower. After, she dressed in leggings and a Renegades jersey. As she pulled the jersey over her head, she heard a knock at the penthouse door.

A ripple of dread disturbed her. She was afraid to see his face, though she didn't know why. It was unlikely that he'd already seen the story.

She opened the door, and when her heart squeezed at the sight of his beautiful face, she understood her fear. She'd grown weary of disappointing him.

Without speaking, he stepped inside the apartment and closed the door behind him. She retreated to the kitchen, and slowly, he followed her.

He'd changed into jeans and a T-shirt, and his super-amazing Jack smell reached out to her from across the kitchen island.

He eased himself onto a barstool. "You okay?"

She filled a glass of water at the refrigerator and gulped down a large swallow.

Then she faced him. "The *Gazette* published a story about Bryce's trade."

His gaze became instantly alert. "What did it say?"

As she told him about the possibility of a grievance, she had trouble meeting his gaze.

Maybe she was afraid what she'd see in his eyes if she looked too closely. Would there be accusation, like so many who'd seen her as the villain trying to ruin those athletes' lives by destroy their promising careers? He was one of them, after all. Didn't she have to consider the possibility that he'd side with his peers? Would he see her as the villain now, dragging the team under with her personal baggage?

"You're worried."

She shrugged. "A little."

"He doesn't have a case. The lawyers might play pretend for a while, but that's all it'll be. Make-believe."

Maybe so, but that wouldn't change the fact that the entire world would know about what had happened to her at the college party.

"You look tired," he said softly.

Exhaustion seemed to hit her all at once. "I am."

The leg of his barstool scraped the hardwood floors when he stood. "C'mon, let's get you some sleep."

❧

He reached for her in his sleep. Finding only emptiness, he blinked open his eyes in the darkness. He lifted his head.

She was gone.

He padded down the hall to the living room, where the obnoxious glow of a computer screen cast an eerie light over the room. He tracked its source to the kitchen island.

She looked up when he approached. Her huge brown eyes brimmed with tears and notched a chunk out his heart.

He balanced on the barstool beside her. "What are you doing?"

She sniffled. "I wanted to see what they'd written." Her chin trembled. "But then I started to read the comment section."

"Oh, Haven...."

She wiped her cheek with the palm of her hand. "The women were the worst. They defended those boys. They blamed me. They said I shouldn't have been at a party like that, and I shouldn't have been drinking so much. I shouldn't have been dressed like that. It's not like I hadn't berated myself already for all of that, and more."

Devastated dark eyes clamped onto his face and threatened to blow his world apart.

"But now they're defending me." Her tears spilled over when she pointed at the computer screen, but they came too quickly for her sleeve to sop them up. "I can take their hostility, but I don't think I can handle it if they're nice to me."

He knew what it was to look in the mirror and detest what he saw there. It destroyed him that she'd taken on their violence and hatred and turned it toward herself. Maybe it was an inevitable result of the helplessness. Hell, what did he know about it? He knew nothing at all, except the feeling of his heart breaking for her.

He reached over and closed the laptop. "Come away from the computer, Haven."

☙

The next morning, he left her in bed when he headed out for his run, and that's where she was when he returned to the penthouse well past dinner, after the activity in the building had settled down for the night.

He crawled under the covers and lay beside her in the dark, thinking he'd give anything to hear her pop off her smart mouth.

After his morning run the next day, he returned to her bedroom to find she still slept.

He used her shower and when he emerged from the steam-filled room, she remained burrowed beneath the covers.

A towel wrapped around his waist, he sat on the edge of the bed, next to her bare foot sticking out.

"You going to work today?" He kept his tone conversational.

"I don't want to." The blankets muffled her voice, yet she sounded wide-awake.

He'd opened his mouth to tell her he understood when she threw off the covers and fixed grave, serious eyes on him.

"You think I should go."

He picked his words carefully, but didn't get the chance to share them because she rushed ahead without him.

"You think there's a crap-ton of work to do, and without Darby there, who the hell's going to do it?"

He scrubbed a towel over his wet head while she pressed her case.

"You think what's happening with this team now is more important than something that happened over ten years ago."

He stopped her there. "I would never say that." Reaching out, he wrapped his hand around her ankle. "Please, don't ever make light of what happened to you."

Her dark eyes shimmered with unshed tears. "I can't go out there," she whispered. "I can't... go through that again."

His heart couldn't take much more. "You don't have to do, or say, anything. You're doing a good job with this team, Haven. Just keep doing what you've been doing and let the chips fall where they may."

"You think I'm doing a good job?"

With the pad of his thumb, he stroked the soft skin over her anklebone. "I do."

She rubbed her forehead, as if massaging an ache. "I'm so tired. I can't think straight and I can't catch my breath and-and I just...." Her sad eyes pleaded with him to understand. "I don't know if I can do this anymore."

He squeezed her ankle. "I know. I've been there."

"You have?"

"More times than I care to count. It's late in the game. You're down and momentum has swung to the other team. Their fans are going crazy, and their cheering is raining down on you, drowning you. You're treading water, just trying to stay afloat."

Lost in his memories, he stared at the floor. "There's no logic in those moments. No reason. Only chaos and pain. You have to trust yourself, and quiet your mind, and then you'll see the way through it. Not all at once, not clearly, but little by little, you'll see it. An opening.

"So you make your move. You try to make the play. It might not lead anywhere, but it's a chance, so you take it. And you take the next one, too. You fight, and you keep on fighting until you see the edge of the chaos, because the only other option available to you is defeat."

He brought his gaze back to hers and smoothed his hand up her calf.

"But defeat is not an option. You can't give up. You can't just give the game to the other team. Make them beat you. Give it everything you have, and then, even if you lose, you know you did all you could do. You fought, and even though that day you lost to a better team, you've learned a lot about yourself. Those are the moments where you grow. You work harder. You get better. You live to fight another day, and the next time the storm comes and you're down late in the third period and all seems lost, you're ready for it. The storm doesn't break you. You become the storm."

For a moment, she was quiet, but then her hand came out to cover his. "Thank you, Jack."

He felt her smile in the center of his chest.

Yet, she didn't get out of bed.

Instead, a ripple of doubt puckered her brow. "Any way we can just get rid of the media? I mean, what do they even really do?"

He shook his head. "I wish I knew. We might love the game, but we don't love all that comes with it."

"I don't love the game."

"Yes, you do."

She didn't argue.

Holding the towel in place at his waist, he stood. "You ready?"

"For what?"

"Time to get your game face on, baby. We got a hockey team to save."

With a huff, she kicked her legs free of the sheets and climbed from the bed.

His heart sang.

Chapter Twenty

The final horn sounded on another Renegades win, this one on the road in Tampa Bay.

Adrenaline flowing, Jack hit the tunnel and followed his teammates into the visitors' locker room. He smacked Milo on the top of his helmet. The kid was playing his best hockey the past two weeks, and he was a big reason for their six-game win streak.

A six-game win streak. An incredible feat in the highly competitive league.

The team was clicking. Personnel changes and a few line adjustments had altered the team's chemistry and given new life to their power play. The young guys were getting better and more confident every day. They'd bought in to what Coach Chambers was trying to do. They were focused, and now they'd clawed their way out of last place.

Jack matched their enthusiasm, but not with his sights

set on a Stanley Cup run, for that remained an outside possibility. No, this time he derived his motivation not from within, but without.

It resided with Haven, and if Haven wanted this team to win, then win they would. She got him, and for that, he wanted to help her. He wanted to win for her, though his reasons were less than noble.

He wanted revenge on everyone and everything that made her feel helpless. That robbed her of her self-worth. Stole her peace and gave all women a reason to be suspicious of all men, but most especially men like him. Men revered by society for no reason other than their ability to play a game, and giving them all but a free pass for doing so.

Someday, he'd get his vengeance. Somehow.

But for now, he'd focus on Haven.

On making Haven happy.

Whole.

They'd begun their affair almost three weeks back, and the more he had her, the more he wanted her. Already he'd grown weary of their need to sneak around, as though what they were doing was dirty or wrong.

Being with Haven didn't feel dirty or wrong to him. It felt right, and it hurt, being so close to her and yet being unable, forbidden, to be with her, to ask her simply how her day had gone, for fear he'd talk too long, or too familiarly, that his gaze might linger, or that he'd do something that'd somehow tip somebody off to the truth about them.

He had eight weeks until the playoffs. They'd need to win more than half of the games remaining on their schedule, probably a lot more if another team got hot down the stretch.

But he now believed this team could do it. They had the talent and the drive. Whether or not they had the stamina remained to be seen.

He would do everything in his power to get them there. He'd push and claw, harass and nag his teammates all the way to the end. With nothing but the sheer force of his will, he'd get them there.

For Haven.

⦋

Haven cracked open one eye. She caught a glimpse of Jack's incredible backside before he pulled a pair of jogging pants over his hips.

She turned her head to read the digits on the clock. 6:22 a.m.

Rolling to her side, she watched him finish dressing for his run.

He'd returned from a road trip late the night before, and during lovemaking, she'd discovered his newest battle scars. A small cut on his cheekbone. An angry bruise over the left side of his rib cage.

She marveled at his drive. "How do you do it?"

He turned his head. "Do what?"

"Stay so motivated."

A lazy smile pushed up one corner of his puffy mouth, but he didn't provide her with an answer.

"It must come from having four brothers. Did you guys always try to one-up each other or something?"

He shoved his arms through the sleeves of his sweatshirt. "I'm not busting my balls so this shitty team can be slightly less shitty for my brothers."

He crossed to the nightstand and worked at fastening his activity monitor around his wrist.

She rose up on her elbow. "Then why are you doing it?"

Without lifting his head, moss green eyes latched on to her face.

221

"I think you know why." Bending over, he dropped a kiss on her forehead. "But if not, I'm not going to tell you."

Then he disappeared through her bedroom door.

⁊

The Renegades continued their solid play, and with the poor play of late of several other teams in their division, by the end of the second week of February, nearly seven weeks after Haven had taken over ownership of the club, they were set to claim the wild card spot.

A win in Milwaukee in regulation over Chicago combined with a loss by Winnipeg in their matchup against St. Louis would move the Renegades into the last remaining playoff slot.

Though they remained more than a month from the end of the regular season, that they were even in contention to squeak into the playoffs amazed most pundits and analysts. To be honest, it amazed most everyone within the Renegades organization, including Haven.

All the winning had the added benefit of making certain the fans and media remained focused on the team and not on her. So far, no grievance had been filed, and she'd secretly begun to hope it was all behind her.

To start the game, the Renegades came out playing fast and frenzied. Her heart in her throat, she tracked Jack's movements at all times, whether he was in the game, taking and delivering punishing hits, or on the bench, where his mouth moved constantly as he coached and cajoled his teammates.

Midway through the first period, Jack buried a one-timer in the back of Chicago's net and the crowd erupted. They continued making noise and, at the first intermission, sent the team to the locker room on a wave of deafening cheers.

In the second period, Chicago struck first, tying the game at 1-1. Shortly after, the refs whistled the Renegades for a penalty. Down a man, Jack, Gabe, and the Donovan twins formed a defensive front before Milo. Jack inched out to challenge the Chicago forward, who attempted to sneak a pass across the ice to his teammate. Anticipating the move, Jack had a step on them. He picked off the pass and charged up the ice.

All alone on the breakaway, he faked left and put the puck in the net behind the goalie's right side.

Haven thought the crowd's cheers might bring down the rafters. The energy in the building remained impossibly high, and every time Jack touched the puck the crowd roared with unruly abandon. Or maybe it was the dollar beer promotion running that night.

With three minutes to the close of the second period, Chicago evened the score at 2-2.

In the owner's box, Haven's nerves wound tight. She sipped Diet Coke compulsively and kept her eye on the TV over the bar where Winnipeg was down a score as the third period got underway.

When the puck dropped in the third, the Renegades went on the attack. They beat Chicago to the loose pucks and played more physically against the boards. Kai scored on a pass from Gus, but Chicago answered with five minutes remaining in regulation.

Just as the game in St. Louis ended with a Winnipeg loss.

Haven stood staring down at the ice, murmuring encouragement to the team as though it could somehow help them get the win.

For the next five minutes, both teams played with breath-stealing urgency. Her heart thundered as the tension ramped higher with every second that ticked off the game clock. As the time left to play slipped under the one-minute mark, it appeared the teams were headed for sudden death overtime.

Then one of the twins fired a shot at the net. The Chicago goalie knocked the puck down and every man on the ice lunged at it. The black disc squirted out and Jack, with a short windup and swift strike, slapped it with enough force to send it hurtling past the goalie and into the net with 3.4 seconds remaining.

The horns blared. Wild, drunken cheering from the crowd released the tension in the building as hats began to litter the ice. Jack returned from the tunnel and skated out on the ice to collect a cap thrown to honor his incredible three-goal game. A hat trick.

He removed his helmet, pulled the baseball cap over his head, and with a wide smile, lifted his stick in the air. With the crowd's answering roar, all the pent-up nervous energy in Haven erupted.

She fled the owner's box, flinging open the door and charging down the corridor.

Though breathless from her sprint through the arena, she pushed on, desperate to get to Jack. In the hall outside the locker room, she spotted the back of his jersey. Nolan, number seventeen, stood beneath the glare of camera lights, giving an interview to the Renegades' broadcast network.

Players and team personnel congregated in the hall, the atmosphere lively as they mixed with reporters and family and friends.

His interview complete, Jack turned from the camera. He looked in her direction and a broad grin split his beautiful face. All white teeth and bright eyes in his dark features.

Her heart ballooned, filling with all the pride and joy in his smile.

Just then, a mass of bodies surged into her path. She tried to move around them but found no space, so she squeezed between them. A shoulder bumped into her, knocking her off her course to Jack.

He held up his arm in a wave, and she struggled forward.

Only a few yards from him, which might as well have been a canyon, she realized his gaze fixated not on her, but on some point behind her. She turned, just as a blur of blonde hair streaked through the crowded corridor and launched into his outstretched arms.

He lifted the woman off the ground while her light laughter speared Haven like poison-tipped darts. Watching them, her feet grew roots to the spot while bodies bumped against her.

Jack returned the woman to her feet and smiled down at her. Haven recognized her then. The woman from the elevator. Sutton.

The balloon in her chest burst, her heart deflating as if it'd suffered a betrayal.

Someone called out his name, and Jack lifted his head.

That's when he saw her.

His smile cracked and faltered. The already heightened color on his cheeks deepened.

Sutton extracted herself from his arms and pressed a cell phone to her ear. "Omigosh, Dad, did you see it? Yes. I know, I know," she said, laughing. "I can't believe it. I'm with him now. I will. I'll tell him."

Sutton recognized Haven then and greeted her with a bright smile. "Wasn't he incredible?"

The beauty laid her hand over Jack's abdomen.

Haven nodded. "Nice game." Silly words to conceal the treachery of her silly heart.

"Thanks." His kaleidoscope eyes burned intensely, willing her to understand the thoughts he couldn't speak. Not to her. Not there.

Sutton's vivid blue eyes shimmered with her delight when she looked at Haven. "My dad is freaking out right now."

"I'm sorry, who?" Haven dragged her gaze away from the place where Jack's arm tucked around Sutton's small waist.

"My dad. Neal Thompson. He's the GM in Detroit."

Neal Thompson, the man Jack considered a father figure, who he credited with his success, was Sutton's dad?

Haven's heart threw up.

Sutton looked down at her cell phone and, with a tiny gasp, smiled up at Jack. "It's my brother." She cradled the device to her ear. "Hey, Jace, did you ever get a hat trick? No? I didn't think so." She laughed at his response. "He said you cheated. Your skate was in the crease on that second goal."

"Bullshit," Jack said, smiling.

"Did you hear that?" she asked her brother.

A dark jealousy wrenched the knot in Haven's stomach. Sutton had a dad that called her just to say nice things, and she had a brother who was still alive.

She had everything Haven once had, but lost.

And she had Jack's arms around her, without a care in the world for who might see them together.

It shouldn't hurt this much.

Why did it hurt so much?

Jack hadn't betrayed her. He wasn't even hers, not for keeps. She didn't do "for keeps." "For keeps" was against the rules.

"For keeps" was for people with loving families.

Whole families.

She wasn't those people. Love wouldn't bring her brother back, or make her parents notice she hadn't died that day along with him.

She was the other people. The ones who love didn't favor. The ones men fucked but didn't invite to the dance or take home to meet their mothers.

A large body knocked into her. "Oops, sorry, boss. Didn't see you there."

Still dressed and in skates, the player lumbered over to Jack. "My man, you were on fire."

Jack's smile flashed wide and bright, and when he began to introduce Sutton to his teammate, Haven turned away.

Chapter Twenty-One

The team traveled to Dallas the next day for a Sunday afternoon matchup, and then went on to St. Louis for a late-night showdown on Monday. When Jack finally returned home early Tuesday, he dropped his bag inside his apartment door and made his way back down the hall to the elevators. He punched in the code to take him to the twentieth floor.

He hadn't seen in her three days and hunger gnawed at him. He didn't care if he could only bury his face in her hair and inhale the scent of her shampoo for a while. It mattered only that he was near her, for a little while, at least.

Then the elevator doors pulled apart and she stood before him.

"Jack." She drew up at the sight of him. "You're back."

"I was just coming to see you." The magnetic force pulled him toward her.

Her arm came out to hold the elevator door. "Actually, I'm on my way out."

Unease prickled up his spine.

He searched her face. "Is everything okay?"

She nodded. "I'm just busy today."

Maybe it was the way she held her shoulders, high and tight, or how her gaze never quite managed to find his face, but he knew he couldn't let her get away or he risked losing her.

"I'll come with you." He slipped back inside the elevator.

"You don't even know where I'm going."

"Where are we going?"

Her lips pressed into a tight line. "You just got home. Why don't you relax?" She pressed the button for the eighteenth floor. "I'll be back later."

She was trying to get rid of him, and he didn't even care to know why. He cared about only one thing.

"I want to be with you, Haven."

She stared straight ahead. "What if we're seen together?"

His lips pressed into a tight line. Dammit, she wasn't his dirty little secret. Nor was he hers.

He pressed the button to take them to the lobby. "We were seen together plenty of times before we started this, and no one thought anything of it."

She lifted one shoulder. "Fine. Do whatever you want."

He narrowed his eyes at her. "What I want is to get you naked and kiss you in all those places that make you soft and slippery until you tell me what's bothering you. Until then, I'll be happy just to hang out with you." Reaching over, he plucked the car keys from her hand. "But I'm driving."

In her sedan, she directed him to get on the highway headed south, and a few exits beyond the city limits, she guided him off the freeway and onto a rural road. They'd driven less than a quarter of a mile when she asked him to turn in at the entrance of a mobile home park.

Uneasiness settled between his shoulder blades as he steered them through the vast park.

Near the far perimeter, where the interstate ran parallel to the boundary line, she pointed to a white trailer with a small front porch. "It's this one here."

He followed her up the porch stairs, where she rapped on the door once and entered the trailer. Ducking his head, he followed her inside.

The living room, dining room, and kitchen all flowed into one space, giving the cramped trailer a much larger feel. Still, Jack's head came within a foot of the ceiling, and he wasn't at all sure that he wouldn't be able to touch the two walls running lengthwise at once.

Haven moved toward the sofa where a dark-haired woman lay covered by a colorful afghan.

"Hey, Mama." She bent down and pressed a kiss to the woman's chubby cheek.

"Hi, sweetie." The woman was slow to sit. "What a nice surprise."

"We didn't mean to wake you up. Go back to sleep."

Haven's mom had the same olive skin and dark eyes as her daughter. She removed the afghan and, with much effort, pushed herself up off the sofa.

Once steady on her severely swollen feet, she lifted her face toward Jack with a smile. "And who's this?"

"Mama, this is Jack Nolan. He's a hockey player. Jack, this is my mom, Beverly."

Beverly shuffled forward. "What position do you play, Jack?"

"I'm a right forward."

A spark of light came into her eyes. "My son played hockey. He was quite good at it, too, wasn't he?" When Haven nodded, Beverly turned back to him. "We lost him in a car accident a few years back now, but he was a real good player."

"I'm very sorry to hear that," Jack said. "What position did he play?"

A wrinkle between her brows, Beverly twisted to look at Haven.

"Right forward," Haven said.

Beverly reached for his arm. "Come on over here. I'll show you some pictures."

He helped Haven's mom to the dining table and she cracked open a large photo album. While she pointed to the first picture, Haven moved into the small kitchen where she flipped on the faucet and filled the sink with soapy water. She then set to work washing a stack of dirty dishes piled high on the laminate counters.

For the next hour, Beverly regaled him with stories about her children as she flipped through the pages of her photo album. A smile played on Jack's lips as he peered into Haven's sweet, little girl face, but Beverly's obvious love and longing for the son she'd lost, while the daughter who'd survived the accident stood only a few feet away, battered his heart and obliterated his smile.

When it came time to go, Haven helped her mom to the sofa.

She laid the afghan over Beverly's legs. "Are you taking your blood pressure medicine?"

"Oh, yes, yes." Beverly fussed with the blanket. "Well, sometimes, I forget."

Haven retrieved a pill from a bottle on the end table and handed it to her mom with a cup of water. "Do you need anything else?"

"I do fine all on my own." Beverly squeezed Haven's hand. "You'll come see me soon?"

"I will, Mom. I promise."

Quakes of despair and resentment reverberated through Jack as he climbed behind the wheel of her car. In trembling silence, he steered them through the winding streets of the run-down park and eased into traffic on the highway as Haven laid her head against the headrest. She watched the scenery pass by for a time.

His mind a mess, he didn't see the road for the scrambled thoughts running through his head. Until her quiet voice jolted him.

"Everything all right?"

He struggled to keep his voice even. "That's where you grew up?"

"No, my mom and I moved there after she and my dad divorced. I grew up in Granville." A smile touched her lips. "In a permanently parked house."

His knuckles turned white on the steering wheel. "So you moved to the trailer park while your dad moved into his mansion with Kristen?"

She stayed silent.

"Why didn't he help you?"

She bristled. "I didn't need his help."

"You did. You do." To soothe the bite in his tone, he grasped her hand. "He should've... protected you."

She made a noise. "That's not how it works."

"It should be how it works."

"He has a family to worry about."

Why was she defending him? "Dammit, Haven, you are his family."

"Believe it or not, I don't want a Lexus or to live in a penthouse downtown."

"The man is shitting money." Jack didn't know why he was so pissed. "The least he could do was get you and your mom a nice house in a nice neighborhood. Maybe pay for you to go to college."

"It's not such a bad place. And he did offer to help me with school, but I didn't need it. I had a full ride." The distinct ring of pride in her voice lessened his fury somewhat.

"I knew it," he grumbled. "You're a smart girl."

She smiled. "It was an athletic scholarship, not academic."

"What sport did you play?" The pad of his thumb brushed over the spot between her thumb and forefinger.

"Volleyball."

A visual of her tight ass in super-short volleyball shorts ricocheted through his body and settled in his groin. He shifted in the seat. "Aren't you a little short to be a volleyball player?"

"I was a defensive specialist, and I'm not that short."

However tall she was, she was the perfect size. She was perfect in a lot of ways. Strong, smart, loyal. Hot as hell.

"I just wish he'd tried a little harder to make things easier for you. I guess that's all I'm saying."

"He doesn't know me," she said quietly. "I see him once a year, at most. After Ryan died... he just stopped paying attention to what was going on in my life."

He pulled her hand to his mouth and pressed a kiss to her fingers.

Right then, he didn't need a wife, but when he retired and got serious about looking for one, he wanted to find someone like Haven.

؃

They snuck upstairs to the penthouse, and because she abhorred cooking as much as cleaning, she ordered them a pizza. Settled at the dining table situated before the windows overlooking downtown Milwaukee, a strange sort of awkwardness colored their conversation.

It was her fault. Four days later, the memory of Jack with his arm around Sutton still irritated, pursuing her like a drunk creep at the bar, though she knew she had no right to the feeling.

"Do you like the pizza?"

A suspicious glint in his vivid eyes, Jack studied her face. "The pizza's good."

She might've just told him what was troubling her, except no words would come that didn't make her sound needy and clingy. Like a committed girlfriend.

On the coffee table, his cell phone buzzed.

He didn't move, but continued to eat.

"Do you like the new uniforms?" she asked. "They're nice, right?"

He narrowed his eyes at her.

Another buzz sounded from the coffee table, but he only flipped open the pizza box and dished himself another piece.

"Do you need to get that?"

"It's a text." He snuck a glance at her. "I don't usually bother to read them."

Understanding wrenched her heart. "Because of your dyslexia?"

One of his wide shoulders hitched higher.

His phone buzzed again.

She chewed her bottom lip. "It sounds like something might be going on. Do you want me to read them?"

As she spoke, yet another text buzzed.

With an annoyed scowl, he flicked his hand toward the coffee table. "Go for it."

She crossed to the phone and located the icon to open his text message. "The first one's from Eli." She tapped the screen. "He says 'LOLOLOLOL.'"

Jack's eyebrows lifted.

Haven shrugged. "The next one's from Sebastian. It says 'Oh captain, my captain, teach me your ways!'"

Jack frowned. "What the...?"

Haven opened the next message, from Milo. "He says 'Does she have a sister?'"

Jack and Haven stared at one another.

Her mouth suddenly dry, she swallowed hard. "You don't think...?"

"They found out about us," he finished while shoving to his feet.

She opened the next text, and the next one, both from his teammates, both with similar comments.

"Reply to Ezra." He came to stand beside her. "Ask him what the fuck he's talking about."

Haven typed Jack's exact words into a text and hit Send.

They stared at the device in her palm. When it buzzed a moment later, she startled and then opened Ezra's response.

"He sent a link." She clicked on the web link and waited for the page to load.

The site, some kind of tabloid or celebrity gossip website, brimmed with photos.

She scrolled down the page.

"Top 10 WAGS of pro athletes," she read. "What's a WAG?"

She scrolled a little farther, and a picture of Sutton came onto the screen. Surrounded by painfully normal-looking people, she appeared to be in the stands at some kind of an event. An arena.

Below that picture was another of Sutton standing in water up to her knees, wearing a string bikini and smiling her incredible smile at the camera.

Confused thoughts cluttered Haven's mind as she scrolled to the last photo of Jack, in his Renegades jersey, with Sutton nestled in the crook of his arm while he smiled down into her face.

Her heart spasmed in her chest and she read the text below their embrace with dreadful reluctance.

Jack Nolan of the Milwaukee Renegades snags our

number two spot with this sultry lass. Swimsuit model and budding actress, she keeps puck-slapping lucky lad Jack warm at night after a frostbitten battle, and melts our frigid hearts.

"What does it say?" Jack asked.

Haven handed him the phone. "Hottest wives and girlfriends. WAGS."

She watched his face as he viewed the pictures of Sutton and pieced together their meaning.

His gaze snapped to Haven's face.

She arranged her features to imitate a smile. "Sutton, right? She seemed sweet."

"She's not my girlfriend."

Haven crossed to the dining table and scooped up her dinner plate. "She's a hugger."

"You're mad."

"I'm not mad." She carried the plate to the kitchen sink.

He moved to the kitchen island. "You say the words, but your tone doesn't match."

"I'm not mad," she repeated.

Sick with jealousy, maybe, but not mad.

He dragged a hand through his hair and it stood up on end. "She sort of latched on and... wouldn't let go. I didn't even see her coming."

"You have no one to blame but yourself. You can't leave yourself out there like that, just so... huggable." She loaded her dirty plate into the dishwasher.

"I'm sorry."

With her foot, she pushed the dishwasher door closed. "I didn't say it was your fault. I said I'm blaming you."

A smile quirked his lips. "I'm sorry if she upset you."

"You don't look sorry."

He sidled closer. "I like that you're jealous."

She folded her arms over her abdomen, guarding against his delicious-smelling cocoon of warmth.

His expression grew serious once more. "Though maybe it isn't the worse thing in the world if people think she and I are... together."

His words hit her like a punch to the gut.

He watched her closely. "They'll be less likely to suspect anything is going on between us."

Jealousy snarled through her. "You're right. No one would suspect you'd want to sleep with me if you could have her." The words escaped before she could stop them.

"Hey." He brushed a strand of hair off her forehead. "You can't possibly think that."

But she did. She wanted him to tell her how horrid he found Sutton's appearance, and even though it'd be a lie, she'd fall into his arms and let her insecurities melt into a puddle at their feet.

It was a ludicrous thought.

She sighed, defeated. "Does she have to be so pretty? And snuggly?"

He bent his head to nuzzle the side of her neck, below her ear. "You're pretty. And snuggly."

She moved toward his touch. "You don't have to lie to me, Jack. No promises, no regrets, remember?"

He drew back.

When he looked at her, the playfulness left his face. "That was before."

Her heart beat with light, furious palpitations. "My dad will be out of rehab and back with the team soon. In thirteen days."

"Then what?"

"Then I guess I'll go back to my life."

His eyes remained carefully hooded. "You don't have to."

He was so handsome. So sweet to her mom. So

perfect in every way that mattered.

She touched his cheek, and he pressed his forehead to hers. Eyes closed, she breathed him in. His fingers danced along her collarbone. Pulling aside her shirt collar, his warm mouth tasted the bare skin of her shoulder. She shivered.

She wanted these last days with him, before she went back to being her and he went back to being him.

She slid onto the countertop and opened her legs to him.

Chapter Twenty-Two

Jack feared he might not survive the grueling six-day road trip. Without her, his body withered. He grew edgy and short-tempered, which helped his play on the ice if not his relationship with his teammates in the locker room.

He thought about her constantly, wondering how she was doing. From his hotel room, he called her on the nights his road roommate went out, but hearing her voice without seeing her face or touching her body only enflamed his want of her.

The Renegades won three of their four games before flying home Tuesday morning. Their flight touched down at 3:00 a.m., both too late and too early to go to her.

He'd prowled his apartment, unable to sleep with the starvation feasting on his flesh, only to doze off and miss the chance to catch her before she left for work.

He arrived at the arena in the late afternoon for

practice. When he suited up, a strap broke on one of his elbow pads, so while the team headed to the ice, he found the equipment manager for a replacement.

New pad in hand, he headed back to the locker room to finish dressing.

He spotted her from behind, walking away from him down the hall. She must've sensed him, for she turned and looked back.

Her lips parted, and her hand came up to offer a tiny wave.

Caught in her gravitational pull, he was moving toward her.

"Hey," she said. "You had a good trip. You guys are playing great."

He didn't want to talk about hockey.

He wanted to snatch the flimsy blouse from her body, tear the confining bra away, and set her large breasts free. He wanted to watch them bounce and sway to the rhythm of their joining. He wanted to lay her on a bed on her stomach, grip her round, lush ass, and enter her from behind.

He drew close, as close as he could get without touching her. "How are you? You okay?"

Her breathing hitched a little higher and she nodded. "I'm okay."

She took in his appearance, dressed as he was in only his black undersuit and shoulder pads.

"You're missing some of your clothes." Her voice trembled.

Without making the conscious decision to do so, he reached for her, his hand finding the curve of her waist.

He slanted his head closer and her scent teased his nostrils.

She whispered his name next to his ear.

At the desperate snag in her voice, a lick of fire stirred in him, awakening his hunger.

His grip on her waist tightened. "I need you."

"We shouldn't...." Her big brown eyes darted left and right.

A nasty curse ripped from him. "I don't care, Haven. I don't care what happens. I have to have you. All of you. Now."

He hated the concern in her eyes when she gazed up at him. "Okay."

That she trusted him, even knowing—probably better than him—what their discovery would mean, sent a surge of affection roaring through him.

He walked her backward into a meeting room. Before the door shut, he was reaching for her. His hands rushed over her body, caressing the lush mounds and soft hollows of her tantalizing form.

He knew her body. Knew it naked. Knew what it craved. What it sought. What it couldn't endure without.

He took her face in his hands. "I can't get enough. It'll never be enough."

"Please, Jack." Her mouth pressed against his with soft urgency. "I need you. Inside me."

His body's desperate, throbbing need for her pushed out all thoughts of exposure or self-protection.

If he were to be burned by the fires of his lust, he would dance merrily in the flames.

ℝ

Haven's intoxicating musk lingered on his skin when he stepped onto the ice and joined the team in their warm-up drills.

As he picked up his speed, trying to catch up with the rest of the guys, his thoughts remained in that room where he'd had her. On the desperate way she'd clutched at him when he hiked up her skirt, and on the sounds of her soft panting and moaning while he drove deep inside her.

Skating around the ice, he experienced a moment of heart-pounding, ball-busting unreality.

What was he doing, fucking his boss while they were at work? Only an unlocked door between them and discovery? It was madness, and yet he wouldn't stop himself doing it.

He didn't know what was happening between them, but they'd certainly gone beyond a hookup. And he wanted to keep it going. See where it led.

What was so wrong with wanting to be with her? Wanting to give them a chance? They were good together. Really good, and there wasn't a damn thing wrong with him enjoying sex with a smart, beautiful woman.

In fact, he wanted to have sex with her every day. For as long as it was good.

Even if that meant forever.

The thought stunned him momentarily. He didn't even see the puck until it was by him.

"Time to wake up, Nolan," Coach offered by way of advice.

"He's in la-la land," Gus called out in his thick Czech accent. "Thoughts of Blondie running in his head."

That pulled some chuckles from his teammates.

They thought he was lovesick.

Over Sutton.

Sutton was sweet, and there was no denying how gorgeous she was, but she would never electrify him the way Haven did.

Jack ignored his teammates' laughter. Let them go on thinking Sutton was the woman dominating his thoughts and commanding his cock. It'd only help protect Haven.

He turned to head back up ice, but drew up when he caught sight of Coach.

He wasn't laughing with the rest of them. Chewing the inside of his cheeks, he was watching Jack.

So when practice ended and Coach called him over, a nugget of dread lodged beneath Jack's breastbone as he skated toward the edge of the rink.

"What's up?" Jack kept his tone casual.

"How are things going?" Coach watched the last of Jack's teammates disappear into the tunnel. "Things going okay?"

"Things are going just fine."

Unwilling to look Jack in the eye, Coach gazed out over the empty ice. "You seem a little distracted lately."

"I'm not." Jack bit off the words.

"The captain thing's not too much for you, is it?"

The captain thing was awesome. Jack had a great rapport with his teammates, and they respected him.

"Is there a problem, Coach?"

Coach dropped his gaze to the floor and scratched the back of his head. He pushed a huff of air through his lips. "You and Haven aren't... you know, involved, are you?"

Though not unexpected, the words knocked into Jack with the force of a physical blow. A black stain of regret began to seep through him.

Coach's serious gray eyes met Jack's then. "Because that would be bad. For both of you. If the media found out...."

Jack saw no condemnation on the man's face, only concern, and the reality of what they'd done slammed into him.

If the media found out he and Haven were sleeping together, the disaster that'd ensue could, likely would, derail the entire season, messing with this young team's frail focus and distracting them from their goals. All their hard work, and all the fragile hopefulness he'd seen in Haven's eyes when she'd asked him to help her, would dissolve like cotton candy on the tongue.

Worse, it'd thrust her back into the spotlight. His reputation might survive, but would hers? Would they rehash her past, dissect her every behavior? He could only imagine what disgusting things they'd say and write.

Their cruelty would crush her. He recalled how, only a few weeks back, she struggled to get out of bed she was so devastated by their words. He couldn't let them do that to her. Not again.

Whatever it took, he had to keep his relationship with Haven a secret. No one could know.

Starting with Coach.

Jack arranged his features into a derisive sneer. "C'mon, Coach, do you honestly think I'd risk the entire season, my entire career, for a little meaningless sex with her?"

At the soft sound behind them, both men twisted.

To see Haven hovering at the entrance to the tunnel.

Watching him with wounded brown eyes.

ଔ

Her heart crumbled to dust inside her chest. God, how his words hurt.

He made their affair sound meaningless, which made her feel cheap. Slutty. She knew she wasn't, but she hated that that was the first place her mind went.

She hated that he chose those exact words.

She hated that she'd put herself in the position to feel denigrated. Again.

Sick with humiliation, she put a hand on her hip and gave Jack a cheeky grin. "I'm glad you set him straight. I mean, can you imagine? You and me?"

Jack's laugh sounded tight. "It's ridiculous."

Splotches of red broke out on Coach's face and neck. "I'll admit it, I'm relieved." A sheepish smile touched his

244

features. "And completely mortified. I'm sorry, guys."

Jack's green-gold gaze burned into her. "How about we pretend this conversation never happened?"

"Done," Coach agreed.

Unable to play along, Haven turned away.

She lifted a hand. "Thanks for the laugh, Coach. Good luck tomorrow night."

She stumbled back down the tunnel, Jack's words haunting her steps. She could forgive him the words, though they hurt, but she couldn't forgive herself for letting them hurt.

Her feet carrying her away punished the concrete floor.

She knew better than to let this happen. She had rules.

Even so, there was no rational reason for this to hurt so badly. No reason, except one.

She'd fallen in love with him. She'd given him her heart when he didn't want it. Never asked for it.

She'd thought she could handle it. Thought she could walk away from him when her time with the team was over, as she'd done on the island, her heart untouched.

With the back of her hand, she wiped at the hot tears running down her cheeks.

She'd let him break every one of her rules. Why? Why had she done that?

Because she thought he was special, and with him, so was she.

But if he were special, she wouldn't be feeling like the other woman right now. The woman she used to be. Cheap. A throwaway.

He was no different from all the other men who'd enjoyed her body only to be careless with her heart.

Immediately, her heart rejected that notion, even as her mind tried to outrun its logic.

So what if he was different? She was the same Haven

of two months before, and *that* Haven knew what she had to do now to put her world back to rights. To save her heart from one last fatal blow.

She had to end the relationship. Sever the bond.

Destroy it beyond repair or recognition.

Beyond the point worth saving.

Chapter Twenty-Three

The sounds of revelry and blues music grated on Jack's nerves while the smooth brewed beer sat heavy in his stomach. His shitty day had taken on a new level of sucking when some guys from the team bullied him into going out with them for drinks.

So while the party raged on around him, he descended further into the chaos inside his mind.

In his entire career, he'd never given a coach any reason to sit him down and have an awkward or embarrassing conversation. In college, he didn't skip classes or drink too much. He never did recreational drugs or sniffed around the wrong crowd, and the women he'd chosen to be with didn't cause trouble because he didn't give them the chance to do so. Everything he'd ever done was with the express purpose of becoming a better hockey player.

Except Haven.

He never should've gotten involved with her, and now everything between them was complicated and messy and—shit. Wasn't this exactly why he'd avoided relationships all these years? A relationship with his boss should've been a deal breaker.

Though, if he were completely honest with himself, he couldn't say he regretted all of it. Just the part where his coach had to ask Jack if he was sleeping with the boss, and the part where the woman in question had overheard his response.

What would he say to her later when he saw her, knowing she'd overheard? The words were callous, cruel, and she'd heard them.

By now, Jack knew her well enough to know they had to hurt her. He also knew she'd deny that they did.

Inside the dark bar, bodies mingled around their table while Jack stared into his pint.

Until a prickle at the back of his neck caused him to lift his gaze.

And there she was, across the room by the bar, looking directly at him. The brown in her eyes melted with gooey warmth when her gaze tangled with his.

A shuddering breath eased from his body. No, he didn't regret it all.

He recalled the night she'd challenged Avery to chug a beer with her and won. Despite his sour mood, a smile touched his lips at the memory, though all he could do at the time was scowl for his erection pressing against the fly of his jeans.

But now, he watched as she seemed to draw herself up and a mantle of resolve settled around her shoulders.

He frowned. Unease listed through him.

She showed Jack her back and leaned across the bar to shout her order to the bartender. She wore the black skirt that showed off her curves, and on her feet, bright red "fuck me!" pumps wailed with intent. The bartender placed a shot glass in front of her and she threw her head back when she drank it.

He'd never seen her drink liquor.

Abruptly, she turned to the man beside her. Whatever she said to him, Jack watched the man's interest in her change, from cordial to sexual.

His heart started to pound.

She twirled a length of her hair around her forefinger, and when she laughed at something the asshole said, she flipped her hair over one shoulder.

Her hand touched his arm.

What. The. Fuck.

At the asshole's other side, a woman appeared to stare daggers at Haven, and the asshole let the woman pull him away.

Haven faced the room, her wide mouth pulled down at the corners while her dark, desolate gaze searched the crowd.

Then another man stepped in front of her, his big back blocking Jack's view until he moved to stand beside her. With a gesture to the bartender, he bought her another shot, which sat on the bar top less than a fraction of a second before she scooped up the glass and tossed back its contents.

The man leaned close and said something near her ear. She nodded and another shot materialized before her.

A wrench of nausea turned his stomach.

What in the hell was she doing?

The guy's hand moved to her back and slid lower. She slipped off the barstool and he led her onto the dance floor. She pressed her body against his, and Jack experienced a blinding flash of possessive rage.

She belonged to him, dammit. Now and forever.

At his side, Sebastian sipped from a pint. "You all right, man?"

But Jack didn't register his teammate's concern, for just then, the man's hand smoothed over Haven's round bottom.

Jack gripped his pint so tightly he might've fractured the fragile glass. Why didn't she slap the creep's hand away? Why did she let him grope her like that? When she knew Jack was watching? Did she seek to punish him? To hurt him the way he'd hurt her?

Then the man's grotesque hand squeezed one of Haven's firm butt cheeks.

A roar of white-hot fury exploded inside Jack's skull. The rage pushed out all else, until he no longer cared what twisted logic guided her. She'd gone too far.

"Uh... Jack?"

His gaze locked on his target, Jack climbed to his feet. As he approached them, the man dipped his head and his fat tongue came out of his mouth even before he claimed hers.

"What are you doing?"

Haven startled and blinked up at him, pretending she'd only just noticed him. "Oh, hey, Jack." She gave him a wink. "Don't worry, I got this. I know my part well."

"What are you talking about?"

Dropping her voice, she leaned close. "In case anyone else finds out you and I are, you know, fucking, I figure I better be doing it with half the men in here. Fucking a bimbo you picked up at the bar can't ruin your career, can it, Jack?"

She slashed his heart. "Haven, don't."

"Why not?"

His anger spiraled out of control. What did she want him to say, there, in that shitty bar? To come away with him? To be with him? Him and no other?

"You're better than this," he finally said.

She flinched as though he'd slapped her. "I'm really not."

The man tugged on her arm, like a child competing for her attention, and she turned back to him.

"Go back to your table, Jack." Her voice held no heat or vexation. Only a gut-wrenching sadness.

The man leered down her top and she tilted her face up to his. His tongue came out again.

Violence whipped through Jack. "I wouldn't do that if I were you."

The guy drew up and fixed Jack with a blurry-eyed stare. "This doesn't concern you."

Jack bared his teeth. "I'm going to enjoy kicking your ass."

"You think so?" The prick pushed Haven aside. "Let's go, then."

Another man walked up behind Fat Tongue and clapped the creep on the shoulder. "Dude, relax. That's Jack Nolan."

Fat Tongue's face fell.

Another buddy appeared and pushed his way in front of Jack. "How the hell are you, man? Hey, great game the other night."

Haven rolled her eyes and threw up her hands. "Are you kidding me?"

Jack took her by the elbow. "Excuse us, fellas."

She twisted around as Jack dragged along. "Next time, use a little less tongue," she called over her shoulder. "That was sloppy."

Out on the sidewalk, Jack hauled her down the street while his anger slashed and ripped at his chest. As though a jagged shard of broken glass, it hacked and punctured. He dragged her around a corner, and a few yards down the darkened alley, she yanked her arm free of his grip to whirl on him.

"Why did you do that?" The anguish in her voice destroyed him. "Everyone's going to think—"

"Why did you let him touch you?" He closed the

distance between them in two strides and his hands smacked the wall on either side of her head, pinning her between his arms.

He wanted to scrub that man's touch from her body.

He reached for the hem of her skirt and tugged roughly. "He doesn't deserve you."

She threw her arms around his neck and gasped as he exposed her heated flesh to the cold air.

"He doesn't love you." Pulling aside the crotch of panties, Jack quested for the heart of her. He found her humid flesh open and wet, ready for the invasion of his fingers. "He doesn't know your heart, or the taste of your sweet pussy."

On a sob, she clutched fistfuls of his shirt and pulled him to her while he stroked her hungry opening. Tears streamed down her face and he kissed them away.

"No one knows those things, Haven." He freed himself and pressed his throbbing cock to her warm hollow. "No one knows you like I do."

Gripping her bottom, he lifted her and her legs came around his waist. He pushed inside her. A guttural groan tore from his chest.

He started to pump, his hips pinning her against the wall. "No one knows what your body craves the way I do."

She squeezed him with her arms and legs, and her forehead dropped to his shoulder.

"No one but me." His voice rasped with his desire as he slid all the way inside her and back out, before plunging into her again. "Only me."

With all the fierceness and desperation colliding inside him, he drove into her in a storm of lust and anger and heartache until each thrust pulled a savage moan from her.

If anyone were to discover them, they'd see two people fucking. They'd see only the carnal possession, the gritty, greedy quest of two bodies striving for connection and release. They wouldn't feel the tempest of emotions their joining whipped up. Longing and fear, arousal and anguish.

They wouldn't know how his heart called out to hers, begging for her surrender.

"Why?" He plunged again, and again. "Haven, why?"

"Because it doesn't matter." Heartbreak filled her voice as she ground her hips against him. "It could be him, or someone else. It doesn't matter, Jack, if it isn't you."

A sob wrenched from him.

She cried out with her release, and when her quivering center milked the orgasm from his body, she took his heart as well.

They remained entwined while their breathing slowed, her body clamped around him and her head lolling on his shoulder.

"I'm sorry," she whispered.

He laid his arm over her head and kissed her moist temple.

His heart bleeding.

Chapter Twenty-Four

Sitting at her dad's desk, Haven blinked at the date on the calendar. That morning, her dad flew home from California with plans to resume his duties as the Renegades' owner and president immediately.

She'd served her sixty days, and in a matter of hours, she'd be free.

The pang in her chest was relief. What else could it be?

It wasn't her misery over Jack. That sat like a heavy pit in the bottom of her stomach.

After what had happened in the alley two days before, he'd taken her home to Hamilton Place, but when they stumbled into a couple of his teammates in the lobby, she'd slipped away and returned to the penthouse alone. She'd been too shaken to talk anyway, and Jack must've felt similarly, as he didn't come to her that night.

The next morning, the team had left on a road trip.

Now, unable to focus her mind, she slipped another paperclip onto the growing length of chain.

Her phone rang and she picked up the receiver.

"Neal Thompson's on the line for you," Mel said.

Haven straightened. "What does he want?"

"To... talk to you."

Haven worried her bottom lip. "Any chance Darby is here?"

"Mr. Thompson asked for you specifically."

"Oh. Okay." Haven's heart fluttered with light, frantic beats. "Hello?"

"Ms. Callahan, this is Neal Thompson. I'm sorry to bother you. I know how busy you must be."

She pushed the paperclip chain away. "It's no problem. What can I do for you?"

"Not a thing. I just wanted to call and tell you I think you've done a great job for your dad. I'm impressed with the way you've gotten your team to perform."

"Uh... thank you."

"And...." After a brief pause, Neal's deep baritone carried through the phone. "Well, I can only imagine how difficult it's been for you. Just know, those of us who understand the job, we know what you've accomplished over there." He laughed softly. "And we know we probably wouldn't have been able to pull it off. Kudos to you, Ms. Callahan."

She sat motionless and mute, unable to comprehend his words.

"That's all I have for you. I'll let you get back to your busy day."

"Wait." The word flew from her heart.

He waited.

She licked her suddenly dry lips. What did she want to say?

Jack. She wanted to ask him about Jack. She wanted to know everything about him.

What was he like as a teenager? Is your daughter in love with him? Is he in love with your daughter? Because I am in love with him. I just thought you should know that.

She was in love with him. The knowledge sloped through her like a warm southerly breeze after the harsh winter.

She recalled the look on Jack's face when he spoke about the man who'd become like a father to him. Reverent, but with a touch of vulnerability, as though he feared he might one day say or do something to spoil the man's good favor. Jack needed Neal in his life, the same way a child needed the affection of a parent.

The same way she'd needed affection from her parents, who, instead, had withdrawn into their own pain after Ryan's death.

Jack deserved all the love that existed in the entire universe. He did. He deserved her love, too. She wouldn't berate herself anymore for giving it to him.

But she knew herself, and while she was surprised to realize her heart hadn't died along with her brother that day on a country road in Wisconsin, or as a result of the cruelty those boys had done to her, it had been severely wounded by both.

And now, so many years later, her heart remained damaged. Disordered. It still beat and pushed blood through her veins, but it had trouble processing properly, and everything that should've been clear and straightforward was instead backward and out of order.

She and her dyslexic heart were simply not capable of giving Jack Nolan all the love in all the world, which was nothing less than he deserved.

It was bittersweet, her love for him. Like the wound and the balm at once.

"If you have a moment, Mr. Thompson, I wanted to talk to you... about Jack Nolan."

C3

The Renegades traveled to Minnesota for a prime-time matchup on Saturday night and returned to Milwaukee to play host to Detroit for a Sunday afternoon puck drop.

The compressed game times on top of the travel conspired against the Renegades and they came out flat in the first period. They rallied in the second and managed to stay competitive the rest of the way, which kept the home crowd on their feet and electrified.

But with a minute to go in regulation, Detroit went up two goals, effectively putting the game away.

With the goal, exhaustion overcame Jack. Hands on his knees, he circled center ice and waited for play to resume. He looked over to the bench, but the Renegades weren't making any adjustments at such a late point in the game.

He spotted Haven in the tunnel and his chest ached at the sight of her. He hadn't seen her since the night at the bar. Beside her, Neal stood with his hands in the pockets of his suit pants. She said something to him and he grinned.

Despite himself, a smile tugged at one corner of Jack's mouth. Neal would like Haven. He enjoyed a smart-ass as much as anyone.

On the ice for the faceoff, Jack chased his man to the corner and battled him, because he didn't ever give up, no matter how unlikely a win may be. He kicked and poked at the disc with his stick, and when it shot out, he gave chase. Taking possession of the puck, he charged up ice, but Kai on the left wing was a step ahead of him and they skated into Detroit territory offside.

A whistle trilled, stopping play.

He peered up at the game clock. Ten seconds

remained.

Then the ref signaled a timeout taken by the Renegades.

It was an odd timeout. Maybe Coach wanted to use these last seconds to work with the young guys?

When Jack skated to the bench, Coach leaned over the boards.

"You're with Detroit now," he said.

Jack shook his head. "What?"

Coach jabbed a finger at the Detroit bench. "You've been traded."

Jack recoiled. "Wait, what?"

That didn't make any sense. He'd been traded? To Detroit? Now? His sluggish mind failed to grasp the pieces that'd make this puzzle fit together.

Around him, a couple of his teammates murmured to one another. The crowd, which had gone quiet with the game out of reach, seemed eerily devoid of sound.

The captain for Detroit, a guy Jack had known and respected for years, skated over to him.

A broad smile on his face, he gave Jack a whack on the back. "Good to finally have you onboard, Nolan."

What the...?

Then Jack's head snapped around. In the tunnel, Haven watched him with her big dark eyes.

She'd done this.

A lump wedged in his throat.

More back pats and mumbled salutes landed on him from the Detroit players. Then, from his Milwaukee teammates, came murmurings of a different nature. The murmuring spread to the crowd, and grew to a steady rumble.

She did this. Behind his back, she'd struck a deal.

He looked to his teammates, who looked back at him with varied expressions. Some confusion, frustration, disappointment. Jack felt them all. Was overwhelmed by them all. He skated down the line of the Renegade players, giving a fist bump to each man. At the end of the line, his new teammates folded him into their midst.

Knowledge of the trade seemed to ripple through crowd. There was a groundswell of surprised chatter, which rapidly slid toward aggrieved.

But then, someone started to clap.

It started slow, reluctant even, but with each passing moment, the applause strengthened and built. Emotion tightened his throat. He lifted his stick and the crowd roared. A classy sendoff for a favored player. A leader.

While the players took to the ice and the last seconds melted off the clock, Jack, in a daze, hit the tunnel.

Neal greeted him with a wide grin. "Welcome to Detroit, Jack. It's good to have you home."

From her spot behind him, Sutton squeezed forward. She grasped his arm with both of her hands and gave him a small shake. "I'm so happy for you, Jack."

Then *she* stood before him, and her huge brown eyes locked on his face.

How could she have done this to him?

Her soft smile suffered a crack when her gaze slipped to Sutton, and Neal, and then back to him.

"Congratulations," she said softly. "You have everything you want."

Chapter Twenty-Five

In the rankings, the Renegades hovered near the wild card spot. On any given night, they popped into or out of that last playoff slot, depending if they, or the other teams in their division, won or lost. But with seven weeks to go until the postseason started, anything could happen.

The fact was they had a chance, a real chance, to get into the playoffs, and any team that earned a spot in the postseason had a shot to win the Cup.

So as Haven arrived at her dad's office Monday morning, real pride bloomed in her chest. Around the aching hole that'd blown wide open when she sent Jack away.

She shook off the thorns of doubt that tried to sprout and draw more blood. It was what Jack wanted. It was what he'd earned. She would've been wrong not to give it to him after promising him she'd do so. So what if she loved him? Love wasn't enough.

Love couldn't keep someone with you, or keep them safe, or bring them back once they'd gone. Love couldn't make her parents stay married, or even realize just how much their child who hadn't died still needed them.

"Hi, Dad."

Hank stood in front of the flat-screen TV, watching the hockey channel, his hands in the pockets of his dress slacks. He'd already shucked his suit coat and rolled the sleeves of his dress shirt up to his elbows.

At his appearance, a wisp of optimism stirred in her. The color had returned to his face and his hair shined. He looked hale, healthy.

Even when his features twisted into a furious scowl. "Why in the hell did you trade Nolan?"

"Oh, uh...."

At the sound of a derisive snort, she turned her head to see Darby lounging in an armchair.

"We needed the cap space," she lied.

"He was our best player!" Her dad's voice boomed.

At least he was feeling better.

"Jesus, Haven. I asked you to do one thing—keep from burning the place down—and you couldn't do it." He threw the TV remote into the sofa cushions and stomped toward his desk.

"We're in fourth place in the division," she pointed out. Up from last place.

"Not for long." He yanked open the door of the mini-fridge.

Haven's breath caught in her throat. Her heart hammered in her chest while her dad stared down into the fridge, empty except for a few cans of soda.

On a curse, he kicked the door shut. Turning, he kicked the desk chair and sent it crashing into the wall. Then he lurched forward to smack his palms flat on the desktop and let his head hang down.

After changing her whole life to help him out, and having some success, no matter how little, with the team, she'd expected a different reaction from him.

How silly of her to hope it'd be different this time.

Hope. That was something Haven, the teenager, used to do. Before her father withdrew his affection from her and turned it toward her best friend.

Haven, the adult, knew better.

From his armchair, Darby looked on with a poorly concealed smirk.

She took a step back. "Okay, well, I'm gonna go."

Her dad lifted his head and his gaze fixed on Darby. "What's going on with Marleau?"

Haven slipped from the room.

–

Haven didn't know how long she sat in her car in the parking ramp at the arena. She'd packed up her things and cleared out of the penthouse. Mel was at home with a cold, and Wyatt was in meetings all day. Even Bob hadn't been around for her to say good-bye.

She was free.

But she didn't feel free.

Before the tears closing the back of her throat started to fall, she put the car in gear. At the highway interchange, she headed south out of Milwaukee. In Chicago, rather than picking up the interstate going south, toward Atlanta, she skirted around the basin of Lake Michigan and headed north.

The sun had dropped and a large orange ball hung low in the sky when she traveled along the island's meandering lakeshore drive. As she climbed the front steps of Emily's grand home, a chill breeze kicked up off Lake Michigan and blew a strand of hair across her face.

Her heart stirred with the wind.

What was she doing there? Why had she chosen to return to the place where she could all but guarantee memories of Jack would only taunt and torment her?

Pressure closed the back of her throat but she swallowed the tightness. It didn't matter where she went. There was nowhere to run to escape her love for him. She might as well move toward it.

The door swung open and Emily's pretty face lit up like a beacon in the dark.

Haven burst into tears.

"I don't know why I'm here. There are exactly zero reasons for me to be here. I should've called first or gone someplace else or—"

Emily pulled Haven inside and shut the door on the cold.

"I never cry." Haven buried her face in Emily's shoulder. "I have no idea why I can't stop crying."

"Don't you?" Not one to ramble, Emily had a knack for saying a lot with few words.

When Haven quieted, she dropped her arms and pulled free of Emily's warm hug. She bumped against something unexpected and looked down at the distinct swell of Emily's belly.

Her heart constricted. How could she have forgotten about Emily's pregnancy? Or that bitch at the wedding reception? Or the whole entire reason she ever met Jack Nolan?

She choked back another sob. "How far along are you?"

Emily's smile held enough warmth to melt the ice at Hank's Pizza Haven Arena. "Five m-months."

"And you're doing okay?"

A man's voice ripped her world apart a moment before he bounded into the foyer and shredded her heart.

Her mind grappled with the sight of him. The same

dark hair, though a touch longer on the sides. The same mouth, just a little puffier, and the eyes a brighter shade of green. His face changed with his smile, the same way Jack's did. The smile that popped dimples into his cheeks and crinkled the corners of his eyes. The smile that tickled her heart every time.

Though a little leaner, he moved with the same fluid grace as he walked toward her.

Emily's husband, Luke.

Not her Jack.

Why, oh why, had she come?

"Haven, isn't it?" Luke held out his hand. "We meet at last."

Haven shook his outstretched hand. "It's nice to finally meet you."

He pulled Emily into his side. "I'm sorry we didn't get a chance to at the wedding."

Heat rushed into Haven's cheeks. "Weddings are so hectic."

A knowing light danced in his bright green eyes. "That they are."

"Can y-you stay, at least a little w-while this time?" Emily rested her hand on the plane of his stomach.

Haven's throat seized. With difficulty, she swallowed. "I don't have anywhere else to go."

Emily tugged on her arm. "Come," she said softly. "Help me get your room ready."

Haven followed Emily upstairs, to the bedroom she'd shared with Jack. With the bed where he'd touched her with heartbreaking gentleness.

Once again, she burst into tears.

໑

Jack had lost his passion.

In Detroit, he'd transitioned into his new role with ease. Top to bottom, the roster was loaded with talent. They played sound, fundamental hockey, and with weapons at every position, they could match any style of play and never beat themselves. They had good chemistry, a professional work ethic, and best of all, no drama. Barring a plague of injuries or some other form of fatal bad luck, they could be a special team.

The team was great.

He was not.

He was... tired. Uninspired. Bruised. Over it.

The travel was a nuisance. The media junkets, always tedious, had become a downright menace. He didn't want to talk to reporters who were always trying to dig up dirt about injuries, game plans, distractions, dramas. So much tired bullshit.

He had no right to feel that way. In ten seasons, he'd made it to the postseason seven times and had advanced to the final round of the playoffs once, only to miss out on the top prize.

Likely, this would end up being his best shot.

And he could hardly get up for it.

Because he'd lost his passion. Left it in Milwaukee.

His passion had walked out of his life with her.

CB

If she'd thought to escape to the island to mend her aching heart, secluded and alone, she'd sorely misjudged.

The men who looked like Jack were everywhere.

Besides Luke, Noah, the professor, lived in the carriage house on the property while he and his wife renovated a house somewhere on the island, and the man Haven remembered as the handsome, frosty-haired bartender at the wedding was Shea.

One last brother, Leo, had arrived at the inn shortly before Haven. The bad boy type, which a younger, far stupider Haven probably would've fallen in love with on the spot, this brother was a little more pensive and protective of his solitude than the others. So she liked him the best.

Drawn like flies to honey by Luke's baked goods and other culinary works of art, the brothers convened at Emily's inn with annoying frequency, typically around dinnertime. It was never agreed upon. No one ever said, "Hey, you want to get together tomorrow night for dinner?" They just showed up, every two to three, but never more than four, days.

Without fail.

Still, the weeks passed, and yet, she didn't leave.

She did, however, become enamored with taking walks on the beach just to get away from all that Nolan testosterone. To pull the fresh air into her aching lungs. To let the lake's majestic power fill her with the strength she lacked.

That day while on her walk, she ventured farther than she ever had before, in the direction opposite the lighthouse and public beach. That way, the terrain beyond the sandy shore sloped upward with a drastic incline. There were no houses up on the hillsides that she could see.

Until, when she'd almost reached the limits of the distance she could walk, she spotted something. A steep staircase led up the hill and tucked away in the trees high above the pristine beach, was a house. Actually, it was not quite a house yet. Still under construction, the home had a frame and the walls were just starting to go up.

Gooseflesh broke out over her skin as she gazed up at the structure. She knew that house. She'd seen it before, but only in her mind. That day at the hospital when her dad asked her to take over the team. Well, not that house.

The house she'd seen in her mind had taupe cedar shingle siding and a bright front door, but the landscape and the view matched her vision.

When she returned to the inn, she asked Emily if she knew who the house belonged to, but her friend hadn't known the home was even being built.

That night, Haven lay wide-awake in the bed she'd shared with Jack, thinking about that house by the sea. Too wound up to sleep, she flung back the covers and padded downstairs.

The house was dark and quiet when she slipped into the kitchen and flipped on the light.

Movement out of the corner of her eye pulled a strangled shriek from her throat.

Leo blinked into the bright light.

"Oh shit." Haven sucked oxygen into her starved lungs. "I'm sorry. I didn't know anyone was in here. I...." Her voice trailed off when she looked into his green-gold eyes.

Jack's eyes.

He reached for the glass in front of him, his hand shaking. "It's fine. I'm done." Standing, he moved to the farmhouse sink and set his empty glass in the basin.

As he turned to leave, her stomach clenched at the thought of being left alone to wrestle with the eerie mystery of her vision-house.

She swiped a cookie from the jar. "Sitting alone in the dark in the middle of the night? Kind of weird, isn't it?"

He didn't miss a beat. "Probably not as weird as running around the house turning on all the damned lights in the middle of the night."

Haven grunted. "So... you wanna do something?"

A look of cornered panic stole into his eyes. "It's three o'clock in the morning. What did you have in mind?"

Her gaze flitted around the kitchen, searching, until a thought struck. "You play poker?"

Chapter Twenty-Six

There was nothing like playoff hockey. Fast-paced, high energy, pure emotion and intensity. It took grit, guts, and a reckless determination to make it to through all four best-of-seven rounds, battling the world's top athletes playing at their highest level, laying it all on the line for the glory of drinking from a ridiculously gigantic silver cup.

Too bad Haven had killed his passion and taken away the thrill.

It'd been more than a month since she'd traded him to Detroit and he thought about her every day. Every goddamned day.

Two nights ago, he'd caught a glimpse of a brunette in the premium seating behind the goal. While he searched the stands for her, a Tampa Bay defender laid him out with an illegal crosscheck.

Pain had exploded in Jack's body and he'd collapsed to

the ice.

He hadn't seen the hit coming and had been completely helpless to its brutal force.

The classic dirty play—a blindside hit.

Just like Haven. He never saw her coming. She appeared out of nowhere, the force of her emergence in his life jarring and disorienting, only to disappear as suddenly as she'd arrived while he lay breathless and aching in the wake of her destruction.

As he lay out on the ice, the darkness closing in while he stared up at the arena rafters with the crowds' taunting jeers and cheers raining down on him, he didn't care about hockey. He didn't care about getting up and giving his opponent the payback the bastard deserved.

He didn't care, because it didn't mean anything without her.

At first, he'd been livid with her for trading him. They'd had a good thing going in Milwaukee and he wanted to see it through. At the very least, she should've talked to him about it first.

But as he lay there, dazed and aching, the anger he'd felt, the anger he'd been holding on to with everything he had, gave way to something else. Something sharp and gnawing, as vicious as the hit he'd just suffered.

He missed her. He needed her.

The next day, he failed concussion protocol and had to sit out of practice.

Hanging out in his dark, soundless apartment, he had nothing to do but think. About her. If he could just talk to her, hear her side of things, maybe he could let go of the anger. What had she really done?

Exactly what he'd asked her to do. If he fixed her daddy's team, she'd send him to Detroit. He did, and so did she. That was their deal.

And because she kept their deal, there he was, with his first real shot at winning it all in the last several seasons, and he couldn't get his head in the game. What the hell was wrong with him? Why was he so indifferent to the game that'd given him everything?

Because it didn't matter. If he won the Cup, would he be a better man?

No. He'd be the same man he was now. A shell without the crucial parts. Because he didn't have her.

His head ached and he laid it in his hands. The misery and frustration felt a thousand times worse knowing he'd done it to himself.

Finally, he picked up his cell phone and dialed her number.

It rang, and when she didn't pick up, his call went to her voice mail.

Jesus, her voice. The sound of her warm, low register on the shitty phone speaker squeezed his throat. He couldn't push words past the sudden constriction and disconnected without leaving a message.

He tried her again three times that day. The first two times, it hurt all over again to hear her voice. But when his call went straight to her voice mail the third time, anger took root. She wasn't taking his call?

She wasn't talking to *him*?

He paced the confines of his apartment, trying to think what to do. He had to find her and talk to her. He called the penthouse and badgered the staff person until they admitted she was gone. She'd moved out more than a month ago.

He dropped heavily onto the sofa.

She was gone. She'd left Milwaukee and gone back to her life. Wherever her life without him took place.

ᘒ

In April, Emily's house became game-viewing

headquarters.

Every game day, the brothers piled into Emily's living room. They'd graze over the platters of food Luke prepared for them and spend some time insulting one another. As their playful ribbing carried on, Shea and Noah's distinct Irish accents seemed to infect Luke and Leo's inflections, and the lyrical cadences of all four brothers only seemed to fuel the output of more zingers.

But when the game began, the jawing stopped and they clustered tight around the flat-screen TV hanging over Emily's large fireplace. They never sat down during game action, but instead stood with their faces close to the on-screen battle, barking at the refs or arguing with something one of the announcers had said, or pointing out an adjustment one of the coaches needed to make.

They watched all of Jack's games this way.

Every.

Single.

Game.

Once, during the first-round matchup between Detroit and Tampa Bay, Noah had turned to her. "There's a spot for ye right here, Haven Callahan."

His thick Irish brogue shivered down her spine. All the brothers had taken to calling her by her full name.

She shook her head and ducked her chin, returning her attention to the bottle of blood-red nail polish open on the table in front of her.

She painted a stripe down the length of a fingernail. "I don't like to watch hockey."

That earned her a few snorts and snickers.

She narrowed her eyes at the two women seated on the sofa across from her. Emily's cheeks flushed with her guilt and beside her, her cousin, Mina, who'd struck Haven as a funny, kindhearted woman up until that exact moment, pulled her bottom lip between her teeth to hide her smile.

"Sure you don't," Luke said, turning back to the TV. "That's why you're painting the coffee table red."

Haven frowned and wiped a splatter of polish off the dark wood. "You guys should just go to his games already." And get out of her space for a while.

"Do you have any idea how hard it is to get playoff tickets?"

"Is it hard?" Haven's question hung in the air while the force of four scowls on four ridiculously beautiful faces knocked into her.

"Yes. Very," Luke said dryly.

"Even if we could get tickets, he doesn't want us there," Shea said.

"Why the hell not?" Noah wanted to know.

Shea rolled his shoulders. "I don't know. He says its bad luck."

Haven sat back and gaped at Shea. Bad luck? A memory floated through her mind of Jack's dark scowl.

I don't need luck to win hockey games.

That's what he'd told her, and by smug look on his face when he'd said, she knew he'd meant it.

A loud cheer erupted on the TV and four heads swiveled back toward the action.

Haven's only peace came during her late-night poker games with Leo. They met often in the middle of the night, in the library or at the kitchen table, with a deck of cards and a container of Oreo cookies.

"You ready for your ass-kicking?" Leo asked as he settled into a chair at the kitchen table.

"Aw, aren't you cute. Thinking you actually stand a chance of beating me."

He popped a cookie into his mouth and dealt the cards.

On the surface, he seemed so serious, kind of sad and lonely, but a touch beneath that layer, he had a sneaky smart wit and an active sense of humor. Ryan had been much the same way.

She couldn't recall ever remembering her brother without the suffocating wrench of pain. How sad was that? Ryan deserved all her tears, but he deserved more than that. He was worth remembering with joy and happiness, too.

An hour later, a soft smile curled her lips.

"What's funny?" he asked.

"You, actually."

"Because you've taken all my money? Or is there some other reason you find me amusing?"

"You remind me of my brother. He was a smartass, too." She held up a hand to cut him off. "I know, I know. Better than a dumbass."

Leo's quick smile coaxed twin dimples into his cheeks, taking him from dangerously sexy to also kind of adorable.

But his smile was fleeting. "Was?"

She rubbed the dent in her collarbone. "Yeah. He died."

Before that moment, she'd never told anyone who hadn't asked directly about Ryan. Though she thought about him every day, she never shared his memory with others. Up to now, it hurt too much to talk about him.

It still hurt, but not as much as the thought of Ryan's memory fading away did.

"I'm sorry," Leo said softly.

"Thank you."

He leaned back in his chair, the wood creaking with his movement. "Besides being a smartass, what was he like?"

"He was good-looking, and he played hockey."

"Uh-oh."

She laughed. "It took me a while to figure out all the girls at school weren't actually interested in being my friend. They were only hanging out with me because they wanted a chance to get close to my brother."

"That's harsh."

"You don't know many teenage girls, do you?"

"So far, I've escaped that punishment."

Outside, the tops of the trees began to take shape in the dark sky. The sun would be up soon.

She tapped a finger on the table. "You going to ante up or chicken out again?"

A light winked in his shifting hazel eyes. Cupping his hands, he shoveled his tall stack of Oreo cookies into the pile.

"I'm all in, Haven Callahan. What you got?"

Haven didn't care that she'd lost her money—er, cookies, to Leo, and she told him so.

"It makes me feel good about myself to donate to charity once in a while." She closed her bedroom door on the sound of his soft chuckle.

At the French doors, she yanked closed the curtains on the morning light and then climbed into bed. She switched on her cell phone to check the time.

But she forgot all about the time when she saw she had a missed call.

From Jack.

Emotions slammed into her, one after another. They came so quickly they robbed her of breath. Annoyance that he'd waited a month to call her. A month! Followed by a wrenching agony at the way her heart soared with the possibility of speaking to him again. Overriding it all, the sharp wrench of fear that if she talked to him, she'd not be able to stop her heart from bursting with her love for him.

A love so strong and full, she knew if she were ever to lose it, to lose him, she'd not survive. Not that time. It was too painful a prospect. She, too weak.

It'd taken her sixteen years to get to a place where she could remember Ryan without the nauseating, soul-destroying wrench of grief and regret. She couldn't go back to that place of ultimate vulnerability.

Jack hadn't left a message, and she didn't call him back.

Chapter Twenty-Seven

She'd disappeared off the face of the earth.

He'd spent hours on the Internet, trying to find her. A name. An address. In any city. Anything at all he didn't already know about her life.

But there was nothing outside the articles written during her time with the Renegades.

She was gone.

For someone who'd never lived in one place long enough to call it home, he felt bereft. Homesick. Haven was his home, and she was gone.

He called her cell phone every day for a week or more, and she never picked up or returned his call.

Panic took hold.

His chest ached from his heart's constant banging against his breastbone.

Where the hell was she? Had he never asked her where she lived? Seattle, hadn't she told him at the wedding? Shit, he couldn't remember, and there were no signs of a Haven Callahan that he could find living in Seattle or a half dozen other major metropolises.

Then a thought struck.

Luke. Maybe his brother knew where she was. Or, more specifically, maybe his brother's sweet little wife did.

☙

Haven's nails were polished, black that time, as were her toenails. She'd read all the magazines in the house and several books from the inn's library.

Left with nothing, she paced in front the large picture window, trying to pretend she wasn't holding her breath until she caught a glimpse of Jack on the TV screen or heard the announcers make mention of his name.

It was game seven of Detroit's first-round matchup, with the winner advancing to the second round.

She chewed her thumbnail as players took to the ice for the start of the third period and the brothers clustered around Emily's TV.

All except one brother.

At her side, Luke appeared, a freshly poured Guinness in his hand.

She kept track of him out of the corner of her eye. He was a sneaky sort. At first glance, he seemed so relaxed and easygoing, but every once in a while she caught him watching her. Not with sexual interest or anything that would've made her kick his ass for eye-cheating on Emily, but more like a partner in crime. As if she and he were old friends, sharing a joke no one else was privy to.

Except Haven didn't get the joke.

She caught him doing it then. "What?" she snapped.

"My brother, he likes you."

Haven's spine snapped straight.

Jack had talked to Luke about her? Now that she was no longer his boss, they didn't have to hide their relationship anymore. But that didn't mean he wanted people to know about them, did it? Was there still even a "them" to speak of?

Her heart lurched. "He-he does? Did he tell you that? What did he say?"

Luke's expression turned bewildered. "He didn't have to say anything. You're the only one who can beat him at poker."

The air left her lungs in a rush. Leo. He was talking about Leo.

"I was wondering...." He seemed to pull back the words, but then change his mind again. "If maybe you could get him to talk."

"About what?"

Lines of worry pulled at his puffy mouth. "Anything. Does he have friends? A girl? Maybe he'll talk to you about his time overseas. I don't care what he wants to talk about, just as long as he talks."

After that, the puck dropped and they became caught up in the game. It took a sudden death overtime goal, but Detroit advanced to play Ottawa in the second round.

Two days later, the thrill of the win stayed with her while she sipped from her coffee mug and flipped through a celebrity gossip magazine. Next to her at the kitchen table, Luke stirred sugar into his cup.

"Emily still sleeping?"

The softest of soft curves touched his lips. "She's in the shower."

A few minutes later, his cell phone vibrated.

He glanced at the screen. "It's Jack," he said, reaching for the device.

Heart in her throat, her hand shot out and clamped onto his wrist.

Startled green eyes flew to her face.

"Please," she whispered. "Don't tell him I'm here."

His eyes narrowed. "Why not?" There was no surprise in his expression, and while the device continued to buzz with annoying persistence, he appeared unhurried to answer it.

"It's, uh, complicated."

"Okay."

He waited.

She licked her dry lips. "Answer the phone first."

"If I'm going to lie for you, I need to know why.

"It's just..." She bit off with an exasperated groan "If you keep your mouth shut, I'll get you playoff tickets."

That did surprise him. "That's impossible. Even if you could get your hands on some tickets, they'd cost a fortune."

She rolled her eyes. "My dad's a billionaire and owns a pro team. Pretty sure I can manage it."

"Jack doesn't want us there."

"That's a lie. He wants you there really, really, *really* badly. I know he does."

Luke silenced the phone and lifted the device to his ear. "Hey, man, what's up?"

He was quiet while he listened.

"That was a great series. I like the matchup against Ottawa." They talked about hockey for a time, and Haven's heart slowed somewhat, though it couldn't return to its normal rhythm knowing Jack was on the other side of that phone connection.

Her Jack.

Luke's gaze landed on her face. "Oh, yeah, what was her name?"

What name? Whose name? She gulped.

He snapped his fingers. "That's right. Haven. I heard you two hit it off at the wedding."

She kicked his shin under the table.

The bastard smiled. "I don't know if they've talked. Let me ask Emily."

Haven bounded to her feet. With her eyes clamped on his devious face, she backed away from the table.

"You sure? I don't mind," Luke said. "Will do. You'll be the first one I call if I lay eyes on her."

She fled.

With round two of the playoffs set to begin, Jack still hadn't found his passion, but as the two teams took to the ice and he stared down his opponent on the other side of the puck, he found something better.

Pure, unbridled hatred.

It whipped through him with the frenzy of an attack dog that'd scented its target.

Bryce Lovejoy.

Jack didn't bother searching the faces in the crowd, as he had every other night in every other arena. He knew she wouldn't be there. She was never there.

But she was with him, a part of her always would be, and so he prepared to battle for her. His passion.

He didn't know how, or when, exactly, it would happen. Maybe the moment the puck dropped or maybe it'd take him five, or six, or all seven games to find his moment. The timing didn't matter. All that mattered was that Jack would get his revenge.

For Haven.

The guys were right. It was extremely difficult to get playoff tickets, but she did it. Sort of.

She wasn't able to get anything for the current series

being played against Ottawa, but if Detroit won and advanced to the third round, then in game three in Detroit, Jack's brothers would get to see him play live for the first time in his pro career.

But first, Detroit had to put Ottawa away, which they could do that night with the win.

As the family gathered for the puck drop, Emily groaned and rubbed a hand over her now seven-month-pregnant belly.

Luke grew instantly alert. "You all right?"

"I think I'm entering the beached wh-whale phase."

His smile turned devious. Triumphant.

"It's not funny," Emily grumbled.

A flash of pity had him reaching for her hand. "I'm sorry if you're miserable, baby."

"You'll be sorry wh-wh-when I'm fat."

He lifted her hand to his mouth and pressed a kiss to her palm. "Never. No matter what size or shape you are, you'll still be the hottest woman on this island, even though you pee a little when you sneeze." Green eyes shifted to Haven. "No offense."

"None taken." Haven laughed at the pink spots of pleasure staining Emily's cheeks.

The commercial break over, the TV honed in on the players gathered on the ice for the ceremonial playing of both countries' national anthems prior to game action. As the music started, the camera panned down the line of players. The men, sprouting serious expressions behind varying lengths of playoff beards, fidgeted or rocked from side to side with their nervous energy and pent-up tension.

Except Jack. Instead, he stood still as a statue, his gaze focused on his opponents across the ice.

She'd never seen that look on his face, or in his eyes, before. Angry and dialed in. A niggle of unease slithered down her spine.

With the puck dropped, Jack erupted into action. He was faster than the other players and hit harder than anyone else on the ice, and his intensity carried over to the rest of his team.

The Ottawa players grew frustrated early as Detroit took command. With less than a minute to go in the game, and with a two-goal lead, Jack and Bryce Lovejoy squared up for the face-off. The TV cameras showed Bryce's mouth moving as he skated twice around Jack. In the face-off circle, Jack stared straight ahead.

Until Bryce made one last comment and Jack snapped. With a flash of movement, he shucked his stick and both gloves, and lunged. He took Bryce to the ground with a jarring strike and then he started to hit.

Fist after fist after fist crashed into Bryce's face. The refs trilled their whistles and when that didn't stop Jack, they tried to pull him off Bryce. Players from both teams ventured into the fray, but Jack was relentless. He held onto Bryce's jersey and pummeled him with sharp, merciless blows.

Finally, several Detroit players were able to haul Jack back. He shook off his teammates and skated away while Bryce lay prone on the ice.

Haven felt sick.

Emily's living room had grown deathly quiet. On TV, the Detroit commentators spoke in grave tones about the fight and the fact that Jack would likely face a multi-game suspension for instigating the brutal attack at the end of the game.

"Who is that guy?" Leo asked in a low, lethal voice.

"Bryce Lovejoy," Shea said.

"Played in Milwaukee with Jack," Luke noted.

All eyes turned to Haven.

It was her fault. He'd risked it all because of her.

The Cup, his career, his reputation, his brothers' chance to watch him play, their respect. All of it tossed aside, for what? The pleasure of punching Bryce's smug face? Okay, that was tempting, but seriously, what the hell was he thinking?

She was going to kill him.

Chapter Twenty-Eight

Jack received a two-game suspension, and he couldn't say he was sorry. He was sorry he'd made things harder for his teammates, and Neal, and he was sorry the bastard Bryce skated off the ice under his own power. Eventually.

When the time for game three rolled around and he waited with his teammates in the tunnel prior to taking the ice, he tried convincing himself the passion was there after having to sit out two games. He didn't need the hatred to fire him up. He was a professional. Besides, if he couldn't manufacture a little passion for a Stanley Cup semifinal game, with the series tied at 1-1, then he should hang it up right now.

The teams ran through a few warmups, and as Jack skated behind the net to pick up a loose puck, fans started banging on the glass near his head with the fervor of game action.

He looked up, and then stumbled back at the sight of them.

His brothers. All of them.

But also his seventeen-year-old nephew, Finn, and the little ones, Maisie and Connor, plus two of his three sisters-in-law, Isobel and Mina. All decked out in the team's red-and-white gear. With flags and towels and pom-poms. They were downright obnoxious.

But they were all there. For him. To watch him play. And they even appeared to be sober.

His heart lifted and a smile tugged up one corner of his mouth. With a jump in his step, he took to the ice with enough fire to melt ten rinks, and three periods of frenzied playoff hockey later, Detroit came out on top with the win.

In the tunnel, Jack's brothers leaned over the railing and he smacked their hands.

"What are you doing here?" he called out to them.

"We got lucky and some tickets landed in our laps," Luke said. "Figured we might as well come see you play."

"Nine playoff tickets just landed in your lap?" Jack laughed. "I need your kind of luck."

"We've got connections," Luke said.

"Where's your wife?" Jack teased him. "Lose her already?"

Luke's green eyes glittered. "She has a friend staying with her and couldn't make it. They're happier without me around."

An electric shock zapped Jack, snatching the breath from his body. The hairs lifted on his neck and arms. "What friend?"

"You remember Haven, don't you?" he said casually.

Jack couldn't even be pissed at the smug smirk on his brother's face. Triumph roared through him.

He'd found her.

"Your connection, I take it?"

Luke lifted one shoulder.

Haven had done this? She'd brought them all there, with their ridiculous amount of fan gear, to watch him play. For the first time. As a whole family.

But why would she do that and at the same time refuse to return his calls? Did she know how much it'd mean to him?

Of course, she knew.

She got him. She understood what made him tick, and she cared enough to try to make him happy. Because she loved him.

His heart soared.

She. Fucking. Loved. Him.

Then why the hell wouldn't she pick up the phone and call him? What was she so afraid of?

Understanding hit him like a punch to the gut. That was just it. She was afraid.

Well, tough shit. He was afraid, too. That didn't grant them permission to give up on each other. To throw away the best thing that'd ever happened to either one of them.

Jack charged down the tunnel. He had to get to her.

In his rush, he knocked into a man wearing a dark suit and holding a vodka tonic in one hand. Jack apologized even as he registered the man stood with a group of league executives. Semifinal playoff games were a big draw, and everyone associated with the game wanted to be there, no matter their title or team affiliation.

The man turned, and Jack recoiled.

Hank Callahan.

Haven's dad recognized him. "Jack, congratulations." He held out his hand. "I'm still pissed my daughter traded you."

"Honestly, so am I," Jack said carefully.

Hank laughed. "Good luck the rest of the way." He started to turn away.

Jack hesitated only a moment. "Your daughter's a great girl, Mr. Callahan."

Slowly, Hank turned back. His dark eyes narrowed. "Do I have any reason to kick your ass, Nolan?"

"Not one."

"Let's keep it that way, shall we?"

"Sure thing." Jack headed down the tunnel.

"She's gonna throw a lot of crap at you, you know."

Jack twisted back around.

Hank sipped the drink in his hand. "If you can put up with her bullshit, she just might be worth it."

Might be?

Jack forgot all about contracts and trade deals when he faced Hank Callahan. The man had disappointed his daughter in countless ways and yet there he stood, two months out of rehab sipping an alcoholic beverage, while passing judgement on her.

His voice shook with his fury. "Oh, she's worth it, but it takes a real man to love her."

Unbelievably, her dad just smiled. "You're probably right about that. I've been trying to give her the apology I owe her for weeks now. If you see her, tell her to return my calls, would ya?"

Jack bristled. His weren't the only calls she wouldn't return? She was avoiding her dad, too? Who else was she hiding from?

But he already knew the answer to that question. She was hiding from the world. Hiding because she was hurting, and she thought if she ran far enough, stayed far enough away, the hurting would stop.

His heart ached for her, a dull throbbing pain in the center of his chest. Damn it all if the whole world didn't owe her an apology.

He met Hank Callahan's gaze. "I can do better than that."

☙

With the brothers gone, Emily and Haven stayed up late talking and eating cookies. Haven asked about the bed-and-breakfast and found out some of Emily's first guests had begun booking rooms for the fast-approaching tourist season.

"I should probably think about getting a job," Haven mused. The money from her dad wouldn't last that long, and she'd need to move out soon to get a place of her own.

"Wh-What do you do?" Emily asked.

Haven experienced a little beat of hesitation. "I bartend." She snuck at glance at Emily from beneath her eyelashes. "But I think I might want to try something else. Maybe finish my degree."

The possibility might never have occurred to her if it weren't for the phone call she'd received from ESPN asking her to appear on a late-night talk show.

A regretful smile touched Emily's lips. "You didn't finish either?"

Emily had dropped out the semester before Haven did to move home and take care of her ill mother.

Haven shook her head. "Maybe we should go back to school together."

"Oh, lets. Except let's skip the dorms this time."

"Deal," Haven said.

Emily picked an imaginary fuzzy off the armrest of her chair. "Actually, I w-wanted to apologize to you."

"Apologize? For what?"

"For not w-writing or staying in touch after I left school. I w-was overwhelmed w-w-with my mom." She swallowed convulsively. "Little things like checking in w-with my friends became too much."

Haven gave Emily's hand a quick, tight squeeze. "Don't

you dare apologize to me for that. I didn't exactly stay in touch either."

"So w-we're even."

They shared a smile.

"But, Em, I do want you to know how sorry I am about your mom."

A whole bunch of words tangled and twisted in Haven's mind, condolences and such, but she knew not a single one of them could possibly heal the hurt.

Instead, she just held onto Emily's hand. "I hate death," she whispered.

"Me, too," Emily whispered back.

A soft jingle disturbed the quiet in the room and Emily checked her cell phone.

She read a text message and the soft, secret smile Haven had grown used to seeing on her friend's face reappeared.

"That's Luke. They're on their w-way back from the game."

Her chest aching, Haven pointed at the phone. "How did you do it?"

Emily's smile faded. "You mean, how did I catch a man like him?"

Haven frowned. "No, not at all. I mean, how did you fall in love? After losing your mom, wasn't it... hard?"

Impossible.

It was impossible.

The damage her heart had suffered all those years before meant if she were to love someone again now and lose them, the way she'd lost Ryan, the weakened organ in her chest simply would not survive it.

After her initial surprise at Haven's question, Emily's expression turned thoughtful. "I was in a dark place for a long time, years, wh-while my m-mom was sick and afterwards. But then I m-met Luke and...." She lifted her shoulders in a bemused shrug. "The lights came back on."

Her watery laugh bubbled up. "He lit up the wh-whole w-world. I didn't have a choice to love him or not. I couldn't not love him."

"Didn't hurt that he's hot as hell," Haven said dryly.

"No, it did not." Emily's laughter faded and she turned serious once more. "No matter wh-what the future holds, I'll always know I loved him and he loved me. W-We love each other, w-w-with all of our hearts, and nothing can ever take that away from us. Certainly not death."

Haven started to cry.

Chapter Twenty-Nine

Haven dreamed of Jack, and of those magical days they'd spent together in the bedroom at Emily's inn. In all his dark, fierce gloriousness, he approached the bed—though dream-Jack sported his playoff beard—and peered down into her face.

Her heart ached with longing and grief.

Long ago, she'd vowed not to let anyone steal her heart. She'd spent half her life running from the fear, but in that moment, from within the shelter of her own dreams, she realized how truly lost she was.

Gazing up at Jack's dream face, perfect and filled with love, a shaky sigh eased from her. "I miss you, Jack."

A tender smile curved his beautiful mouth, and then her dream talked back.

"So why don't you get your hot little ass out of that bed and show me."

Instantly wide-awake, she bolted upright.

"Jack!" Her feet tangled in the sheets when she tripped from the bed. "Wh-what are you doing here?"

He straightened and eased his hands into the pockets of his blue jeans. "You have something that's mine, and I'm here to collect it." His features hardened into concrete. "I'm not leaving without it."

A chill chased through her.

She shoved a hand through her sleep-rumpled hair and hiked the wide neck of her sleep shirt over her bare shoulder. "I don't know what you're talking about."

The sliver of light glittered in his eyes while he waited.

One of his dark eyebrows lifted in challenge.

With a huff, she thrust her hand under her pillow and yanked.

"Fine. Take it." She flung his lucky T-shirt at him.

He snatched it out of the air. A smug smile played over his lips as he fingered the soft fabric.

His unsettling gaze remained fixed on her face. "I wasn't talking about the T-shirt."

Disconcerted, she gave her head a small shake. "Then what are you talking about?"

"You." He edged closer. "I'm talking about you."

Her heart started to pound.

"You belong to me, Haven."

Her hands started to shake, so she crossed her arms. "You're cocky."

"Damn straight, and I'm also right. Admit it."

She lifted one shoulder and looked away, pretending a great interest in the pattern of the quilt on the bed.

"Admit it, Haven."

She meant to avoid the torture of his eyes, but instead, the memories of their time spent beneath that quilt wrenched her injured heart. Her vision blurred with the terror clogging the back of her throat.

"I can't, Jack." A tear spilled over to stream down her cheek. "I can't love you. I can't... I can't... lose you."

A ripple of alarm disturbed his features. "You won't lose me."

"You don't know that." Her voice broke. "You can't promise me that you won't want to leave me one day." She pressed her clenched fist to her breastbone, trying to rub away the ache beneath it. "After Ryan died... my heart... it broke. Jack, I can't go through that again. I just can't."

Just thinking of it shattered her, and started her feet moving under her. She strode past him and down the hall, her retreat slowed by the slipperiness of her slouchy socks on the hardwood floors. At the landing, she slid to a stop.

"Dad?"

Sitting on the bottom stair, Hank pushed to his feet and turned to look up at her. "Hey, pumpkin."

"What are you doing here?" But by the time the words left her mouth, her scrambled thoughts had sorted it all out. She turned slowly to gape at Jack. "You brought him here?"

Jack dipped his head. "Your dad has something he wants to say to you. Don't you, Hank?"

Hank's face clouded with uneasiness. "You, uh, flew out of my office so damned fast, I didn't get a chance to tell you what a great job you did for me. Thank you."

She stared at him, baffled.

At her silence, an unpleasant blush swept over his features. "Also, I'm looking for a new General Manager and I wanted to run a few names by you, see what you think."

"What happened to Darby?"

He shoved his hands into the pockets of his dress slacks. "I fired him."

Surprise rippled through her, which she quickly concealed. "Good move."

"A little overdue, I know." He studied her face a

moment. "I heard about the offer from ESPN."

She moved one shoulder in a shrug. "I'm going to turn them down."

"You shouldn't. You'd be great at it."

Uneasy with his compliments, she folded her arms in front of her. "Yeah, well, I've decided I'm going to be a lighthouse keeper."

Hank nodded. "You'd be good at that, too."

Her arms dropped heavily to her sides. "Stop agreeing with everything I say. You're confusing me."

"I'm sorry about that, too." He scratched the back of his head and stared down at the floor. "The thing is, kiddo, I know I haven't been the best dad to you." He looked up at her. "After Ryan...."

His expression twisted and he ducked his chin, but not before she glimpsed the slash of pain contorting his features. Her breath caught and she eased back to lean against the wall. All the grief and heartache in the world lived there, on her dad's face.

She knew that pain. Knew it well. For it lived in her, too. It was that pain that had kept him from loving her after her brother died.

She used to think there was something wrong with her. That she wasn't good enough to deserve her dad's love, but he was the one who wasn't good enough for her. He'd been too wounded, or scared, or weak to love her.

That same pain kept her from loving Jack now. Rendered her wounded and scared, and weak. So very weak.

She gulped hard, and a hot tear tracked down her cheek. "It's okay, Dad."

And it was. It really was, because, quite honestly, she didn't need her dad's love anymore. She had Jack's, and that was all that truly mattered.

Jack.

Her dad's smile didn't reach his eyes. "It's not, but I

appreciate you saying so."

She swiped at another tear with the back of her hand. "Hey, did you see the flat-screen TV in the living room?"

Hank perked up. "Is it big?"

"Huge." She pointed in the direction of the room. "Check it out."

Her dad disappeared through the archway. In the silence that followed, she took a moment to find the courage to face Jack. He hung back, watching her with green-gold eyes that shimmered with uncertainty.

Looking at him, her heart ached, as though a fireball burned in the center of her chest. The fire of Jack's love. And as she gazed upon his beautiful face, the two halves of her heart, broken apart the day her brother died, fused together again.

At the pang of sweet relief beneath her breastbone, a tiny gasp slipped through her lips. The old familiar ache eased suddenly and she drew a deep, fortifying breath.

With her new, whole heart, she went to him.

"Okay, fine, I admit it. I belong to you. And you belong to me." She sidled closer. "And I hate you."

His smile put the stars to shame. "I know you do, baby."

He caught her around the waist.

"I'm serious, Jack. I hate your guts."

He nuzzled close to her ear. "Tell me more. What do you hate about me?"

"I hate your face and your body." Her hands gripped his arms and smoothed around to his back. "I hate the way you make me laugh and how I can't breathe when you're too close."

He kissed the side of her neck. "Like this?"

"Yes," she said, breathless.

"Is that all?"

"Not even close. I hate your big heart, and the way you stand up for me." She pulled back so that she could see his eyes. "Did you fight him because of me?"

His silence told her everything.

"Why did you do that?" she whispered. "You could've lost your chance to play for the Cup."

"Because fuck the Cup. What happened to you—" He swallowed hard. "You deserve better than this world's given you, Haven, and that pisses me off. I need you to be safe more than I need to win a hockey game."

"It's not just a hockey game. Jack—"

"Don't." His hold around her waist tightened. "You won't change my mind, and I can't take it back anyway."

"Promise me you'll never do something like that again."

"I can't promise you that. I'm sorry." His hand came up to brush her cheek. "I'll always fight for you, whatever that means, and whether you want me to or not."

She took his hand in both of hers and pulled it in front of her face. Her fingers trailed over the knuckles where the skin remained raw and irritated from the fight a few days back.

"I'm sorry I can't take away the pain for you." His voice rasped with emotion.

She pressed her lips to his pink knuckles. "You already have."

He pressed his forehead to hers, and together, they breathed.

"I don't want to love you, Jack."

"I don't want to love you either. I don't have room for you in my life. I travel all the time. I'm in training most of the year. It'll never work."

Their soft laughter mingled.

Her fingertips traced the outline of his jaw. "I'm probably going to love you for the rest of my life. I'm sorry."

"Why are you sorry?"

"Because I'm the worst person to have love you. It's

going to be ridiculous. I'm going to be clingy and needy, obsessed and possessive. I feel sorry for you. I really do."

"Don't." He dipped his head low. "Sounds like heaven to me."

Then his mouth claimed hers.

03

Jack scanned the crowd. He spotted her immediately, right where she always was.

It's where she'd been when Detroit went down one game to Pittsburgh's three in the third round, and it's where she was when they clawed their way back into the series and won in game seven in sudden death overtime to advance to the Stanley Cup finals. It's where she stood now, watching Jack take his turn lifting the Cup above his head as he skated across the rink to a cacophony of the fan's wild cheers.

As he rounded to her side of the arena, she came down the stairs to stand at the glass. He passed the Cup off to a teammate and though he couldn't touch or hear her through the glass, he skated over to her. She pressed her palm flat against the Plexiglas, and he laid his hand over hers.

He could get lost in her eyes, at the way their centers melted with warmth when she gazed at him. The sadness he'd so often glimpsed in them hadn't been evident these last few weeks, replaced instead by a soft sparkle that tugged at his groin.

Then her wide mouth slipped into a crooked smile and she lifted her other hand between them, showing him the backs of her fingers. At first he didn't understand, so she pointed at the silver band hanging loose around her ring finger.

It was a man's ring. A wedding ring.

Understanding knocked him back and his gaze swung to her face. Her smile turned sweet and her eyes filled with a hesitant hope. She lifted her shoulders.

His heart lurched and he reached for her, but his palms came up hard against the glass.

"Are you sure?" he shouted over the noise and glass barrier.

Dark eyes shining, she laughed and nodded.

With the thrill of having just won the Cup still zinging through him, his feet moved under him. He skated along the boards, slow at first so she could keep up with him, but as he neared the tunnel where the glass partitions ended, he couldn't contain the love in his heart.

He charged toward the edge of the rink, and when she came around from the other side, he hauled her into his arms.

Her arms clamped tight around his neck and she buried her face in the crook between his shoulder and throat. "Marry me, Jack?"

"You don't do commitment, remember?"

She took his face in both her hands. "I don't want to run, Jack. Not anymore. Not from you."

Her mouth touched his lips and pure, sweet joy erupted inside his chest.

"And look." Pulling back, she shoved the sleeve of her hockey jersey up past her elbow. "No hives."

Laughter burst from him and he enfolded her in his arms. He'd won the Cup, and he'd won the smartest, strongest, most amazing, hot-ass wife imaginable.

He'd won life.

Chapter Thirty

When it came to marriage, Haven Callahan had rules.

Well, one rule.

One soft, squishy, gooey in the center rule.

Rule Number One and Only: Screw the rules.

They didn't do her any good anyway. One by one, Jack had broken every single rule she'd ever constructed to protect her fragile heart. He blasted right on through her defenses and claimed the battered organ. Rescued it, really.

Her arms loaded down with dirty dishes, she used her hip to push open the back door. Inside, she rounded the scarred walnut dining table and passed through the kitchen to the farmhouse sink.

As she bent to stack the first dinner plate in the dishwasher, the door to the back deck opened and Jack ducked inside the house.

Their house.

It was the Cape Cod from her vision, the one being built a few miles up the beach from Emily's inn. Turned out, that was Jack's house, which he'd had built on a hillside tucked up in the trees high above the waters of Lake Michigan.

A month past, they'd added her name to the deed.

"Sorry," he'd said, a wide grin splitting his handsome face as he'd waggled the paper deed. "You can't run now. You're committed."

She'd laughed. Like she could ever outrun her love for Jack.

"You need some help in here?" he asked her now.

"I'm good. Go visit with your brothers."

"My brothers would kick my ass if I weren't in here trying to flirt with my wife."

His hand found her waist and she twisted in his arms. "Is that what you call this, flirting?"

He dipped his head while his hand roamed up her side. "It's the best I can do. I've never been able to slow myself down around you long enough to flirt."

Her pulse raced.

A frustrated growl reverberated in the back of his throat, and he pressed his forehead to hers while he visibly struggled to bring himself under control.

After a moment, he gave up trying to conquer the pull. "I like your dress."

A blush of pleasure warmed her cheeks. "Thanks."

She'd found the ivory sheath wedding dress at the boutique downtown and fallen in love with it immediately. It was the perfect dress for their small, late summer wedding on the beach in their backyard.

His fingers clutched at the delicate fabric, inching it upward. "When can I take it off you?"

"Not until everyone's gone?" His mouth found her neck, turning her statement into a question.

"Never stopped us before," he murmured against her

sensitive skin.

She gasped. "At least wait until my dad's gone."

Along with Jack's family and the Thompsons, Beverly, Mel and Harlon, and Hank, Kristen, and the boys had come to see Jack and Haven exchange their vows.

Jack pulled back, suddenly serious. "Did you talk to your mom? What did she say?"

"She said she'll think about it, but I think she'll say yes." Haven dropped a kiss on his cheek and brushed away a smudge of lip-gloss with the pad of her thumb. "Thank you, Jack."

It'd been his idea to ask Beverly to move to the island. He'd offered to buy her a house or build one for her anywhere she wanted on the three acres he and Haven now owned.

"Did you tell her we need someone to watch the house while we're away during the season?"

"I told her."

He frowned. "I thought for sure she'd say yes to that."

"She will." Haven smoothed her hands down the front of his dress shirt. "She needs a little time to get used to the idea, that's all."

"Well, tell her not to wait too long. Training camp starts in a month."

"I'll tell her." Her fingers played with the hair at his nape. "How does it feel to be a married man?"

He buried both his hands in her hair and kissed her. "You wanna know the truth?"

She nodded.

"It's better than winning the Stanley Cup, and I'm not gonna lie to you, that was awesome."

While she laughed, his expression grew serious. "How about you?"

She pressed the tip of two fingers to the crease between his brows. "I have some good news."

"Oh yeah, what's that?"

"I've settled on a brand of shampoo."

A slow smile banished the worry from his features. "Have you now? Will I like it?"

"You're going to love it."

She'd spent her adult life afraid to look to a future that didn't have Ryan in it, but she wasn't afraid anymore. With Jack, she'd found the freedom she thought she craved. True freedom. The kind that comes only with surrender.

"It's light and weightless," she said. "You'll never have a bad hair day again."

"I've never had a bad hair day."

"So you won't notice anything's changed."

"Well, one thing is going to have to change."

"What's that?"

"The name of your TV show."

She'd taken ESPN up on their offer, and what started as an occasional appearance on a late-night talk show had morphed into her own weekly program. She now got paid to talk about sports, with as many smart-ass comments as she could pack into a half-hour segment, to a small, likely drunk, middle-of-the-night audience. It was the perfect gig for her.

"'Dirty Play with Haven Callahan' isn't going to cut it anymore," he said. "What do you think about 'Dirty Play with Haven Nolan'? Or 'Dirty Play with Haven Callahan Nolan,' if that's your thing?"

She slipped her arms around his neck. "You are my thing, Jack. Only you."

THE END

ABOUT THE AUTHOR

Amy Olle is a USA Today bestselling author of sexy contemporary romances filled with charmingly flawed characters and cozy settings. Her debut novel, *Beautiful Ruin*, is the first book in the series about the five Irish-born Nolan brothers sent as children to live with family on a remote island in northern Michigan. She is delighted to put her Psychology degrees to good use writing romance.

Amy lives in Michigan with her longsuffering husband, brilliant son, and (female) turtle named George.

Amy loves connecting with readers! Find her on the web at www.amyolle.com.

www.ingramcontent.com/pod-product-compliance
Lightning Source LLC
Chambersburg PA
CBHW051644180726
48284CB00006B/1857